THE GROUP

KHURRAM ELAHI

Published by Khurram Elahi Publishing

The characters and events portrayed in this book are fictitious. Any similarity to real persons, living or dead, is coincidental and not intended by the author.

ISBN: 978-1-739303-10-5

www.khurramelahi.com

Also by the Author:

A Change of Seasons

Contents

THE GROUP

‘Gambling only pays when you're winning’

Genesis, 1973

PROLOGUE

A round of anger.

An episode of regret.

A bout of remorse.

Jagat Singh felt like he was born to suffer. He slapped himself on his sweaty forehead, feeling enraged and regretful with himself. His clumpy black quiff bounced up and down with the force of the hit. The slapping sound echoed in his ears, mixed in with the internal jeers that spat blame into his mind.

This was the emotional place he was at.

To others, he was a man with no problems. To them, he was simply, Jag.

Jag, the British Indian, who had married a beautiful English woman. He had it all, or at least it seemed that way. Great job, wife, and angelic daughter. That was, until he came across The Forex Group.

CHAPTER 1

Jag tapped on the keyboard, fingers dancing from letter to letter frantically in search of the right words. His flawed typing skills frustrated him, even though he worked as an IT Consultant. It was a minor distraction that played with his easily plagued mind.

A few weeks had passed since realising his fears, but he was still reluctant to acknowledge them. How had he fallen for it? He was normally so thorough and diligent in all his worldly affairs. Scrupulous, even in ensuring his child's work was done on time, Jag had really let his guard down on this occasion. And this also bit at his mind, making him feel more and more vulnerable.

His failings began at a young age, but he had always spent his youth arguing with himself that in fact he was not really all that gullible. Most times he had been successful in convincing himself he was better than he actually was, but he possessed an immaturity far beyond his years. Often feeling reluctant to face the limitations he knew of himself, he would hide behind the successful career he had dug for himself so far. There was no masking it. He had been easily deceived, almost like a puppet playing into the hands of its master.

Just a minor act of naivety, one that the most rational would happily overlook. It had been a costly bout of inexperience. Jag would always feel like turning back the pages of his life, regret, hoping to make sure his biography be kindly written. The pen waits for no man. By time, man is in loss.

The seconds of his hand were ticking, marking a weary indulgence into a grey unpredictable world, fearful of falling into that trap again. This time it had been an expensive mistake and a formidable trap. He now had to somehow squeak his way out and find salvation.

Jag sat back in his chair, as it too, displayed metaphorical discomfort from his actions. The chair groaned in unison with his mind. Was it really only the pressure of his weight on the aging reclining office chair? Or was it the psychological trauma passed through from Jag to this normally inanimate object? A sigh followed him leaning back into a world he now hated to think about.

Sipping on his green tea he found himself taking in an unprepared amount, resulting in him coughing in reflex, almost choking as if he had swallowed the liquid down the wrong pipe. Quickly putting down his mug with a bang, he spent the next thirty seconds trying to recover from a bout of spasmodic convulsions and uncontrollable neck pressuring jerks. At least it took his mind away from the disastrous financial decisions he had made of late.

There was a silence; a silence that came with unwanted regret and a man in the back of his mind intent on reminding him again and again of his unwitting mistakes. It was like an angry parent spouting nothing but anger, teaching in a way only a disappointed parent would do.

You were born to make wrong choices, Jag. Born loser!

The little man in the back of his head, did he really care about Jag? Like a grumpy old woman prodding him with a stick. Or a child continually chiding him into capitulation. Jag had become fed up with these voices in his head. Yes, he knew he had made a mistake, but enough is enough. Paying the price now was enough; a costly affair from his love-hate relationship.

CHAPTER 2

It had been about six months ago when Jag had stumbled upon The Forex Group's website. To say he wish he hadn't would be a huge understatement. The subsequent sleepless nights that followed had been a nightmare.

The flashing lights and attractive website had enticed him like the windows of a pawn brokers to someone going through tough times. Where to look on the screen was the question, there was so much going on? Which window to look through? Which link to click? Each item there for window shopping, waiting to be dragged into the basket. All that glittered may not be gold, but it certainly seemed that way to Jag.

It was all part of the game. Like a black widow, or maybe window, enticing its pray into its lair, it was a sticky affair. That game of addiction; addiction for the thing that pushed the right buttons. With the heart of a gambler, Jag had fallen right into the wide web, now unable to free himself from the clutches of technological confusion. An imbroglio of greens and reds on a screen that had derailed Jag's mood like a real Black Friday.

It all seemed so innocent, welcoming, and rewarding at first sight; a win-win situation. Just invest a small amount, as much as you want, as much as you can afford. Then watch the greens light up emerald eyes. See the glittering attractions in the window, shop till you drop!

Just a simple click for Jag to satisfy his immediate desires. That's all it was for him.

So easy.

Like clicking without consequence, as if clicking on the mouse was divorced from the fact that each click was a transaction. It was all too easy. All too easy to swallow then, but too difficult to digest now. It would take more than a Gaviscon now to alleviate this pain.

The flashing online sign-up form had been too tempting and too easy to complete. A golden buzzer filled with anticipation. As he had filled in the online form, he had no idea what was in store. As he hit send his heart did not even flutter a second. Now though, butterflies had overloaded his stomach.

About six months ago Jag signed up, completed the verification process, then began trading on the foreign exchange market. It was a market new to him despite his good general knowledge of business and its models.

He'd spent much of his working life in project management so was familiar with how to run a project but had never delved into investments beyond the customary Robin Hood trading that had become common place. Robin Hood trading, aka home for Mickey Mouse traders, feeding off hype and overindulgence. Traders who would do anything for their cheese.

The internet had transformed the way the world did business, made things easier and complex at the same time. Easier to transact but with more complex repercussions. A simple click, hardly audible, the squeak of a mouse, had led him down a deafening path of regret. And not at all a straight path, but one he still found himself meandering along aimlessly and reluctantly.

Reflecting, Jag returned to the task at hand. As he composed his message, he tried to compose himself at the same time. His emotions had not really recovered. For much of the day, he did feel fine; the times of the day when he was preoccupied with something else. That was the good thing about having a wife and kids. It simply meant time away from thinking about The Group. Any free time he got, it seemed he would devote to them so... bring on the family. It wasn't fun and was reason enough on its own to spend more time with the family.

It had become a strangely muddled episode in his life; needing his family to take his mind off the disturbances that occupied his mind. Any spare time he got was stressful time. An idle mind leaves room for questions. When his mind was idle, he was being bombarded with questions, the ones with no answers. It wasn't fun being Jagat Singh from the Indian Subcontinent.

His dark hands rubbed his dark brown eyes, premature bags of disappointment and sadness forming. His instinct was rubbing away the tiredness, but deeper strands of his emotion were working on those finer fibres of anxiety. His darkly tanned skin had been the victim of sporadic racism, though to him it was part and parcel of being an Indian living in the UK.

Satan doesn't need much to find mischief. Just offer an idle mind and the devil will do the rest. It certainly fitted Jag's circumstance as of late; idle hands are the devil's playthings. And his fingers, well, they had become like crooked sticks, blunted by the passions of a gambling addict. So, he went along awaiting the welcoming, ever smiling embrace of his wife and child. A smile that wiped away many tears; that erased silly lapses into uncontrollably addictive actions. These were actions his hands were forced into, he often convinced himself.

To Jag, even the mirror lied. To his family, well he had kept them in the dark; kept them in a darkness shadowed by intractable desires yet a natural gleam of hope to keep at least their lives balanced. Many times, he thought about his life and the situation it was in; discussed and disgusted at the same time with himself. Sometimes even tears came and others, he kept them out. He had at least some control left to manage certain aspects of his life.

There was very little fun left in Jag's life and in his financial and emotional rollercoaster.

CHAPTER 3

He finally hit send. The email was gone, and Jag hoped it would be a return to better days. It was an email to the National Fraud Office, based in London. It was also a strand of hope amidst a cauldron of calamity burning his insides. Despite him not really feeling particularly positive, it was still a straw that he clutched to, keeping him chained to this world, his world of false hopes. He knew that, despite the desperation, there must be hope.

He did still hold some hope in the chambers of officialdom, that just maybe, the policed yet politicised segments of the country could somehow offer a way out. It was a long shot, but one he had to take. Logically speaking, The National Fraud Office should deal with fraud.

He was learning to live, though sometimes felt like a blind man having been taught braille. He'd walked blindly into this abyss, and was now trying to stumble out.

Jag combed his hair with his fingers. His thinning hair, already receding despite only being in his late twenties. Grouped together into a side parting, if combed back, his hair would have revealed much more of his impending baldness.

So, he followed the guidelines of his newly found friends in the same boat as he; drowning together with no orchestra to help them pass the time. There must have been about thirty of them that Jag new about. All scammed by the same scammers. All of them wearing metaphorical life jackets. All of them starting to realise that they had been made a fool of. All of them knowing this did not help the situation. It made Jag and the rest of them in fact feel worse. The penny dropping slowly to the floor in a clatter, ironically turning some of them into paupers. Presently, none of them knew of each other's misery.

At the same time Jag's gifted Cross ball pen fell to the floor, a heavy instrument of beauty. He remembered receiving it as a leaving gift from former work colleagues who had passed it to him as a token of appreciation for his years with them.

He had wished for a better gift after five years working together, but that's life. They even had his name engraved along the middle of the silver pen. Perhaps a nice touch. Sometimes he thought they had probably paid per letter.

Three letters, he thought. Cheapskates.

He was just a little bitter he had not received something more useful like a tablet or smart watch. He consoled himself with the fact that it was better than a kick up the backside.

Picking up the pen, he croaked at the same time, his body starting to show signs of disappearing youth. It took him two attempts to retrieve it, the first missed attempt made him feel more frustrated. Then he slammed the laptop shut with a view to also slamming shut the thoughts of regret that plagued his mind.

Jag had managed to keep the secret away from his family. To keep from his five-year-old daughter had been easy. It was always like he was in a different world when he spent time with her. That's why he loved her company, any time of the day. It let him take his mind off his financial misfortunes. But with his wife it was different. That was when reality bit, and bit hard. It was tough at times trying to hide things from Jenny. She could read him so well, and at times, he felt like releasing it all, not holding back. But he never could summon up the courage.

CHAPTER 4

He had begun trading with The Forex Group some months ago and initially it all seemed to be going great. To start with he was advised to trade on the platform in practice mode only, to get familiar with forex trading. It seemed easy to use and friendly. The trend is your friend he would think to himself, remembering the phrase from trader talk.

Soon he took the plunge to move into actual money rather than fictitious trading. Why else did he sign up? He remembered the disclaimer now. It was horrible when he thought back to the disclaimer that he, nor anyone else ever read then like he did now, as he scoured the internet for details on what he had invested in...

> ...Trading foreign exchange on margin carries a high level of risk and may not be suitable for all investors. Past performance is not indicative of future results. Before you decide to invest in foreign exchange you should carefully consider your investment objectives, level of experience, and risk appetite. It is possible that you could sustain a loss of some, or all of your investment and you should not invest money that you cannot afford to lose...

It was now all too obvious to him. When something is too good to be true it probably is. It ended up being too bad to believe. Who reads the small print? Everyone knows you can lose but no one believes it. It was all marketed in such a way that losing money was very unlikely to happen. Like small, small print. Jag was forced to face it though. Forced to face his mirror that never lied, and that like himself, was not smiling back at him.

Initially, he enjoyed the practice account where he nonchalantly bought and sold like a millionaire's wife. Not a care in the world occupied him as he clicked his way to glory and a positive experience as well as a hypothetical bank balance. It didn't take much to impress Jag, his financial naivety ensured that. The paradox of having this financial incompetence seemed at odds with his IT and business background where he specialised. Such awareness of IT risks and related security pitfalls, yet so far away from the required knowledge of share trading, financial institutions and the manipulated chasms that followed.

Despite having Indian roots, Jag was as integrated as they came. England was his home, and he knew no other. He had only really known England, with India being a faraway land where he had been a tourist on a few occasions. Those roots had dried up a long time ago. The only fruit that remained was the indelible colour of his skin. Thankfully for him though, British society had become so multicultural that even he had become part of the painting on the wall, blending in like another dot on a William Turner landscape.

Coming from the Indian subcontinent often meant he, and those from Pakistan had become synonymous. To outsiders there was no difference. Cosmetically, it helped of course a little, being Indian as opposed to Pakistani. For him, religion didn't get in the way, and, despite occasional uncomfortable moments, he found that benefit of not having religion as a hurdle to his western materialistic lifestyle.

Setting himself up against a plethora of assaults on IT systems and devices he felt comfort, confidence, and full awareness. Despite this, when it came to his financial affairs, accounting, and investments he was lost, lost in a world of colours and numbers. Within a week Jag had decided he would transfer over an initial five thousand pounds. He didn't want to overdo things but was tempted by an offer The Forex Group had. The blurred lack of analysis was simply staggering. Jag, getting blinded by dollar signs, also ended up blocking his normal analytical logic from taking part.

Account Manager, Mark Goldsmith had given him a call. With a strong Cockney accent, Mark had been clear to Jag. 'For our new clients we're having a promotion now. If you make a transfer to begin trading with us for at least five thousand pounds, we will double it and give you an extra five thousand as a starting bonus. So far, the offer has been taken by so many clients that we have had to cut the deal short, and you must transfer your money by the end of this week to get the promotion. It's the first time we made an offer like this to our clients, and I don't expect we'll be doing it again. Such big demand you know Jag.'

Five thousand, he thought to himself, was a fairly high figure, but did not have any expectation of anything going unexpectedly wrong. He could have been told to invest fifty thousand, he would still never have thought that it could go wrong. He just saw bags of cash in his eyes.

Despite his comfort level, he traditionally was one to play it safe. He agreed with only five thousand pounds thinking it was not too much considering he would be getting another five thousand free, so already having a hundred percent profit without even lifting a finger from the mouse. Jag really felt lucky that he had stumbled upon this opportunity. Thus far it had all been his little secret, indeed one where he saw no negatives.

Mark had been honest with him. It also seemed like he had gone out of his way to offer this free bonus promotion and that it was way too generous; that's probably because it was. Funny thing was that at the time he never thought anything of it. How often do you get a free five thousand pounds? Jag just assumed that it was The Forex Group's way of developing business. Not that odd he had convinced himself. Business strategy, simple as that. Well, it wasn't the first time Mark Goldsmith had given away free money. Probably not the last either.

That had been Jag's first exposure to his new Account Manager, Mark, aka The Cockney, confident and convincing.

CHAPTER 5

For the days that followed, Jag got on with his life, and Mark, his. Many phone calls followed, with Jag asking for the occasional clarification, receiving the right answers to confusing questions. Of course, Mark was there to give the answers Jag wanted to hear. These were more administrative questions rather than related to trading in general.

'So can you explain what it means by multiplier trading Mark?' Jag had quizzed.

'Well, that's a detailed question Jag, but I'll try an' explain the friendliest way I know.' It almost sounded unprofessional as the Cockney accent was the most striking thing that Jag would always initially take from any conversation with Mark. It was like speaking to Del Boy and that didn't help things. Mark had the gift of the gab. Jag himself, had a London accent but it was not a strong accent, probably because he only came over from India in his youth and his exposure to London's youth, although plentiful, was diluted by visits from extended family from India. Furthermore, his parents still fortified his immigrant label with their broken English.

'Look Jag, if you were to buy dollars for example, you can choose a multiplier to trade at. For example, if you say you want to buy at a multiplier of 1 that means if you'll trade at 100 for example, you'll potentially gain the exact percent that your trade goes up. So, if you trade and it goes up 10% then you'll get back 110. If you choose a multiplier of 20 then that means you can effectively make 20 times the amount. It's a simple concept Jag but keep in mind that you could effectively lose the same higher amount that you could make. You can make more with a multiplier, but you can also lose more. That's why we don't recommend you use high margins. Can be risky. But it's up to you, you know.'

'Thanks Mark. Good to know and appreciate your honesty.' Jag was learning and was like a sieve. His quest for knowledge though, was starting to blur the rational nature he normally possessed. Forex trading was starting to take a logical twist to Jag. It was starting to seem like common sense to him, especially as he had made over fifty percent gains in a few days of fictitious trading on his virtual account.

Now, Jag was ready for his step up to currency trading with real money. His trading balance looked sweet at ten thousand pounds without yet having made a trade. The candlesticks on his account page lit up his imagination; seeing potential patterns as he stared hopefully at the screen.

At times it was a little confusing, relying on luck, but at other times he felt lucky; like he knew where it was going next. The trend, he thought, is my friend. With real money on the table Jag traded for the first time and he felt nervous. Ironically, the nerves multiplied after making his first trade. He felt as if he was walking along a line like a tight rope walker; time seemed suspended. He felt on edge, nervous and as if in a precarious situation he had no control over. Dealing with real money changed the game entirely for Jag.

As time passed, Jag did get more comfortable, steadied by the fact that his trades were generally quite successful. He stuck to stop losses and took profit where recommended. Soon his balance had gone up more, and with that his emotional balance improved too. His ten thousand pounds had moved onto twelve soon as his scales were getting heavier.

His discussions with Mark became less and less frequent, as a once dependent slave was breaking free from his chains. Jag felt happy at the thought of a heavier bank account, as if a weight had been lifted off his shoulders.

Wishing to seize an opportunity further, Jag transferred more and more money over the coming weeks into an already swelling foreign exchange trading account. It seemed that this was just what he needed to get his life moving forward, just the catapult to move him along the green line of hope emotionally and financially. It wasn't like he was short of a few bob, just that no amount of money is ever enough. Give man a million and he'll want a million more. When will he be happy?

As his trading balance continued to swell, and as he continued to add more and more funds to allow it to balloon even more, it never even struck his mind why The Forex Group had their bank account and business set up in the Marshall Islands. Also, why did they always ask him to transfer the funds to Slovakia. There were moments when he did consider why, but they were only fleeting moments amongst a room full of satisfaction and greed.

Slovakia! To be honest, he hardly even knew where that was! All he cared about was the fact that his balance was swelling like a city bankers' stomach.

It was the convenience as well. Often financial investment companies would not allow you to transfer via credit card. But with The Forex Group, that was no issue. They were happy to receive payments any amount, any way. It was just so convenient for Jag; making money had become so convenient. Too easy.

It was only later that it struck Jag how easy and painless the account set up process had been. Normally there was a million forms to complete and statements to give. Normally letters from the bank or verified passport copies or bill statements. But not this time. It had just been so damn simple, addictive, and friendly. Jag never knew making money was that easy, until he found out it wasn't. There was simply a form to complete and one bill statement to submit. Nice and easy.

CHAPTER 6

A month or so had passed, and Jag had a swelling trading balance partly through successful trades but also due to the number of bank and credit card transfers he had made.

There had been other bonuses Mark Goldsmith had given him, despite previously mentioning the company had given too many bonuses and would need to withdraw this promotion. You could say conveniently, at least for Mark, but Jag had overlooked that little detail and had been transferring repeatedly partly due to the bonuses on the table. Jag just got blinded by the figures rising and rising in his online balance.

It seemed to be a happy time for Jagat Singh. To be honest it was, but he did not realise the web of deceit he was living in. He was just living in a dream he didn't want to end.

The first signs that things were not as he thought were about month after opening the account. He'd transferred via credit card and bank transfer into various trust pay accounts. He did think it a little odd why the receiving account changed on more than one occasion but again, the dollars in front of his eyes blinded the peripheral glimpses of reality in the distance.

In an email to Mark, he wanted to see the trading balance statement of his account. It seemed like a normal request, and one which should have been set up to begin with by Mark. But this time, his request was treated a little defensively by his account manager. The amity between the two of them kept things civil, but Jag did raise an eyebrow as if in a little discomfort. Jag never got a reply from the email so took his mission onto the phone.

'Hi Mark, as I've been trading for a few weeks now, is it possible to get a statement of my activities and transactions? I mean just to give me a picture of things?' It was a polite, almost timid request for something not out of the ordinary at all.

'Hi, Jag. I'm sure we can provide a statement for you to let you know how things are going. But why do you need it? You can see your balance online?' Mark was right, though Jag was not exactly asking for anything out of the ordinary.

'Also, Mark, could you arrange monthly statements so that I can track how things are going? Again, it's only so that I can manage and plan things better.' This time Jag was a bit more forceful, as he was taken a little by surprise by the reluctance of Mark. All he wanted was a simple account balance statement that, in Jag's eyes, probably was automatically generated anyway.

'Not a problem, Jag. Let me discuss with Accounts and I'm sure we'll be able to get you that, mate.' It was the usual casual interaction that Mark preferred, keeping things as informal as he could. He realized that Jag was being a little more forceful and wanted to appease the situation.

A few days later Jag received an email from Mark. It was a simple one-line email with no footer, signature or electronic business card. It was something Jag had grown used to, unprofessional emails from Mark and his team. He was used to it by now. Attached in the email was an Excel file called 'Statement_jag.xlsx'. A few clicks and it was downloaded. The balance was correct and other details too, but it just seemed too unprofessional. Anyone could have created the statement. There was no company stamp or logo or pdf style download. It was simply what seemed to be a basic spreadsheet that a child could have made.

That was the first time that Jag started having doubts about his investment, and the people he was investing with. He'd never met Mark or anyone from The Forex Group. Their website was good, no doubt in that. But their style of business and interaction left a lot of room for improvement.

Jag had invested sixty thousand pounds of his hard-earned money into the trading account by now and despite having a trading balance of over a hundred thousand now, he was starting to feel a little uneasy. Uneasy because he had now so much invested, but also the amateurish way that his account manager dealt with him.

The tingle of an alarm bell way in the distance put a few questions into his mind. He had a lot of money resting with the trading company and felt something was not quite right.

The bells got a little louder the following month as the supposed monthly account balance statement from Mark never arrived. Things were starting to feel more and more uncomfortable as Jag's trading balance swelled more and more. There was no apology or even acknowledgement from The Forex Group. As if it had accidentally, conveniently, or even intentionally, been forgotten. It all added to Jag's disappointment as well as his alarm at the company's antics.

CHAPTER 7

The bells that rang inside Jag's head got him to change strategy. Admittedly it wasn't exactly a hostile relationship he was having with Mark, but one of caution. Mark had guided him nicely and helped in this extremely successful venture so far. But, as was becoming more and more clear, something was not right. Subsequently, Jag gave a call to Mark the following Monday.

'Hi, Mark. How are you doing? You had a nice weekend?'

'Good morning, Jag. All good from my side. Just suffering from allergies, you know?' Allergies were common in the UK and the greater London area was no exception. As Mark spoke, he continuously sniffled, as if trying to prove his point. Jag didn't need the sniffles, he believed Mark, though that could not have been said for all sides of their relationship.

'Yes, Mark. You don't need to tell me. In the summer I get it myself but I'm good at the moment. Listen, I wanted to ask one thing about the account. It's going great now I know, but I was wondering about withdrawing some funds as I just needed a few things, had a few commitments. What you think, when can this be arranged?'

An awkward silence followed. It was only a second or so, but felt much longer, especially to Jag. He didn't really need the withdrawal funds. He was just starting to feel a little unsure with the company and needed this as a kind of reassurance. He felt he needed to test the water. There was also no need to give his reasons to Mark.

Why on earth do I need to even explain to Mark why I need the money?

It's my money to start with!

Why am I even beginning to make it look like I'm begging him for my own money? Jag knew full well why. It was clear to him right from the beginning. He had become nervous about this whole investment venture. He didn't want to rock the boat in any way and felt like being as polite as possible to get the outcome he wanted.

There was a hesitation. Maybe it was the phone line or maybe the allergies? Maybe it was just a natural delay? Or maybe it was his old friend, Cockney Mark, who was weighing up the request, not that he even had the right to do so. In his mind, Jag was playing a million storylines, all potential disasters that of course did not have happy endings.

'Well, Jag, it's a bit difficult to withdraw funds,' Mark finally said, breaking the heavy and painful silence. 'The problem is that you took so many bonuses from us after the transfers you made. Because of that it's kind of impossible to withdraw any funds. It's a little precarious but part of the policy and one of the implications when you take advantage of the transfer bonus option. Not sure what we're able to do, Jag.'

It was a real shocker for Jag who really did not need that excuse from Mark. What the hell did he mean, '... kind of impossible?'

'So, when can I withdraw my money then?' It was the inevitable follow up question. Almost sarcastically Jag stressed the word '... my.' It was a question Jag knew he had to ask, and one Mark knew was coming, but Jag didn't like the way this dialogue was going.

'Well, we must keep the funds related to the bonus for at least six months, Jag. It's just so we're able to invest as positively as possible for you, Jag. I hope it makes sense. It's for your benefit.' But to Jag it neither made sense or logic. It just felt like a random response from thin air; thin air to go with the tension, thick with scepticism.

Even before the conversation had started, Jag was brimming with doubt and suspicion. His whole reason to call Mark in the first place was because he wanted some tangible return in his bank account. His whole state of mind was overdosed on insecurity and lack of clarity. The last thing he needed was to be drugged even more by man in a suit.

Six months! Six months! Six months!

It didn't change regardless of the number of times his conscience was going to tell him the duration. At least six months!

Well, at least over a month had passed so far. Another four and a half months, he consoled to himself, was not too far away.

Not too far away! Are you mad, Mr. Singh?

It was that high pitched voice again adding to the alarm bells resonating in his ears. Despite his yearning, and lust for some salvation, he could not find any; like he was looking for a needle in a needle-less haystack.

'So, Mark, what can I do now?' It was like a man in an Escape Room knowing the time was up and having used up all hints. It was time for Jag to take the hint. The bottom line that kept staring him the face.

You're not going to see any of that money, Jag. All gone, mate, all gone...

It was a thought that Jag knew he couldn't keep hidden forever inside is tiny little brain. A brain polluted with marketing and false promises. A brain diluted with the dust of green lines that now looked more like lines of envy and hatred to a company that up till now had not paid him a penny, despite over a month of regular transfers Jag had made.

He was in a delicate situation. What could he do? He couldn't start screaming foul for the risk of things going even more distressing. Clearly things could get worse. Taking a step back he analysed the situation. He had invested sixty thousand pounds, and now with over a hundred thousand as his balance, he could just patiently and perhaps subserviently wait only a few more months and he could be rich. Things could be worse, a lot worse.

With this he consoled himself as the green lines of envy turned a little less erratic.

CHAPTER 8

A few more months passed as Jag's trading balance continued to swell. This high frequency trading was effective, but niggling in the back of his mind was the fear that all his gains could turn into nothing if The Forex Group folded or just shut down their operations, or even if they just turned around and blew a raspberry in his face.

It was only in hindsight that some logical thoughts tried to warn him. Before that, in the real, he simply happily went day to day, comfortably numb, consulting in his day job whilst spending evenings engrossed with his green and red lines, spending less and less time with his wife and child.

There were moments in the day when he would sit back and reflect, reflect in fear. But those moments were fleeting and seemed to cause him only little lasting discomfort. He was clearly oblivious to the gravity of the situation, in denial. It never really struck him until it was too late. It was as if his mind was playing snakes and ladders with himself.

It never struck him as odd that some days he was transferring money to Bratislava to some random Trust Pay account, and others to the Marshall Islands, a place he had only vaguely heard of. To him it was just a remote island. It sounded like a deserted island that he had never heard of before. Well soon, he was going to wish he never had heard of it again as it would come back to haunt him; a shipwrecked survivor on a desert island.

And it was ironic. Each time Jag made his transfers from his personal account to his other somewhat fictitious account with The Forex Group, he didn't even give it a second thought, despite that little man in the back of his mind screaming angry reminder after reminder at him. It was like the voice of reason amidst the cauldron of deception.

Jag seemed to have found Neverland; a place that only existing in the confines of his own head. A dream that could not unite with the day. Well at least for a while, it was in fact a happy place.

CHAPTER 9

And then close to eight months had passed. Eight months since his first dealing with The Forex Group. This eighth month meant that Jag could request some of his investment back. It was a milestone month! Eight months was what he had been waiting for. Eight had become his favourite number!

There was a mixture of nervous excitement and anticipation as Jag started on his email to Mark in expectation of his payment. Even at this stage he only wanted a token transfer to be made to himself. He was happily making big bucks with The Forex Group, so why would he want to take too much out when he could use that money to make even more money? The so-called penny, (or pound) had still not dropped for Jag. It might sound amazing, but he was so engrossed in life and was making so much money that it did not even occur to him.

Email: Transfer

Hi Mark,

I hope you are well. Just a request that as we are approaching the eighth month of my investment, could I request a transfer to my personal account for £20,000.

Thanks for the support and hope we can continue with the successful trading.

BTW, I stopped receiving the monthly trading statements some time ago. Can you please set this up again?

Regards and Thanks,

Jagat Singh

Jag sent the email. He had called Mark also, but the secretary who answered said he was not available and would get him to call back. That had been in the morning and no call was forthcoming. It didn't concern Jag too much as over past few months he had grown used to this erratic behaviour from his account manager.

***

Jag refreshed his email. A new email had arrived.

```
Email: Re: Transfer

Hi,
This is an automated response.
I am just on my month of gardening leave. Therefore,
I am unable to directly help with this matter.
Please contact the office directly, or send an email
to admin@theforexgroup.com

Kind Regards,
Mark Goldsmith
Senior Account Manager
```

It was a bit of a surprise. Mark had never mentioned any plans to be away, and gardening leave, well that was just a façade normally to say you were not going to be available for a long time. More dauntingly, it suggested his old Cockney friend was not hanging around for too long at all. This, again, took him some time to realise. The penny (or pound) was again slow to drop. This time though, it dropped with a clang.

For the first time Jag did not like it. There had been alarm bell moments in the past few months, but his mind had managed to dismiss those away. He was not sure what to do next. First thing he did was check what exactly was meant by 'Gardening Leave'. He wished he hadn't checked, especially after realising that it meant Mark had, for some reason left the company or been told to leave. He had left without any words for Jag, and to be honest, that left him speechless.

All he could do for the first few minutes was imagine Mark sat there in his back garden on a deck chair soaking up the sun, fresh from an afternoon of getting his fingers lovely and green. Worse still, he saw Mark smiling at him, lifting a drink with the words 'Cheers' being the only supposedly friendly, yet sardonic words that escaped his mouth. It was like the ironic grin of a fraudster, proud of his accomplishments.

A bead of sweat dripped from Mark's brow as he took in the beautiful English weather. Don't be fooled; it was not the sweat of a guilty or laborious worker, rather that of a man knowing he'd hit the jackpot whilst his collar remained white. Jag thought he could find an insolent grin right across Mark's face that bled a tone of someone chuffed to bits.

Now it was Jag's turn to feel that familiar moist perspiration form on his head. This time though, it wasn't due to warm weather or in any way connected to the somnolence of summer. There was nothing refreshing about the beads of sweat that strangled Jag. It was a perspiration coupled with palpitation, that he could only twin with anger and antagonised rage. But still, a rage caged up like a controlled psychopath.

This was the quagmire he found himself embroiled in, up to his waist and rising. This was the pathetic realisation that was swallowing him up like a great swamp creature. It was the daunting floods of a monsoon that he found himself drowning in at increasing speed.

Jag had always been a level-headed kind of guy, and this situation, despite being above average in terms of importance, still left him not caving into emotional suicide. Often his surroundings did hit him, but only after some time, and he always found some bright side to look at. He had to keep things together for his wife and child. It was the way he lived; the only way he knew how. So, despite the internal turmoil, he never let these financial disturbances get in the way of his artificially stabilised life. It had been his approach and it worked well, or at least he pictured it that way.

Why had Jag waited so long to realise something was wrong?

Well, his mind did have the odd feeling that something did not feel right. The other part of him, the more predominant part, had convinced him otherwise. The eight-month trigger had been a milestone. The point at which he could request a payment from his investment. And that was what Jag was holding onto. Holding onto a glimmer of hope.

Hoping… dreaming… willing… praying that The Forex Group would come good and make their payment.

CHAPTER 10

Bloody Gardening Leave!

What was going on? He would have to find out. He began by emailing as many people as possible he knew from The Forex Group, and probably most importantly, the support email for the company. A part of him, the part that dreamed, still had hope that things would turn out okay. He just needed to keep communicating with them until they got back to him.

His emotions were so flipped at this point that he was willing to side with the emotion in his head telling him that things will turn out just fine. The thought of losing that much money! It just jarred with him. There was no logic to it. Put it down to the difficulty of accepting making a silly mistake. A huge mistake! Part of his mind just did not want to go there.

The next day an email came in from Mike Goodchild, Head of Administration. He gave his sincere apologies to Jag. Explaining that Mark had left the company, Mike confirmed that things would get back to normal soon as there was restructuring going on in the company. That though, was the last email he would receive from Mike!

For some time, things went silent on The Forex Group front. His money was stuck, and it seemed they had all gone incommunicado. Each time he went to his trading platform he was almost expecting something to go wrong. It was no way to live. He was expecting a HTTP or website error, half expecting the website to go down any day. There was nothing but negativity.

So, Jag decided enough was enough. Into the Google search bar, he typed in the words 'the forex group scam'. A huge part of him did not want to do it; did not have the courage to see what was on the other side. But as so much time had passed, he really had no choice. It was one of the worst moments of his life, stepping into the unknown where one would not want to step into even if you knew what was behind that door… or Window.

Hitting ENTER was like allowing to worst thoughts and feelings to come and embrace him like Satan. The kind that made Monsters Inc. look like real child's play without any Chuckles... or maybe with!

His reluctant fingertips brushed the ENTER button with hesitation mixed with that familiar craven edge that always taunted him. The results of the search, well it was partly what he expected, exemplifying the asinine behaviour he had inside him. That almost juvenile ability to fall for the most obvious of tricks. It was not the first time he had been fooled and shown that gullible trait. His fingers had stuttered over the ENTER button like a scared rabbit staring into lights, minute shivers gliding over letters.

Just the thought, even more than the actuality of writing the word 'scam' hurt and embarrassed him. Having to contemplate the repercussions of being a victim of fraud was a place he did not at all want or expect to ever enter. Doors and windows to that place, plagued with viruses and worms, malicious and insecure.

Enter at your peril, to a web-tangled world of lies and deceit, where no one knows me from you. Where men can become women and bots long to become your best friend. A world of information overdosed on misinformation.

Enter the world of the scam; a world of the entrepreneur from the circus of the underworld, making clowns out of gullible fools. Roll up, roll up, buy your tickets to enter this tent of travesty. The superhighway of information blurring avenues of hope and honesty. Tarantula claws, so unwelcoming yet enticing, allured those looking and tempted by the idiom 'No Pain, No Gain'. Jag had been one of the tempted; one of the ones coaxed into this plexus of nerves like red and green webs, sticking to him, allowing no escape, and in fact opening more and more windows of false ambition, whilst at the same time closing a plethora of dreams.

Here come the clowns!

CHAPTER 11

Jag finally hit the button. Then he felt that claustrophobia that had drained him on occasion. That emotional congestion that had blocked his mind. Jag had a history of suffering from claustrophobia, suffocating and terrifying.

His mind drifted...

He recalled about fifteen years back following long term headaches with no explanation. He remembered so many days of unanswered questions, migraines for no apparent reason. It all led him down the familiar uncomfortable path to the doctor for his cure. The cure never came, but thankfully a potential solution did. In the end, following numerous visits he eventually was sent for his MRI. It was an experience he could never forget, one which often came back to haunt him.

Many weeks of unexplained headaches and migraines had invaded Jag whilst on an IT project. He had put it down to a few possible reasons. Perhaps the long-distance driving or the lack of sleep. Though he didn't think it was the long hours at the office, that did not help.

In his youth he had been plagued with these migraines, but just got used to them. They were a part of him, and he had learned to live with the burden. At the onset of a migraine, he would head to his medicine box for his salvation going under the name of Micure, his cure for migraines.

Those killer migraines. There was a yellow tablet to take initially with the onset of a migraine. Sometimes he caught it in time, if he was lucky. On those occasions it would be his lucky day, and he knew that catching it early would nip it in the bud and the day would play out much more auspiciously. Once caught, he would be fine for a few days or weeks, waiting for the next time his ailment would pounce on him. It was like a Rottweiler waiting in the back of his mind.

If not caught on time, or if he did not have that wonderful yellow pill to hand, he would have to move onto the powerful red pill. Rottweilers must not like red for some reason. The red pill was bigger than the yellow pill, perhaps intentionally, knowing that it was more efficacious. That red pill even looked more like the real deal but came with alarm bells. No second chances when it came to that bad boy.

When it came to the red pill, Jag knew that there was trouble ahead. He knew that if the red pill was needed there was going to be collateral damage. The kind that resulted in agonising pain that would normally last days rather than hours. Sometimes he wondered what the point of this infamous red pill was. It didn't stop the pain, that much was sure.

The pangs that remained, elongating his torture, a throbbing, pulsing, rhythmic pain often to the beat of a Neil Peart solo. Mystic rhythms beating as an after-effect, head banging and brain numbing. That was how the migraines felt to Jag. Sometimes it felt like the headache was never going to go away, like an acquaintance you just can't shake off. Someone you've known for years yet hated having to stop by and say hello to. Someone who could natter you to death, literally!

His migraines, yes, they were severe, especially in his youth, but they had become less so over time, and that was something to be grateful for; life rejuvenated in a beat. But he knew another one could be just around the corner to drive him around the bend once again.

The migraines that antagonised him for years had suddenly become less frequent.

But some time back, when he was on his IT project in the south of England, he had an extremely severe attack. His headaches still lurked in the back of his forgetful mind, waiting to pounce.

Well, this day, the tiger had been unleashed.

Yellow, or red, nothing worked; blinded into darkness. It didn't matter what damn colour they gave these pills! This time it lasted for days; a familiar resonating beat consistently struck at the top right of his head. It was a gremlin that was stuck inside his head trying to escape. That gremlin, that quarrelsome gremlin, thinking that the only way out was via the top right of his head. To Jag, it did not want to get out. Maybe it was someone chiselling away trying to get into his mind? Either way, the pulsating throbbing was incessant.

Release me, release me... or I'll continue to hammer away on my anvil.

Palpitations breathed through the hair follicles that adorned Jag's head, but no relief was in sight.

And thus, the headache that started as a migraine of stars imprinted into his vision had become like a galaxy of pulsars feeding off him. This time he had no choice but to go to the doctor. And, after a catalogue of visits, he found his story only got worse.

The headaches subsided but the history remained, and Jag was requested to have the MRI to try to analyse why he had experienced such a severe migraine. Part of it was the fact that Jag had private health insurance, which was pretty comprehensive, and where private insurance was involved, there was almost always a financial desire for as much invasive treatment as possible.

Almost directly opposite to the NHS, his private consultation almost inevitably resulted in him being requested to have further analysis. For Jag, it was not really what he wanted but he did not object. If a doctor tells you to do one thing you are reluctant to do the other.

'Please change into the gown, Mr. Singh,' the nurse requested casually. Jag just followed orders. At this stage he was a little uncomfortable, not one to enjoy the inside of a hospital any day of the week.

It had been about five days since his migraine hit and finally subsided, and it was amazing just how quickly he had managed to get the appointment for his scan. One of the wonders of private health and the financial pleasures that came with it. He recalled never having an MRI before but knew a little about MRI machines and most notably doughnut shaped ones as well as full body machines. He was just hoping it was a doughnut. Be a nice, sweet doughnut, please!

It was like a puzzle trying to figure out how to put the gown on. Jag was discombobulated, figuring out even where to put his arms. Which was the front and which the back? It didn't help to allay his fears and confusion prior to the scan.

Eventually he figured it out, a sigh of relief accompanying his achievements, as if he had just completed a two-thousand-piece jigsaw. Still, the knots tied on the various strings of the gown were probably tied wrong he thought to himself. His self-inflicted straitjacket was starting to look at least a little bit more secure though. The knots that tied his mind and constricted his emotions, they were a little more concerning.

On his return from the changing room, the nurse's greeting from her eyes told him that yes, he had, as expected, messed up putting on his gown. But what the hell, it was something she had seen a million times and more.

Why were operative gowns made so complicated anyway?

He fiddled nervously with the strings and tassels that hung loosely and unprofessionally. For a second, he felt like Oliver Hardy fumbling with his tie. It sure felt like a fine mess he was in.

Moving into the MRI scanning room it hit him immediately. Like an electric shock combined with expectant fear that then turned into trepidation. It was there, pretty much in the middle of the room, just to make sure you don't miss it.

But who could miss it?

It was an MRI room, wasn't it?

The magnetic resonance imaging machine sat there plain to see. It wasn't intimidating to most, but to Jag, it was not what he was looking forward to seeing.

You did come for an MRI scan, Jag! What were you expecting, a garden full of sunflowers?

Jag did not like it one bit. Certainly, did not smell like roses, or sweet sunflowers for that matter. The reason he wanted the Open Unit MRI machine was clear to Jag but not to others. More specifically, the medical staff, of course they noticed his hesitation.

Jag was claustrophobic, and was unsure, having seen the shape of this machine. His fidgeting now had become a little excessive, palms beginning to sweat. Trying to persuade himself to breathe, he started in the direction of the machine, having to remind himself to breathe. Wow, that was a challenge considering it was normally the last thing you need to do.

Breathe you fool, breathe!

But it was like trying to teach a child algebra. Each step seemed like a marathon, the tickertape in the distance. With each step the sounds of Vangelis grew stronger. There was irony. As he approached the tickertape and got closer it should have been a victorious feeling for Jag. Instead, with each step, not only did the music rise, so did his heartbeat! And the keyboards roared him on, unlocking his way to victory.

Each step forward was like an emotional step back, feet getting heavier with each step. His lead feet seemed stuck to the floor, as the most menial of tasks became monstrous. He felt like Thor would feel if unable to lift his hammer. Yet each step, despite being a challenge, was in fact progress; the grip on the hammer feeling more comfortable with each passing second. It was like he was trying to convince himself of that as well. Not doing a great job though.

Glancing around for support and guidance he gestured towards the nurse for the next instruction. He was like a mute in a room of blind people. 'You want me in this side? Should I take my slippers off?' They were normal questions but by now Jag felt small, weak, and useless, like a blunt pencil. The words just stumbled out of him, like an even more unsure Mr. Bean.

'Oh, oh it's fine, Sir. Just come over to this side please, Mr. Singh and lie down here please.' She directed him kindly, sensing a kind of unease in his actions to ameliorate the situation. She said, 'lie down,' to him, but she easily could have said 'lay down,' such was his resemblance now to something almost inanimate. Regardless, it was a relaxing friendly tone and was welcomed by Jag. He obliged, hesitating but naturally compelled to follow suit.

Despite him asking about the slippers, there had been no response from the nurse. As he sat on the hard plastic bed, he just automatically started to take off his slippers, as if settling into a good night's rest. 'That's fine, Mr. Singh, you can take off your slippers.' He had guessed right, a tiny victory for him in his decathlon-like mission.

As he considered the bed, a thought came to him. How can you even call this a bed? More like a table he thought... and he was like the slab of meat, awaiting the slaughter. He half expected to look left and right and find cleavers, blood and that horrible stench that accompanied the proximity of a butcher's shop.

Then he lay down and was given some huge, completely unfashionable headphones that you would never even be seen dead wearing! Fitting, as he was starting to feel like the living dead!

He moved the headphones towards his ears naturally, finding very tinny and unattractive music. It was almost like an additional portion of torture being asked to listen to the loud sounds of some dance music that he wouldn't listen to by choice. Jag coerced himself to at least try to listen.

Lying down, he heard the sound of motion. The sound was the vibration of this so-called bed retracting back into position, its final position?

Simultaneously, the image of the world seemingly saying goodbye as he was being caged into his box. It was a feeling he had never felt before. Pure and simple, it was like he was being pushed into his grave.

Being pushed into your grave, well that is a feeling you're not likely to have often. A once in a lifetime experience, unforgettable, yet at the same time unrecognisable. Unrecognisable, simply because having happened, you are not alive to recollect it!

He felt like he was being buried alive!

That was the only thought that swallowed up his mind; that suffocated him. That, and the feeling of drowning. That horrible feeling of spending too much time under water with nowhere to go, but down.

It was a combination of emotions, all devastatingly horrific. And when the covering appeared above his head, that was pure and simply the lid of the coffin.

Nothing more, nothing less!

Nothing but negative thoughts reigned as the dull metallic sound tortured him as a side effect. A head banger drifting into never-never land.

The sliding lid above his head seemed to Jag like it was literally touching him, literally shaving the tops of his eyebrows. It wasn't that close, but it felt like it to him. There was no silver lining he could envisage, only the lining of the hard plastic top of the MRI machine.

Suddenly the headaches did not seem that bad anymore. The migraines, confused vision, pulsating pains; they all seemed to be heaven compared to this. Anything could be bearable in comparison to this!

How do people choose to do this he thought? How did I choose to do this? A self-inflicted sadistic punishment out of this world, yet real and in it!

And in that moment, he realised that the grass was not greener, not at all. It was just a mirage of reeds that looked secure, but that in fact simply shielded the deep swamp below. Life was not better on the other side, he now realised.

He closed his eyes as the drums blurred on and the sliding roof droned forward. Was it the drums of the music on his old, antiquated headphones or the drum roll of the beefeater beckoning the inevitable?

The Master of Puppets was pulling his strings now. The drone of the MRI machine roof, or that of an unidentified flying object from a Martian landscape coaxing him into the unknown. Either way, it was a journey into an unknown world for Jag. One he was not welcoming with open arms.

CHAPTER 12

It was no fun. Not for the doctor. Not for the nurse. And of course, not for Jag.

Who would enjoy being placed inside this tomb? Maybe only an Egyptian? What was supposed to be helpful to Jag and his condition had turned into a psychological nightmare. He tried to settle down and relax, listening to the terrible music supposed to distract his ears from the mechanical resonance.

He only lasted a few minutes. Being given an orange squeezable ball that looked so much like a 1920's bicycle horn, he was told to press it in case attention was needed. It had a tube connecting it to the machine, only to be used in case of emergency. Well, this was an emergency. This squeezable ball felt like his heart, and the tubes, they the arteries; in tandem they had become his lifeline. And he felt like he was having a heart attack.

Not even two minutes had passed until Jag felt his emergency. He squeezed without hesitation and the ride along his road of pain clearly had immovable objects in the distance; cholesterol blocking the path. I don't want to ride my bicycle, he thought.

His journey in his globe of death had come full circle as he found he could take no more. The pump of air he squeezed made no sound, other than the imaginary toot of a bicycle on a Sunday afternoon. Sending invisible rays of hope to outside forces, the hero stood in the sidelines waiting to rescue him. There was also embarrassment tinged with his squeezing, as if self-consciously letting out a great fart. But there was no humour in this release of air, only the odour of awkwardness that had polluted his airways.

It had always been in the back of his mind that he was claustrophobic, but it had never really transformed itself into reality. He liked to call it mild. At least that made it sound better, less headline grabbing. It was like a devil hidden inside him waiting patiently. Today was its big day; a day of reckoning; a day of judgement.

He recalled a time, way back, when he was very young. He must have only been nine or ten then. A time so far back that only momentary clippings of his life were available for recollection. Only significant glimpses of life could be recalled of those times. It was a time when his youth, as anyone's youth, only selected standout moments to save to the hard drive of his life. Like indelible photos of his past, they marked his future.

He would regularly play out after school in the park nearby with some friends. Arguments were normal, as were the confrontations for power and the right to at least feel the most powerful in the tiny democracy that ruled them. Random outbursts and challenges littered those afternoons in the park near his parents' house.

On one such occasion, he was playing a game of Chase the Ace with some of his friends. It had been a game they often played when bored, other than cricket or football. One would be the Ace and the others would have to track him down and make the ace immobile. A bit like rugby without the ball.

He was always a swift runner so managed to evade the others quite easily, but that led to jealously and envy from them. Being the Ace, he usually managed to avoid the runs of the other jokers, and their intentions of catching him. He always wanted to be the Ace and was often inspired to live up to that reputation.

Their only real proven way of catching Jag was through teamwork, collusion, cheating, whatever you want to call it. And even that didn't bother him too much because he usually managed to evade those plans as well. It made him feel superior and always with an upper hand on the others.

On one occasion though, his swift movements as the weight of being the Ace caught up with him, or maybe it was his over confidence. Darting one way then the next, he was like a swallow in the sky, well adapted to his role. A slight misjudgement though, and he found himself not actually cornered, but metaphorically so. He jerked, and overly so, trying to avoid getting caught by Trig, one of his friends. Trig's partner, Curt, first eyed-up Trig, then took his vision to Jag to perhaps hypnotise him. Mental hypnosis of course did not work, but his physical ability and coordination with Trig proved more auspicious.

Once in a lifetime these opportunities came along. Jag was trapped despite swift efforts to evade the attackers. Jerking left and right, up, and down, he only found himself crash into the elbow of Curt, who groaned in pain as his funny bone did not see the lighter side.

Jag was caught between the two, and it took both to get him down and under control. There was clear satisfaction being felt by his two assailants but that was part of the game, why they played it.

The Ace had been trumped. Now face the consequences.

Jag jerked and squirmed around like a dying snake on the grass fighting for its life. When the final pangs are staring you in the face, whatever type of living creature you are, it's the only way to react. But like the inevitable final pangs of life, they too would come to an end at some point.

He was pinned down now by the two of them like nails on a tent, or maybe a coffin. Occasional frantic surges left his body as he tried until the end to break free, almost like a bluebottle trying indefatigably to save its losing cause. But it was no good. They were too powerful, especially when the two of them joined forces. So, he gave in and fell to submission hoping that would be the end of it. Curt was now kneeling over his chest and Trig held his legs down. There was no escape.

But that was just the start of it. Held down, like a nail in a coffin, he suddenly felt a real urgency to breathe. It was like something was being held over his mouth, stopping him from even trying to take a breath. It was real panic he felt. Like his chest had just been filled to the brim with water and all that surrounded him was nothing but, you guessed it, water. Like a combination of drowning and being buried alive, Jag was just stuck in this big mess. There were no thoughts really at this stage, just a metaphorical conflagration of smoke pulverising his lungs.

He simply couldn't breathe. His two friends could have been holding a cushion over his mouth for all he knew, it was that suffocating. At first, they were oblivious to the internal wrangling that had overtaken him. They naturally thought he was still showing a feisty appetite for the game they were playing rather than realising his body was being starved of oxygen and hope. Maybe his throat had got blocked with something or his windpipe was just refusing to work.

There was nothing but alarm and chaos that rang in his ears. Impulsive jerks in all directions were all that emanated from him. It was like he was on the electric chair after the switch had been turned on. The buzz of electricity popping his veins. And it felt like he was almost drifting in and out of consciousness, though only for fractions of a second as the panic still showed itself to be prominent.

Then the two boys began to realise it was not right and they simultaneously realised Jag was not acting. It was as if they were marking the end of the game. Chase the Ace was no more as a silence overtook them all, especially Jag. He just sat there, deflated, and confused. Yes, he had been chased down, and that was a defeat he wasn't used to. But more distressing was the set of emotions that he had felt. He had no desire to discuss the strange fear that had suffocated him just now.

It made no sense to him, so how could he explain it to a bunch of giggling victorious kids? Trying to explain to them that he couldn't breathe under their weight and control would have been too daunting and damaging to his esteem. So, he sat there for a few seconds, finally managing to enjoy some oxygen, though enjoy was no doubt an exaggeration.

He was just, for once, gratified at being alive. It had been the closest he had ever felt to death, or at least not being alive, escaping from a place where he firmly felt like he had been drifting in and out of this world. The sighs of relief were long and hard as he sat on the grass, arms crossed over his bent knees.

He tried to mask his shock, and did a pretty good job of it, though was clearly subdued for the rest of the day. ‘So, what happened, Ace? You the joker in the pack now, Jag.’ Curt spoke in patronising tones, glowing about his victory. He seldom encountered victory over Jag so wanted to enjoy it. He had to milk his moment the best he could.

The delayed response finally came with less emotion than normal. ‘Yeah, this time, Curty, but won't happen again.’ But it didn't have much conviction as Jag gave his judgement. ‘I think I must have slipped or something.’ In the back of Jag's mind that ‘something’ took on another angle and he didn't really understand what. That feeling of walls closing in on him.

For the first time in his life at that young age he felt that bone crushing tension of claustrophobia. It was just that, at that young age, he didn't understand it at all, thinking it was just an isolated emotion that maybe he was just having a bad day. But it would not be his last bad day, perhaps just his first.

CHAPTER 13

Harsh reality, anticipation, reluctance, they all gave way to an inevitable trepidation that could be read on Jag's face like the webpage results. He knew what he would see but that didn't make things okay after seeing them. Forum result displays from the internet page showed the writing on the wall, or window to be precise.

'I have been scammed,' Jag read out aloud to himself. They were the first few words that stared at him as he scanned the page. Wherever he looked, scratching for salvation, those unfortunate words kept the wound from healing. Those words were like the salt on his already lacerated skin.

Now feeling brave enough, he clicked on the link, half hoping it would reveal a clown blowing a party horn, and it all being a big harmless joke. But the joke was at his expense. There were no clowns on the other side of the screen; only the one that looked at him through the window, or on the other side of the mirror.

Then Jag read with a concentration suspended in mid-air, finding himself engrossed in the catalogue of catastrophes that littered the pages of the website. It was like opening the door to his first alcoholics anonymous session, but without any relief. From a human side, it felt like each post was a victim's vomit spewed painfully out onto the page. His stomach turned.

He tried to understand user after user, wrenching out his own heart, placing it on display in a show of open embarrassment, plain for all to see. It was an exhibition without the artistry, a museum without masterpieces. Only naked, humiliated tears of blood in a sordid and candid display of devastation.

And it wasn't just one website. Others followed like rats following the piper, zombies handing over their sob stories like they had done so, their money. The

Forex Group had become a dirty word on parts of the internet, and big parts at that. A dirty word in a dirty world.

But what would they care? The likes of Mark Goldsmith, et al, playing games with people's money and life. Jag figured now that these games The Forex Group had been playing were now so bloody obvious!

Now the pieces of that awkward jigsaw were starting to fit together. Others on the website revealed they had lost their life's savings, all on a whim. And Jag too, now he realised how easy the set-up process had been, how odd the money transfer process had been, each penny dropping like a gold bullion.

Jag was beginning to feel like a penny was starting to drop. He wanted someone to blame, other than himself. How unprofessional and absent the monthly statements from Mark had been and how aloof he had been. Was Jag jumping to conclusions about Mark? Maybe Mark too, was just another pawn in this chess game with no mates?

As his fingers scrolled through the sites, sighs and gulps provided gaps in his realisation. At the same time, he searched attentively for strands of hope, looking for that needle. Haystacks in abundance, but no needles.

Then one post he spent a little longer on. It read as follows...

I have seen many posts and personally know of many of us who have been badly scammed by The Forex Group and have set up an email group to try to plan a way of getting back our money. Join me in this effort. The more of us who can make noise and plan effectively, the more the chances of being successful. Email me.

That post stuck out to Jag, and he read it over and over in contemplation. It gave Jag hope once again, hope and contemplation.

Then the sound of his wife in the distance rescued him from this insanity, from this world far, far away and back into a reality he needed, yet knew was only temporary. 'Jag, dinners ready.'

Jag was often absent despite being physically present, more so recently due to the fine mess he was in. Nothing but monkey business. That was probably why he really loved his daughter's company so much more than that of his wife.

His wife, Jenny, knew him and his mannerisms too well. She knew he had not been himself over the past few months and had planned to ask him. She had just been waiting for the right time. And Jag sensed it too. He sensed that she had an idea as to his aloofness. He had a lot on his mind, and this was only going to get worse with his latest visit to the internet.

Each interaction now was self-examined by Jag, trying often a little too much to make things feel as natural as possible. Instead of being natural, Jag was forcing artificial naturalism into his actions, only resulting in making things look somewhat contrived.

'What's for dinner, Jen?' Jag asked casually.

'Masala pasta!' she gesticulated, waving the pasta spoon like a magic wand. A magic wand would have come in handy for Jag too, to somehow reproduce the thousands of pounds that had conjured itself into thin air.

'Oh, wow, is that the first time you've ever tried that one, Jen?'

'Err, not quite. I made it last month. You forgot already?' It was another example of Jag and the detachment from family life that had been his best friend of late. He really did not remember. There were other things on his mind, private to him and his conscience. 'How's the project going? Is it close to completion yet?'

'Not even close, not even close.' Jag was working as Integration Lead for an IT implementation. These projects often extended, and this one was no exception. He was supposed to have finished this project a couple of months ago but inevitable delays from the business side and lack of resources had meant at least a six-month delay to completing. Still, the delay wasn't his fault so what did he care. It was money in the bank at the end of the day. He just needed to keep calm and calculated during these project delays and keep watching the month end pay come rolling in.

Yes, the project had dragged on, but working as a contractor made it all the better. More delays meant more money for him as he was paid daily for his time. The only problem was that it gave Jag the temptation to throw more and more of this cash into his recently found love affair with forex trading. Like most affairs, it was tainted with a litany of arguments and disruptions. Maybe he should've spent more time in risk management?

'You look tired, Jaggy.' He hated it when she called him that. Whenever she called him that he couldn't help but think of Shaggy. The deep voice of Shaggy singing 'Mr. Lover Lover' would echo in his ears like poison; poison because he hated the song. How could any normal person like that song, he again thought to himself. Bombastic! Argh.

Normally a nickname is shorter than the actual name. But bizarrely, her nickname for him was longer than his name. Ironically, Jag was in fact his nickname and Jenny had gone from full name to shorter nickname, then back to longer nickname. It was bizarre and often nagged at him. With all the peripheral issues hanging over him like a cocked revolver, even the smallest trigger was likely enough to tip him over that edge.

It was one of the things that had started to anger him about Jenny, though tried to hide that discomfort as much as possible. Anger management without the anger management training. He was good at controlling his emotions, naturally gifted in that regard. 'Yeah, maybe the project work. Had to re-plan everything after the delay. It was a big headache.' Jag replied calmly and without even looking at his wife. It was something they had started to get used to.

Not only had his love waned over time but also that emotional bond. 'Big headache,' he whispered to himself. He certainly had one of those. And it wasn't due to the heavy project workload, or his former migraines. He knew what his 'big headache' could be, and it didn't take him any second guesses.

He had become more and more inclined to his own company over time, increasingly so, following his recent financial ventures that he had no desire to open up about. Thankfully, on the side-lines his wonderful daughter Bunny, well she had held the cement to their relationship, or at least kept them grounded.

Bunny was his princess, and priceless at that. She was the one thing Jag looked forward to seeing at the end of a day. At age four she was still at that tender age where innocence ruled and when no question or comment from her was odd. She had clearly taken over from Jenny as the woman in his life, and to Jag, was more potent than any marriage counsellor.

To look at her, Bunny did not appear to be the daughter of Jagat. She had a fair complexion to Jag's dark one. Being an offspring from a mixed-race marriage, she had taken her mother's genes it seemed. She was so pretty, like her mother. She was the angel that Jag always dreamt of, and was fortunate to get. She was his world.

Jag looked towards his wife, then daughter, and felt a sense of relief that at least he was so lucky to have them. And he was weighing up the idea of telling her his big problem. Maybe this was the time to speak up, ask for support, be a real family again. It had to be the right thing to do, he thought to himself. We got to share our problems.

Feeling his heart flutter a little, he had decided he would tell Jenny about his forex mishap. She would understand, wouldn't she? It was a big step in his eyes, to confess, but it was a step he now wanted to take.

'Hey, Jen, there's something I've been... meaning to mention. It's like, been on my mind for a while now, just never got around to it. I... errr... a few months back I...'

'I was also thinking, Jag errr...' Jenny butted in, and then a slight pause from her. For a split-second Jag was then the one doing the thinking. His thought process had been completely disturbed. What could she be thinking? '... well, I was wondering, what do you think about having another child?' Jenny thought she was reading his mind.

Wow, there it was.

In all of Jag's thinking, he had never thought of that one. That was a good one. A good one, but in a sarcastic way. There was nothing good about it, to Jag. That took him by surprise. So much so, that the pasta, floating up on his fork on the way to his mouth hung there for what seemed a lifetime, well maybe the lifetime of a fusilli pasta, twisting its way through his mind. Then, in that moment of suspended silence, a plop, as the fusilli pasta piece dropped from its pierced fork, back into its family on the plate. Relief for the pasta, reunited, but for how long?

'Yeah, yeah, I want a baby brother. I want a baby brother!' Bunny was already hyperactive in her response like it was a thing she needed right now. Like something had just reminded her that she needed this right now. Her urgency was truly innocent. 'Come on, daddy, you know you want a little baby, mama wants too.'

'Okay, calm down, both of you.' Jag had to be a bit stern in addressing Jenny and especially Bunny. 'We'll talk about this later.' Normally that meant no, but it was all Jag could think of. The last thing he wanted now was another child. This time he did look at Jenny. At least that made a change. And it was her turn to look away.

This was the last thing he needed. Jenny sensed how cold he was to the idea of another child, and it surprised her a little. 'I… I'm not sure, Jen,' Jag said, looking around the room at his wife, child, and the blank walls. There was no support from anywhere.

The truth of it was that because of his money hanging in the balance with The Forex Group, he really could not even afford another child. Worst case scenario, that money was gone. Losing all this money, even the thought of another child was too much of a burden for Jag to think about!

'Well… let's all agree to think about it for now. There's no rush, Jag. We already have an angel, don't we, Jag?' She looked smilingly over at Bunny as she spoke, hiding her emotions. Jenny sensed a strong barrier being put up by Jag. She felt a reluctance from him but could not figure out why.

Her instinct had been wrong. Surely, everyone loved a second child, maybe on the hope of a boy to complete their family? Jenny was so taken aback that she never even asked Jag what he was going to ask her a few minutes ago.

The moment was lost. Jag's bravery to discuss his financial problems had given way to cowardice. A sigh of disappointment.

Jenny was finding out new things about her husband she never figured before. Before, there was so much more that brought the two together. Jenny was always the type that loved culture and integration. In fact, the two met at a multicultural cooking event in Hatfield. Jag only really went along because his sister wanted to go, needing company. On the other side, Jenny not only loved cooking, but also different cultures. As Indian food was her favourite, it was a no brainer for her to give it a visit.

Jenny went with her mother to the event. She was amazed with how widespread the subcontinent had become integrated and was really attracted to the culture from the start. It's not to say that she went out looking for Jag or someone at the event, just that both were in the right place at the right time.

That's where it all started. Fortunately, her family, made up of only her mother, all embraced other nationalities. Jenny's father had passed away when she was young of an unexpected heart attack. She was an only child and thus, with very few attachments was open to what the future held.

Jag, hiding behind the open friendliness of his sister, who had a food stall at the event, went along mainly to help out and give support. The Hatfield Food and Multicultural Evening, as well as being a mouthful, boasted a healthy turnout, even though initially things were slow to get going.

'Hi, and welcome. Would you like to try some? We have samosa, puri, chaat. Chaat can be a little spicy, so be careful. We have vegetarian options too. These are vegetarian samosa, and those are chicken samosa. Oh… I'm Sara, and this is my older brother, Jagat.' Jag felt a bit mute. There was nothing he could really add to the conversation. He only came to help out if needed. Clearly, he felt not needed now, only when it came to eating.

'Hi, yeah, I'm Jag.' It was as if he was correcting his sister. He always preferred Jag rather than Jagat since childhood. This was around six years ago, and Jag had just started his first professional role in IT Consulting. 'Please try if you wish,' he humbly offered. All the while he could not keep his eyes off the brown, mesmerizing eyes of Jenny.

'Thank you, both of you. Everything looks wonderful. No idea where to start. What do you think, Jenny?' It was Jenny's mother who offered her introductions. 'I'm Theresa, and this is my daughter, Jenny. Very nice to meet you.' Jag couldn't help thinking of Mother Theresa to himself, just jokingly putting two and two together.

'Hi… yes, all looks so amazing. We should get a bit of everything, I think. I'm a big fan of any Indian food really. I even like the spicy options. Bring them on!' said Jenny, gesticulating as she spoke. It was a bit of an icebreaker and welcomed by all, especially Jag.

There was a chemistry between the two of them from the start, eye contact verifying that. Eventually Jag passed their number to Jenny and her mother, '… in case you needed more Indian food.' That was the guise it went under, just to potentially keep in contact with Jenny.

That was where they first met. They had both been much more cheerful in those days, the early days. Jenny did have a slightly reserved nature to her personality, not only because she lost her father whilst still young, but also being a single child. Whilst not quite fearing for her own daughter as such, she did see the potential for parallels. This was why she wanted more children, one more, at least.

It hadn't been the first time she had brought up the desire for more kids. This time though, Jag’s negativity was palpable. Little did she know the background to his financial problems that shot to the fore for those first few seconds.

Jag’s reluctance for eye contact after the short conversation was clear. Though, the odd glance up into her beautiful eyes and straight brown hair gave him a glimpse into the world he had just wounded. Though he knew she was wounded now, he had no choice but to handle his problems the best he could think of.

Her eyes became glazed over as she fought back her emotions. Glassy pensive eyes with more questions than answers. Reflecting eyes, mirroring her own past, fearing her own history, hoping it did not repeat. It was her fear of the loneliness that she wanted Bunny to escape from. And for that, all she wanted was another child. It wasn’t that much to ask, was it?

Would Bunny grow up to the same world she herself grew up in? Jenny didn’t want that. Jenny loved kids and wanted more. Yes, she loved kids and wanted more, but she also loved her living family to the point that they came first. That was the bottom line.

The last bite of Jag’s spaghetti wasn't as nice as the first, as he headed back upstairs to his privacy and his problems. Thoughts of the relevance of the way he met Jenny and the poignancy that food played the music of that time had all but evaporated.

CHAPTER 14

A yawn greeted her as she bent down to pick up the post, cracking knees adding to the chorus of sound effects of the flapping envelopes like belated applause. Another mundane start to the day was at least interrupted by the auspicious package and numerous letters she now held.

Bunny was already playing with her dolls, foretelling her own fantasy, with Elsa as the heroine, who for sure she could not live without. By now and over time, it never really struck Jenny that the start of a day was the start of a new story, but for Bunny, every new encounter with her dolls was exactly that.

It was almost like a daily vlog for Bunny, a series of encounters under the guise of 'Bunny and her friends'. All her friends and family were present today, as always, sitting and awaiting their instructions for today's performance. Jenny stood there for some time watching and listening to the sound of innocence; the sound of a storyteller whose imagination knew no bounds. Where did this world come from? This place paradoxically confined to Bunny's little mind yet knowing no boundaries.

Jenny's vantage, like a looking glass, peered into the mind of the infinite, her smile broadening with each of her daughter's words, helping to warm up her morning and emancipate her vibes. Lined up like toy soldiers, the dolls stood to attention in ranks, under the auspices of Colonel Bunny.

'How are you doing, baby? When you got up?' The angelic moment was broken by the banalities of life. Awoken from her trance, Bunny turned around, following orders.

'Hi, Mommy, I didn't see you there. You like my dolls? Which is your favourite, mommy?' Jenny came closer, close enough to give Bunny a hug, their morning hug.

‘Oh, I dunno, what do you think? I suppose I like Tinkerbell. Doesn't she fly as well?’ She did used to fly, but the other piece which helped to spin her around to elevate her had been lost somewhere, somewhere on a previous mission. That would be the spinner, the other half of her Tinkerbell doll.

Maybe she had just tried too hard to save Peter. The spinning top, or spinner, used to rotate the dragon fly like wings of Tinkerbell had been misplaced some weeks ago, somewhere amongst the plethora of dolls and cuddly toys, probably now hidden in her toy box.

‘I used to like Tinkerbell, mommy. But she can't fly now.’ That was true and had resulted in a little loss of affection. So, for now Elsa was the winner, the love of her child's heart, frozen in time in her daughter’s imagination.

‘That’s fine, darling, I'm sure we’ll find Tinkerbell's other piece. It'll be somewhere in there. Maybe Peter knows?’ And she gestured towards the big, long rectangular box full to the brim with toys, many smothering and strangling other toys below.

Peter Pan was visible at the top, scrambling for air. It was like the Amazon down there, but this time it was the unnatural plastic toys fighting for light. It was only a hypothetical gesture, knowing she was not in the mood to delve deep into the unknown, deep into the artificial rainforest of dreams and adventures in search of Tinkerbell’s lifeline.

Jenny fanned her way through the letters in her hand but was most allured by the small cardboard box, impatient to see what was inside. It was addressed to her, so she had no second thoughts. She began to try to open it, dropping some letters in the process.

It was always a minor challenge trying to open parcels. Trying to find the end of the tape to begin opening from always antagonised her. Having blunt, bitten nails didn't help either. It had been one of her weaknesses, not being able to control her nail biting and as a result ending up with uneven blunt fingernails.

Eventually succeeding, she started to peel the tape back frantically, finally managing to reveal a wonderful Gucci ladies watch. Then she realised it had been one she had told Jag was nice on one occasion. Looks like he had surprised her. Nice.

She put the watch on right away, feeling good in front of the mirror with her newfound friend. What a great husband, she thought to herself in the reflection of the shiny watch, glowing happily on her arm. She couldn't resist looking down every few seconds with adoration at the beautiful jewellery on her wrist. Then switching the angle, she would look and appreciate from a different view. Each time, she thanked Jag for such a nice gift.

Then her attention passed to the letters, some of which had dropped onto the floor in her excitement. 'CONFIDENTIAL' was stamped on the front of one with Jagat Singh as the addressee. All the other letters that had dropped ended up the wrong way around. It was just this one that was the right way around, staring at her inquisitively. Or was it a reflection of Jenny's own inquisitive nature?

There were no major secrets between the two of them, well, not that she knew of. I often open our letters, she thought to herself. Whilst he normally didn't mind her opening his letters, he could never bring himself to open hers. It was a part of his nature and inevitably a part of hers.

This time though, she harboured a slight reluctance, especially with that 'CONFIDENTIAL' image stamping her in the face. It seemed to get bigger each time she looked; bigger and brighter. Jenny waved the envelope in her hand, having already put the other inconsequential letters down on the side table with disinterest. Then, trying to peek inside and noticing it was sent from Leicester, her guess was that it was from the bank. Bank or insurance or maybe a pension forecast. Could it be a winning lottery ticket letter? Adversely, it could be a parking fine. Well, she thought, only one way to find out.

'What you think, Bunny? Shall we open it, eh?' It was like asking a deaf man in a room with no windows whether it was raining outside.

'I don't know, mommy. Open it if you want.' Bunny replied without hesitation, no idea what she was being asked. She was naturally only interested in what dress Elsa should wear for the day.

Despite knowing that once opened there could be no hiding it, she tried to open it as carefully as possible. After failing, she carelessly tore open the letter, feeling little remorse when opening, but regret soon took over as she read the words. It was regret combined with exasperation and anger.

Looking to her side, then to the new gift on her arm that suddenly was getting older by the second, she returned to the letter. It was ironic that just a few minutes ago the beautiful watch that had been gifted was the most amazing, delightful gift, partly as it was such a nice surprise. Within minutes that had turned like the hands on a twenty-four-hour clock.

Digesting the information in the letter took some effort, and gave her stomach-ache, especially as she only knew half of the story. The other half would have to wait till her other half came home. In the meantime, she dwelled on the issue all day until he returned after work to vomit out the full story for her.

CHAPTER 15

Evening, Jaggy. How are you doing?' Part of her knew that calling him that hit his nerves, and on this occasion, she said it intentionally, as if to anger him a little bit more before asking him about the letter. She was just getting him in the mood, as he gave her a split-second glance with hidden connotations; telepathically trying to strangle her. It was one of those glances you give to someone so briefly, just before realising something is not right.

'Hey, daddy, you're back, you're back!' Now that was a much more welcoming and genuinely warm greeting that reunited a daughter with her father. That natural bond somehow tied by the emotional cord you could never cut.

Bunny was bouncing up and down in reaction to her father coming back from work. And Jag couldn't control his smile for her, despite himself not always being the most expressive person. It was such a stark contrast to the numb welcome from his wife. Bunny, so naturally flowing with love and warmth, and of course, innocence. His wife, no doubt, dripping with that of an experienced henchman.

'Hi, baby. How you been today?' His first attention was to his daughter, Bunny, as she seemingly deserved his full attention and got a warm embrace in the process. Then, 'Hey, Jen. How you been?' The same enthusiasm was not there this time as he hardly even turned to return her greeting. It was more of a casual, routine response that he afforded her. That was life nowadays.

'I've been good, daddy. I cleaned up all my dolls today, daddy, but I still can't find the spinner for Tinkerbell. Do you know where it can be, daddy? I checked all my toys, but it's disappeared.' There was honest disappointment in her voice.

'I'm sure it'll turn up, Bunny.' He really had no idea what she was talking about, just wanted to at least sound like he did. 'Did you check with mommy? She normally knows where all things are.' He knew by now that it was a lot easier to fool his daughter than it was his wife. Her telepathic sixth sense always seemed to catch him out at the best, and worst of times. Jenny knew that he was pretending to know what he told to Bunny. Her sixth sense had turned into a sick sense, far away from any seventh heaven.

'Any letters came today? Any calls?' he asked. It was a normal question but as it turned out, in abnormal circumstances.

Any letters came today? What a wrong thing to say today, today of all days to ask that! Yes, letters came, and in abundance! There were even letters that she had not bothered to open after the main two she had divulged into! Any letters came today? Really?

What a joke, Jenny thought to her herself. There are letters, and then there's LETTERS! Well, Jag, yes today you got LETTERS!

Jenny turned around, as if her neck had been electrocuted. Jag did think her movement a little erratic, shocking and sudden to a question he often asked. Maybe her mind had been preoccupied elsewhere and had been jolted back down to earth? And all the time, Bunny hummed her Frozen, 'Let it Go' tune in the background, untouched by nearby sparks.

'Yes, a few letters came, mostly bills and junk like normal.' But he could see in her eyes there was something else, fireworks in the distance? Then he noticed her arm shimmer, and putting the sums together, figured out that the gift he had ordered a month ago had arrived.

It had been very slow delivery, probably due to a USA despatch point. Ironically, when he did order it, his forex trading woes were far away. Then, he only saw the green lines of hope and progress and, of course, profit. That watch was a careful and welcoming stamp back to the past; the good ole days.

Back then, when he had placed the order for her surprise gift, Mark Goldsmith had not even started his gardening leave, and his woes had not even left the station. Back then there were no chutes of devastation. Back then, his heart beat a little faster with excitement and enthusiasm for a brighter future. Back then, he hadn't had the misfortune of typing hopelessly into a keyboard, thinking the next internet page could possibly give a http error.

Green had now turned to red, as flashing alarm bells belted out a grim image of the future. As he followed her glimmering new watch he saw a time stamp of the past, reminding him of a felicitous future that had been stolen from him.

'A letter came from the bank. Were you expecting anything from them?' It was just a polite enquiry she offered. It broke his nostalgic divergence into a past that he didn't want to leave, as if a child's favourite toy had just been forbidden.

'Oh, okay, not really, just regular statements I guess?' He really had no idea at this stage where she was going, but her style suggested it was more than just a monthly statement he was dealing with.

'Was it a regular statement?' he begged, though managing to sound completely blasé about the topic. It was a tell-tale sign that he was trying to hide something, yet at this point he really did not know what the bank wanted; normally it was more of his money in the form of attractive offers and deals.

Her demeanour did suggest it was something more serious. All these years he had never put his foot down and stopped her opening his letters. It had just been his timid approach to married life. He called it a partnership, but others called it being henpecked. He preferred his definition. Less damaging to his outlook on life.

'Not a statement, Jag.' She handed him the open envelope, the 'CONFIDENTIAL' stamp still beaming red alarm bells at the two of them. For a few seconds, even Bunny stopped humming her happy tune, as if encapsulating the moment. It was clear Jenny was not going to 'Let this Go'. Bunny was just taking a breather, preparing for her next melody, or was it a lament?

As Jenny went to the kitchen in a dismissive tone, Jag contemplated the contents of the letter. He knew straight away what it was, and his flawed plan identified. As he read, the shimmer and gloss of the new Gucci watch on his wife's hand seemed to age very, very quickly.

It didn't seem like only the same morning when she felt the wonderful surprise of being greeted with a new gift from her husband. Instead of shiny silver, it was now aging like an old tin can.

He had so carefully instructed his bank to send electronic letters to his email address rather than paper-based versions, but clearly, they did not take heed. It was supposed to be his own problem that was potentially becoming a family affair.

Sometimes he felt like he was talking to thin air, dealing with the bank, and he half expected them to make a mess, having repeatedly told them not to send details of this issue in the post. Not the first time his bank misunderstood his instructions, and probably not the last. He had been half expecting a mistake from them. Well, his more instinctive half had been proved correct.

The issue stemmed from his forex trading and the transfers he had made to various accounts in dubious locations. In last ditch attempts at trying to rescue his money back, Jag had spoken to the bank to investigate the transfers made over the past 6 months. His desperation told him he should at least try.

Using the banks ever increasing fraud centre, Jag had opened a ticket with them to try to identify and track down the accounts he had transferred money to. It was a last-ditch attempt to claw back the funds somehow.

At the time, Jag saw it as an opportunity for them to be of real benefit to him for a change. As usual though, it seemed they had again become a liability, a blundering liability.

Part of Jag, a big part, thought the bank thrived on the misfortune of its customers. After all, the more problems customers had, the more business for them as well their expanding call and fraud centres. All part of an evil merry-go-round of fun and games: Fraud Centre was an apt name, thought Jag.

After handing him the dreaded envelope, Jenny didn't hang around. She dismissively headed into the kitchen simply as a means of getting away from him. She always knew that he was a bit gullible, and putting the sums together, she simply assumed he had been stupidly defrauded. Subsequently, she was in no mood to hang around to listen to excuses.

Jag had to think quick or risk losing the situation. His last resort would be to admit his forex trading mistakes, though, despite ready to let those beans out before, he felt now was not the time. Jag was good at deflecting attention; thus, he went down that crooked path.

He had to raise his voice as he wanted to remain on neutral ground, rather than in the kitchen. 'Yes, that was an old issue I had with some finance company. They gave these strange bank accounts to transfer money into. You not remember, I mentioned it to you once?' It was an old trick to trivialise the situation, acting as blasé as he could; a common tactic he used but a risky one as he used it too often. 'Well, in the end, the company, Finance Frontiers, transferred back the money after I complained with them so much. The bank is always so slow to update me. This issue was solved weeks back and luckily, I got all the transfers reversed. They shouldn't be sending letters now.'

He deserved an Oscar for his convincing words. He even felt convinced himself. There was great versatility in managing to combine a mixture of lies. First of all, he had never mentioned this topic to her in the past, even though he said he had. Secondly, and more gut-wrenching, he had not got his hard-earned money transferred back to him. That was hard to take but he couldn't risk adding insult to injury by admitting he had potentially thrown thousands down the drain.

The fact of the matter was that he was plain out lying to his wife. Jag had become so engrossed in the embarrassment of the loss he was in, he simply could not admit those failings to his family.

By now Jag had made his way to the kitchen entrance, where he found Jenny staring into the garden through the window. She wasn't really looking at anything, it was her ears that were more aware. 'I might change banks, they always come back so slowly and delayed. Easier to employ a tortoise.' It was his usual attempt to brush aside the potential confrontation and avoid controversy.

'What are these transfers you made? I mean, don't you think these transfer locations sound a bit odd? Where is Bratislava and The Marshall Islands? You sure you got the money back?' Jenny finally asked Jag doubtfully.

It was a barrage of questioning, but thankfully for Jag, most of it was rhetorical. 'Yeah, Jen. I'll show you my bank statement later if you want?' Now it was his turn to throw a rhetorical one into the ring. He knew he was not going to show her any statement, except the one stamped on his face. Jag knew her well enough to realise she would cool down soon.

She looked down at her Gucci watch that was already beginning to look a little shinier again.

CHAPTER 16

It was a close shave for Jag. By now, and with the time that had passed since discovering The Forex_Group, his whole life and circumstance was unfortunately turning towards a cliff edge. As a result, he had gotten edgier and edgier. Rather than a normal person trying not to appear edgy, he had become an edgy person trying to appear normal. And cracks in his performance were beginning to show.

The incident with Jag and the unnecessary mail that Jenny had opened was just a few weeks ago. Jag often found himself reflecting for minutes at a time, lacking his own normal clarity. He had sent his email to the National Fraud Office, more in frustration and desperation, less in hope. The only positive thing this time was that there would be no chance of getting another letter in the post. The Fraud Office confirmed they would reply to him by email, a minor line of hope amidst a plethora of blotches.

His realisation that he had been scammed had sunk in even less succinctly. It was like a penny being dropped from miles up in the heavens, taking a lifetime to touch the ground. The penny, in his case, had been a suitcase full of thousands of pounds, exploding on contact, into dust.

Amidst this emotional rollercoaster, Jag struggled. Normally a balanced personality, he found himself doing things he wouldn't normally do. He would now lie to his wife, perfunctory and unconcerned. At work he rushed things, his mind otherwise engaged. It was only his delving through webpages that engaged his nerves of hope; nerves that had been too enraged and unnerved at the same time.

And so, he sometimes spent hours scouring websites for strands of hope. What initially seemed like a strand, a flimsy spider web-like strand did present itself. During his isolated time spent searching for salvation on the internet he did stumble across a blog. It was a blog, not only discussing scammers, but specifically discussing The Forex Group scam.

This online group was picking up notoriety. Jag was partly surprised, shocked and at the same time found himself nodding his head in shame. He was dumfounded that his predicament, which he thought was such a personal and secretive one, was not in fact unique to him. At the same time, he was shocked by how huge the whole thing had become. From considering himself alone and unlucky, he realised that he had become himself, part of a Group.

He was part of a Group that nobody else knew he was a part of! A hidden Group of selected few, lonely, yet unknowing of how many really are impacted. It introduced a feeling of incomprehension for Jag. Knowing he was not alone yet feeling like an alien. On an emotional level it confirmed to Jag that yes, he and many others, had been scammed.

This was just the beginning of a journey into the cyber world of this Group.

CHAPTER 17

Over the next few months Jag made use of his project working skills. He contacted the others in the blog via the blog itself. Initially, it was simply an attempt to salvage some hope and perhaps a way to search and plan a way to contact these scammers.

His blogging also acted as an alternative way of healing emotional wounds. Maybe his online screams of hope were his way of just keeping himself busy, active, and a chance to munch on this picture of fear?

He knew by now there were few answers to many questions, but still at least wanted to keep in the fight. He still wanted to ask the questions. He knew there were very few avenues left he could pursue, especially as he was reluctant to pour more money into an already pessimistic cul-de-sac.

Jag though, had to take it to the next level, otherwise his family life would end up suffering more and more. He was already turning into a bit of recluse in his own home, his daughter being the only one not noticing his waning concentration. Jenny realised it more and more.

It was becoming commonplace now that Jenny would question his attentiveness. 'Are you listening to me, Jag? Why are you so lost?' she would scream at him, her increased frustration getting more and more evident. It was a far cry from the enticement that she possessed during that multicultural evening when they first met. A lot of water under the bridge since then.

'What did I just say?' she would spit at him; testing him and his concentration. Jag would often fumble around confused and unclear, not able to give correct answers. Sometimes he would guess what she had said. Occasionally he was right, but mostly wrong. He lived for those minor victories when he somehow guessed what she was talking about.

His absent-mindedness only contained empty vessels of a desire to find his life once again. To refuel that mind he decided to take the plunge and contact the online bloggers who seemed to be in a similar position to himself. It was his only way to try, at least, to salvage something from his recent difficulties.

So, he reached out to Martin O'Leary. Before his recent misdemeanour's he had neither heard of, nor thought of doing this kind of thing. Now Martin had become one of the draws that Jag hoped would have some solutions. It certainly did seem that way, as Martin's own invitational blog offered hope.

Martin was in a similar position to Jag. It was just that he had taken the initial step into the web, hoping not to get trapped. As a successful owner of a local business, he had not seen the scam coming. Certainly, it was a little disconcerting to him.

Having dealt with hundreds of customers worldwide over the years, he had seen many dubious and dodgy potential deals. Working in textile exporting, he really didn't think The Forex Group would pull the cotton wool over his eyes. Well, they had, and he suffered from the same reflective thoughts as Jag. For Martin, being more of a social media person combined with that business-like commercialism, he had taken the first step into inviting others who may have gone through the same mangler as he.

He posted his online blog of desperation a few weeks ago.

Hello,

It looks like I have been a victim of a scam. The company is The Forex Group who are registered in London under the names of Fine Deal Ltd. They are supposedly an options and forex trading company.

Their website is https://www.theforexgroup.com.
I invested a portion of my life's savings, a little stupidly, and I have requested an investigation by

The National Fraud Office.
I wondered if there was anyone else out there who had interacted with The Forex Group? Any information and coordination is needed to try to catch these criminals as it is destroying my life and I'm sure many others.
I hope you can help by contacting me so we can discuss further.

Moleary@igniteme.com
Regards,
Martin O'Leary

***

Jag could relate painfully to every word, and that, together with him having no other options, compelled him to get in touch privately with Martin.

Email: Contact

Hi Martin,

I hope you are well. I noticed your details on the internet. You wrote a post regarding The Forex Group. It looks like I am in a similar position to you in that I made some investments with them as well. Now I am not so sure. I haven't heard back from them for over a month now and fear they may have closed business. Where are you based? We can discuss further.

Please add me to any plans you have to recoup our money back. The whole thing is quite distressing, and I have never fallen for this type of scam before.

Not sure what else I can say right now but it is not having a good effect on my family life also.

Regards, Jag Singh

***

It wasn't an easy step for Jag to take, but a necessary one. He had to retain some semblance of hope; something to salvage from his sixty-plus thousand pounds loss. Over sixty thousand pounds! Think what I could do with that? An apartment, top-of-the-range car, wow, so much.

Reflective headshaking from Jag.

He looked blankly into nothing. Dark matter. So much mattered. So shattered.

The following day he heard back from Martin. It sounded at least a little positive. Martin had already set up an email group as a work-in-progress type of thing. Having a small business already, he was well prepared, and had discussed with the others about potential ways forward, keeping in mind that there was a high likelihood that they would not get back their money.

Martin had been realistic with the others, and updated Jag on things. He had advised about The National Fraud office, contacting the bank for help, and keeping spirits up as much as possible. Martin had unfortunately given even more than Jag had to the bloodsuckers at The Forex Group. But in Martin's case, he came across as much more level-headed and took investments in his stride. Some you win, some you lose.

Martin was also older than Jag, at fifty-eight years of age so had seen a lot of good and bad in his time. His balding head had seen tougher times, though this had still been a nasty shock for him. He had a newsreader accent that antagonised a few. From his point of view, it was professionalism and clearly got him places, especially trying to run a business. It contrasted heavily with Jag, whose street style English was a polar opposite to the correctness and grandeur of Martin. One thing they did have in common though. They both found themselves on the same sinking ship. A ship that did not differentiate. It just searched for its next victim ruthlessly.

The two of them had begun taking metaphorical swimming lessons, desperately hoping to float. And despite what some could view as pomposity, Martin was the life jacket that could help save Jag's life.

Of course, the two of them only met over the internet waves, not knowing how different they were, yet brought together.

CHAPTER 18

Whine, whine, whine… but nothing to get Jag out of his inebriated state!

That's all he heard. It was just like that typical broken record. Not music to his ears. Often it was his own fault. He was the one pulling that string, that of a kid's toy. If you keep pulling that string time after time after time, you'll keep hearing the same tune. Like that perpetual crying of a baby. It didn't matter if you fed it, starved it, or even hit it; it would keep crying.

Whine, whine, whine… with no satisfying aftertaste!

Most people learned from their mistakes. Most people, even the least wise, did manage to put one and one together to get two. Even the most stubborn would realise over time how to deal with things. With Jag, he only succeeded in making things worse. Clearly over the years all he had been digesting from his relationship with Jenny was high-fibre ignorance. Medicine for the mad, protein for the impoverished, though none of it ever seemed to work nowadays with their relationship hitting hurdles. He never had learned, except for having to eat his own words on occasion. Muesli for the masses, but for him, he had become a serial offender.

Frustrations on his part triggered by frustrations from her part, or was it the other way around? Learning to live had become less living and learning in a world where they both seemed to speak difference languages.

'How many times have I asked you to change the battery in the clock?' Jag didn't know the answer. A big part of him didn't care, and the other part was too carelessly forgetful to remember.

It felt like twenty-four hours a day she would bleat at him like a nagging kid. As she spoke, she gesticulated over her shoulder and they both instinctively turned to look at the motionless square wall clock now more resembling an old painting on the wall, a timepiece of the past. It wasn't what you'd call a masterpiece, more like ageing graffiti.

In all honestly, Jag had gotten so lazy with the other things on his mind that the clock battery could wait. But wait for what, the end of time?

His mind, preoccupied with thoughts of doom and gloom, and potential plans of retribution, ensured there was little, or no space left in his brain for mental tasks like changing the clock battery.

'I just changed the battery last week, Jenny. Not sure, maybe the clock is not working properly.' And Jag had changed the battery. It seemed maybe its time was up. 'Remember, Jen, I changed the battery last week? Bunny, you remember, don't you?' He was starting to sound a little desperate, and for no real reason as he had changed the battery.

There was just silence as Bunny just smiled and shrugged her shoulders innocently. Maybe it was her way of asking Jag to come clean about his financial misdemeanours? Maybe children can see through the evasive latent emotions intuitively? At least that's what Jag was thinking as he stared blankly through her friendly eyes, seeing only paranoid interrogators trying to break him; good cop, bad cop.

'Well, if it's not working what is it up there for? Every time I look the time is wrong. It can't be that complicated can it, Jag dear? Either change the battery or change the clock?' So, Jag got up, reactively as usual, lacking any ounce of motivation, almost machine-like.

There was desperation and exasperation in her voice, completely fed up with her husband's outlook on life lately. It wasn't just the dead clock on the wall. That was just one of the symptoms she saw. It was a whole suite of ailments that she was sensing around Jag. That dead clock on the wall seemed to symbolise their marriage lately; stagnant and seeming to last forever without any progress.

'I don't know what it is with the clock,' as he picked it off the wall, took the battery out and warmed it in his hands. For some reason he held the battery closed in a fist then blew into his fist as if blowing some magic into it. It was something his daughter would be more logically seen doing, bizarre. Maybe he was trying to blow pixie dust into it? Tinkerbell would've been proud of him. Then he rubbed the battery to warm it up. It all seemed like kind of ceremonial rebirth, the rebirth of that ethereal AA battery.

After the potential heroics, he placed the same battery back into the rear of the clock and gave it another spin just to make sure the magic worked. Then he set it to the correct time and hung it where it was before, on the wall. The second hand began to tick forward, rejuvenated into life. Both Jenny and Bunny had already lost interest, with Jenny in particular, not expecting anything magical from Jag's actions.

A couple of hours later the clock stopped ticking.

CHAPTER 19

Martin set up a Zoom meeting.

From his point of view, it was not before time. Over twenty others had contacted him about their experiences with The Forex Group, all very similar.

Some recalled speaking to Mark Goldsmith with his gardening leave. Others also referred to Matthew Goodchild. Could even have been the same person. They all recalled his cockney accent, bit of a giveaway.

Martin spent much time collecting information about Mark and Matthew, finding surprisingly more details about them online. All that was missing were their partners in crime, Luke, and John. They were members of other LinkedIn groups as retail investors but could quite possibly just have had the same name as the dreaded ones that tainted gullible investors of The Forex Group.

It had become so easy to create fake accounts, fictitious personalities, and multiple users. So much so, that tracking anyone down was really potluck. Martin was not even sure whether the information he had amassed was real or not.

Ironically, Mark Goldsmith appeared elsewhere online in a few places, as if intentionally trying to antagonise the naive and susceptible. Mark supposedly worked for Pluto Investment Solutions as well as Global Investment Providers. These were both self-acclaimed leaders in their industry. Self-acclaimed for self-interest, whilst maybe intent on capitalising on others self-esteem, or lack of? Organisations professing to offer high performance bonds or high yielding housing projects. The smell of money soured even their very existence.

There was a whole web of knowledge around that Martin was beginning to be piece together of these culprits; uncovering a plethora of jigsaw pieces with no-one knowledgeable enough to solve. His problem? Not having all the pieces.

In total, twenty-two registered to attend Martin's meeting. It certainly was a global investment for the simple minded. As one of the twenty-two, Jag felt a little self-conscious and pressured, embarrassed and a little non-committal. He had the additional burden of keeping the whole thing a secret from anyone he knew.

For months now he had kept this big secret little, and the longer this went, the longer it was likely to extend. This all added to Jag's reluctance to confess. It was like an extension to his domestic life; the secret that had become his life. He could just never find the right time to tell his wife.

It was as if he feared opening up on things would mean ballooning the whole dilemma and the cat would be out of the bag. And to him, that would make life not worth living. That was how he saw it. Being henpecked and then suffering the financial misfortune he had been through did not bode well.

Jag was sat in his car, cold and tense with the fine mess he was in. His five-year-old BMW M5 was still in great condition; better than him, that was for sure. It had always been his best friend. Or maybe that was his daughter, Bunny? She still was like a breath of fresh air to him, morning, noon, and night. He needed a nice car for the long project journeys he often found himself on, consulting expeditions.

'Making life taste better,' he read to himself looking up at the orange Sainsbury's logo. He shook his head sardonically, sat there in splendid isolation waiting for the Zoom call to begin. 'Life supposed to taste better?' he spat at his windscreen, the only barrier between him and the logo of capitalistic indulgence. The psychological barrier between Jag and a successful capitalistic endeavour.

All he had planned for was a little financial success. But the barrier, a symbolic car windscreen, was blocking him from capitalisms ideals under the guise of Sainsbury's.

He offered a cynical laugh as he read the words over and over. 'Making life taste better.' One long last resounding reflection as if angrily looking himself in the mirror. 'When will it get better? When will it taste better?' It was like he was talking to his window, or maybe the sky outside, a prayer to the knights of St. Sainsbury. He certainly was going to need some armour for the months ahead, where the only thing certain was uncertainty.

Months of emotional snakes and ladders bit at his mind, each day seemingly moving him another step away from redemption. Weeks spent cruising along on his high-speed rollercoaster; a never-ending black hole offering him no light of hope. This was the vegetation that surrounded him, like Venus flytrap's in abundance, opening and closing with each step he took. There was no easy way out for Jag, who sat in contemplation in his nice but damp vehicle in the suburbs of London.

The car windows were starting to steam up but that was fine with him. The greater the barrier to the outside world, the better. That typical chilled formation of water droplets on the inside of his window becoming more and more smooth with every breath he took.

If Bunny had been here, she would have probably enjoyed drawing images on the window. Probably an angel or living dream she always took with her. Most likely a resemblance of Tinkerbell trying to escape. But where could she escape? Her spinning top had been lost now for so long. Bunny had told him so many times but never paid enough attention. Now she was stuck, suspended and unable to fly.

Jag shook his head in reflection and sadness with how much he loved his daughter. Yet his head shaking was stronger because he never showed her that love enough, just took it all for granted.

He drew an arrow pointing upwards into the canvas that was his car window. Just something to pass the time waiting for the Zoom call to begin. Maybe he was trying to be positive drawing an upwards pointing arrow? Maybe it was the direction of his forex account before it all fell apart? Or maybe it was Tinkerbell's long-lost spinner magically rediscovered? In any case, within less than a minute the window had fogged over, leaving only a shadowy image of an auspicious past.

He felt nervous, partly because it was his first in-person introduction to Martin and the team, and partly due to the surreptitious nature of this engagement. Despite it being a meeting set up from potential strangers from all around, with open access to make any response to an internet blog, it felt like an open secret sat there. It felt like it was very much a closed group he was chained to; chains of hope or those of chastisement?

It was a chilly evening as normal in Borehamwood, and not that busy a night for shoppers. 'Making life taste better, for who?' he whispered and questioned at the same time.

He had intentionally chosen a Sainsbury's further out to be sure Jenny would not even think about visiting. It would've been an exception anyway for her to go to do her shopping at this time, especially with Bunny to look after at home. But he was taking no chances. It was easy to say he had extra work to do for the project, which was what he did. Quite normal and easy to get away with.

It was starting to become like autopilot, the way he would deviate Jenny away from his secretive plans. On a regular basis now, he would not even be able to recognise his own lies from his truths. He was starting to become that good.

A quick telephone call around lunchtime, intentionally planned. 'Oh, Jen, I'll be a little late tonight. There's a project milestone coming up soon. Maybe a few later nights needed to get it done on time.' Normal speak in abnormal times, but she would know no better. It was becoming like a piece of cake for him to make up these lies. The worst thing was that he was starting to like the taste of that cake.

His paper and plastic coffee cup was now starting to get cold. At least it provided some benefit in fogging up the windows quicker, mentally barricading himself from outside intrusion. Not being one to waste, he continued taking sips to pass the time. Had it not been for his body heat and that of the coffee, his heavily receding hairline would have shone against the nearby lamps of the supermarket carpark.

The chilly weather helped to keep any perspiration from his forehead. He often left his hair to grow a little long, thus curls formed naturally, keeping at least some respectable covering on his head. It was just that sometimes that tuft of black hair in the middle of his head would blow around a little on a windy day.

Jag's naturally slim body suited the long shape of his head, and despite not being a smoker, one could have thought he did smoke from his appearance alone. He had the natural slimness of either an athlete or a smoker; but Jag was neither. Even before his financial misadventures his weight was well-controlled, now stress gave more justification to his even better weight control as, quite noticeably, the stress had turned him away from food and the fairly normal life he once led.

There was a shifty semblance he had developed, a little distracting and deviating. Over the past few months these features had been accentuated by outside forces that had manipulated his mind, not to mention his bank balance. Thinning black hair, straight and a little glossy sat on the top of his head, a little greasy and wet looking from the tension he felt in the car.

His dark skin was happily camouflaged with the darkness enveloping outside, nature's way of suggesting a positive portent for the evening ahead. Taking stealthy glances outside now and then, he couldn't help checking his phone every thirty seconds or so, his mobile phone already beginning to manipulate him into this nervous fidgety frenzy.

There was also a depressing tone; a dampness that didn't bode well with someone who had gone straight from the office to a random car park in outer London to take a sneaky Zoom call. He, himself, felt this furtiveness. There was a deception that, even the condensation-dressed windows of his BMW found hard to conceal, leaving the curtains of his private engagements potentially open for all to see. The drawn dullness of the changeable weather suited Jag's character, the steamed-up windows at least partially fortifying that stealth.

Then, as luck would have it, or more honestly, bad luck would have it, he noticed a work colleague in the distance through the steamed-up windows. It was only the previously drawn arrow on the window that allowed him to see through, making the image out.

A very plump James Balden was not too far away, seemingly doing some evening shopping. 'I bet he's not waiting for a Zoom call,' whispered Jag to himself. He couldn't help focusing on James's fat stomach, easily, way too big for his suited trousers. Ironically, they were called suit trousers, but were so tight on his stomach that the last thing you would call them would be suited to him!

James was a work colleague rather than a friend. The pompous appearance and overconfidence that always accompanied James was as apparent as his fat belly and it always made Jag laugh; laugh in a way to try and make himself feel a bit better. It was Jag's way of psychologically getting back at James in his mind.

Why did Jag need to get back at James? Well, no one could argue against how good James was at his job. He was extremely professional, confident, and wonderfully well-mannered, and he knew it. He lived in Surrey too, so felt this self-importance even more as he considered himself above the others. James felt that he had worked so hard and professionally that he deserved this respect. These things got on Jag's mind, along with jealousy and envy.

Very motivated, even at his age of sixty, Balden had his own business in consulting too. He had worked in IT and Business as a contractor for years, certainly as long as his fat stomach had been on display; two decades and more. Two decades of feeding that bloated waist and antagonising anyone who was tempted to challenge his intellect. A bloated waist containing mostly waste.

Travelling around the M25 orbital, James didn't mind where he worked. He was a bit of a workaholic and just loved himself. As long as the contracts kept rolling in, to feed not only his stomach, but his family and spacious detached home in the country. That was one of the things that kept him motivated. He enjoyed his work and took pride in it.

Not only did James have a plump stomach, he also, as him name suggested, was pretty much bald. He didn't care much about that, only about his next contract. And still being so good at his job, he didn't have any issues there. There was always, what seemed to be, a smug smile on his face.

The worst thing Jag wanted was to have to stop and chat with James, especially as the Zoom call was in a couple of minutes. So, Jag tried to hide low down in the car; tried to squeeze himself to be as little, and as low as possible. Even on the best of days, Jag would have done his utmost to dodge that never-ending conversion with a such a psychological enemy as Balden. And today he had more reason to avoid his company.

Being a good consultant, Balden could talk till the cows came home. Jag didn't need that. Fearing it was too late, he noticed the short, overweight James already heading in his direction. Maybe he parked near me, thought Jag, hoped Jag? That turned out to be wishful thinking.

A few seconds later Jag heard hard tapping on his car window. Knowing what it was, he initially tried to ignore it, trying to remain the invisible man inside the car. How he wished he had Frodo's ring, though it seemed he was otherwise engaged. He so wished for Harry's cloak but knew it would not suit him.

The inevitable followed. Repeated tapping on the window, accompanied by repeated smiles. Smug smiles twinned with self-assured jibes. The arrogant Balden welcomed him; welcomed the downward looking disinterested stare of Jagat Singh, pretending he was looking for something near his feet. At this rate it was starting to sound like hard hailstones knocking on his window, inclement signs of things to come.

The hailstones became hail Balden, as his fully bald and very round head beamed in the streetlight stare. It was the equivalent of the night's solar power, except, here, power was coming from the adjacent car park street lighting, then bouncing off his shiny head. The artificial power producing an artificial welcome from a gluttonous co-worker.

Lower your gaze, hail Balden. Like a majestic maestro with light beaming from his head, Balden adorned that Cheshire cat stare and a sheepish grin. And, as if playing his part in the script, Jag bowed down, in reverence and awe, a hallucinogenic matador, hypnotised by the bull. Though, of course, he was trying to hide behind the metal of the car door.

He was low enough to kiss the feet of this man, the man who never spent much time considering Jag as an equal. To start with, he was probably twice the age of Jag, with twice as much experience. As well as that, he was white, upper middle class, to Jag's Indian roots. Though he was not in any way racist, hidden arrogance always occasionally peered out and onlookers could be forgiven for thinking otherwise.

It did flirt with Jag's imagination on occasion, that maybe Balden was racist, but over time, and getting to know James, Jag realised that it was just his apathetic way of dealing with all people, his love affair with egotism.

Living his lie, Jag arose; arose like a defeated and devastated schoolboy, realising his punishment. It was his turn to face his opponent, music he never liked the sound of.

A scene of images came to his mind for a split second, though it played out in his mind for an age. In his own little performance, he took the first step, getting out of his car to go in the direction of James.

He lowered the electric window, removing the arrow of condensation he had paired onto his canvas. That arrow had been his arrow of hope for the night ahead; for the Zoom call to elevate him up into the sky, dissipating his clouds of negativity into another galaxy.

Maybe, just maybe, the arrow had been the long-lost spinner of his beloved daughter, Bunny. The spinner of Tinkerbell. It put a split-second of sadness into his heart as he thought of his daughter. She had nothing to do with his financial tribulations and he always felt he had let her down.

The cool breeze sent in wafts of air into Jag's slightly sweaty face. He had been hidden from outside forces until the portentous visit of Mr. Balden.

Then Jag's imagination took over...

CHAPTER 20

The coolness of the outside air. It hit Jag suddenly.

It should have knocked him back into shape. Not the shape of a plump James Balden, but into the psychologically improved shape to deal with his work colleague. Instead, the absent-minded Mr. Singh went into a daydream, or in this case, night-dream. In fact, you could even call it a nightmare, though there was no sleeping involved.

In his little reverie, Jag had drifted off into another world…

In this world of Jag's imagination, Balden was not tapping on his window anymore…

… Jag finished tying up his shoelaces. It was, of course, the reason for him bending down beneath the steering wheel of the car. As the notoriously plump Mr. Balden had spotted Jag, he was heading Jag's way, and that didn't impress Jag, not one bit. Jag got out of the driver's seat and then the car, then opened the back door at the same side. He was alone in his car as he was going home after work.

Normally you wouldn't need to open the back door. Why would you if you were travelling alone? Maybe he was opening it to offer Balden a lift? Why would he do that, especially as Balden had come to Sainsbury's in his own car?

Jag reached down again, towards the bottom of the inside of the car. It was not the first time he had reached down in the car tonight. Then he closed the car door. Balden slowed a little, that glum smile slightly changing and becoming somewhat quizzical. But he continued because he couldn't quite make out what Jag was holding.

A few seconds later it became clear. It became clear what he was holding, but not why he was holding it.

Jag loved his cricket. Coming from an Indian heritage, cricket was in his blood; it ran through his veins. All his Indian friends were the same. Cricket from an early age was a prerequisite of an Indian childhood. And, he had no problem with that, partly because he was pretty good at it too.

Jag held the SS cricket bat securely in his hands, as if ready to take guard. His coach had always told him to line up the V's of your hands down the side of the bat for a correct grip, otherwise no point playing the game. It had become second nature now; his grip on the bat was perfect. Unfortunately, his grip on his life was not quite as secure.

Jag set off in the direction of Balden. Balden was already heading his way.

It was a duel. A face-off. A battle. Time for the coin toss?

But Balden now slowed a little, wondering what the hell his work colleague was doing brandishing a cricket bat horizontally for. It seemed odd, especially as he was heading his way. But still, Balden was wearing that familiar grin that always seemed to be on his face.

He must want to show me his new bat, of course, Balden thought.

As the two got closer, Balden’s smirk was starting to lose its courage. He just saw his colleague, striding confidently towards him, but felt he didn't recognise him.

Now who was the cocky one?

A sense of aggressiveness came to him as he pondered Jag’s movement towards him. Aggressiveness was the right word, wasn't it? But Jag was never aggressive. He was always controlled and timorous; would never even complain to a fly. Now though, there was a sting in his step.

Balden slowed to a trickle. ‘Hi, Jag. You, okay? How are you doing, Jag? Why do you have a cricket bat in your hands?’ They were all questions without answers, for now. But only for a short time. SS on the bat cover... Sainsbury's Shopping... Suicide Squad... Striding Singh.

Instead of turning, Balden put on his happy face; the face that always gave and showed great confidence. But now it was time to face Jag. It was a risk, the smile, but it was what Balden was best at. Of course... Sanguine Smile. There was a lot of hope in Balden's actions, though his expectations were much less optimistic.

Then Jag let loose. He just swung the bat. Screaming like a madman inspired he acted without hesitation. Bam... Pow... Wham... Bang... He was... Batman, but this was a real dark night and Balden had no idea what to do. He wasn't much of a fighter, always having his vocal cords do the fighting in the past. Tonight, he was looking more like a joker.

No other shoppers even noticed. That was strange. Some just walked by, as if ignoring the beating. Maybe they chose to ignore. Balden screamed for help, but Jag's screams of anger and built-up malice were louder and more potent. The screams of a badly beaten Balden were drowned out by the cacophonous reverberations from his opponent. It was thud after thud, six, followed by four, punishment for an aging man, now feeling his age, and aging faster with each strike.

Balden was on the ground now begging for mercy in the form of a curled-up ball of fat. Jag, on the other hand was now letting out yells of delight and relief; a momentary act of madness releasing a burden of belittled emotion, now over-zealous with the excitement of a child playing a computer game.

Jag had never used the bat so much in a game. From his point of view, it had been a great innings, a good knock.

As he went back to his car, Balden lay motionless on Sainsbury's car park, taking up the best part of a parking space.

CHAPTER 21

'Mr. Singh, I thought it was you down there. How are you doing?' As usual, James's introductions always had that polished welcome, brandished with a feeling of 'You do know I'm better than you, don't you?' Balden would always start the day with 'Mr. Singh,' when talking to Jag. It was his attempt to lighten things for the rest of the day, though it only increased the weight of anger on Jag.

... And Jag was back in reality. He looked at his hands. They motioned to him as if holding something. But all they were holding now was thin air, a vice-like grip of thin air. Jag couldn't figure out whether his hands were holding a pretend cricket bat, or in fact just the frustration that ruled his mind. Either way, there was no sign of a cricket bat, nor were there any signs of wear and tear on James Balden. He just adorned that wonderfully sardonic grin, his reliable friend.

A little embarrassed as usual, Jag tried to look surprised with the arrival of his unwelcome foe. 'James, how you doing? What are you doing here? This is not your neck of the woods, is it? I thought you lived in Surrey? Wasn't it Woking?' It was Jag, trying say 'Why the hell are you here, ruining my day?' He almost said, 'Can't you leave now, and forget we ever met?' But, of course, he didn't.

His mind was a little preoccupied; partly with the immediate memories of the fantasy his mind just enjoyed, but more so with the Zoom call he was due to attend soon. Fresh in his mind was the battering he had just given Balden. He had battered him black and blue with an SS bat, all of it a wondrous experience. That was, until you realise it was all fake, and Jag remained the weasel he always had been.

Jag envisaged Balden lived in this great mansion in the middle of the countryside; the beautiful Surrey countryside that Jag had only ever heard of. He wasn't in the league of those who could even consider saying they lived there, and in Jag's eyes, that's exactly what Balden was; controlled and calculated, living a trouble-free existence.

That was the impression that Jag had built up from the outside, mainly from the inside; the inside of those office walls where the two of them worked. Neither had bothered too much to delve into the personal life of each other. The life of a business consultant generally remained a peripheral thing, not a thing for close encounters. In a few months their relationship would be over, and they would move onto a new project. And that would be the end of it.

'I was just on the way back home, yes. Just needed a few groceries. You know this place, making life taste better. Couldn't resist a few snacks for the journey home. It's a long journey back tonight.' There had been patchy rain around London, and he knew it would be a longer journey home tonight. Often, James wouldn't get back till after nine. Tonight, was one of those nights.

And Balden was one of those consultants who could really manipulate a molehill into a mountain. He knew his business like the back of his hand, often able to give a metaphorical slap in the face to the project sponsors. He knew the ins and outs of running a business and more importantly running a project, so found it easy to mould project goals and milestones like a polished Bill Gates.

As Balden spoke the words 'Making life taste better,' they simultaneously looked up at the orange logo. It was like they were looking up at the eternal sun, this time though, a beacon for the night.

It wasn't the first time that evening Jag had looked up to dwell on the orange slogan; in search of hope and salvation. Both times though, he had not received any inspiration from above. All he got back was the poisonous marketing germs that polluted his mind, less the vitamin D.

It was with the same vitality and enthusiasm that Balden always exhibited, like he could not erase that piece of his identity, whether at work or away. And why would he? It was just that it nagged even more with the nerves of Jag, bitter with the envy of indelible greenery.

'I was just also going inside to get a few things. My wife messaged that we needed a few things, and this place was the nearest I could find on my way home. I was just doing up my shoelaces before heading out, that's why I was bending down.'

There was a catalogue of lies Jag was unravelling. Balden wasn't too fussed or bothered what Jag was doing down under the steering wheel. The last thing he would consider would be that his friendly work colleague would be trying to hide from him.

Over the past few months Jag had become a natural liar, something he never would have thought about himself before his forex days. Trading on the foreign exchange had at least taught him something. It seemed The Forex Group had rubbed their dirt on him.

His guilty conscience had coerced him into giving out more detail than was necessary. What did Balden care what Jag was doing under the wheel of the car? He couldn't care less. Yet, Jag, as if wearing a t-shirt with 'You Got Me' printed in huge letters, couldn't help himself spilling out those beans; Jag and the beans talk.

The condensation had dissipated due to the coolness of the breeze, now inside and out of Jag's car. It was a result of the opened front car window. He was impatiently waiting to close his window to allow for the castle walls of condensation to build up again. The castle walls for Jag were the windows tightly closed, with condensation covering them, clothing them. He felt a kind of false security.

His furtive actions and fidgeting around were clear signs of his unease. Balden, on the other hand, epitomised calmness, confidence, and clarity. But of course, he hadn't just lost sixty thousand pounds on a flimsy financial venture. 'Everything okay, Jag? You seem a little uneasy.' James sensed Jag's impatience, his aloofness.

The street lighting shone onto Jag's head, early signs of approaching baldness glowing in the artificial light. Sweat as well, which James thought was odd on a chilly night like this. 'You... you're sure things are okay, mate?' There was more of a calm concerned approach this time as James looked deeper into the car as well as the mind of his work colleague. There was more genuine concern this time, as he knew Jag was hiding something.

James thought back to when Jag was bending down under the steering wheel. Maybe something hidden there, he thought. 'So, you did the shopping then, Jag?' James was trying his version of the Sainsbury Inquisition. Jag just nodded, mumbling something not so audible. James looked around the car for evidence, clues, then simply shrugged his shoulders, as if to say where is it then? None of your business Balden, thought Jag, trying to teleport his response. It has nothing to do with you, Balden. Just go home.

'It's in the boot. I was just going to head off myself now.' More lies. Jag was becoming an expert. I'm sure I've also got a cricket bat in the boot as well. If you don't go soon, Balden, I really am going to use it. This time it won't just be my imagination, mate!

For the third and final time, James asked, 'So, you sure things are good, Jag?' He knew they weren't, but it was clear he wasn't going to find out.

'All is good, mate. All is well. You better head off, you've got a long drive ahead. I'll see you in the morning.' Despite the normality in his words, there was a depressing abnormality Jag expressed, a mundane and routine feel to his tone.

It was lie upon lie. Like a house built of straw. The little pig was not looking good. Jag had lied to his wife that he had extra work at the office. Then he'd lied to Balden that his wife had asked him for shopping; a web of lies and deceit, painfully intertwined. Ironically, he had inadvertently bumped into the plump James Balden. So, in his own twisted little mind, he could perhaps at least try to convince himself that it was a kind of work; sort of work; work-related. But that was just the little man inside his head making up excuses for him to carry on his little charade, to help keep his wife happy.

It seemed a lifetime, but in the end Balden finally went into the superstore. Jag was taking no chances; he drove off to a nearby street to take his call. He was already a little late now.

CHAPTER 22

The conference call details had all been prearranged and sent to him by email. Part of Jag still had a bit of mistrust but what else could he do? How else could he get in communication and have at least a sliver of hope to cling to? Mistrust, of course remained.

Firstly, he never actually knew anything about the others. They could all be axe murderers for all he knew, even the women. Furthermore, the recent fraud he had encountered had made him a little paranoid, at least in the short term.

The call connected efficiently, as Jag joined the call, already in progress. He felt a little embarrassed, part of him still thinking about the cricket bat and his old friend, James Balden. But he was more embarrassed about the fact that it was his first introduction in person with Martin and the others, yet he was late.

It was the first meeting set up by those unfortunate enough to have been the ones caught up in this fraud. Yes, they were the unfortunate ones, but, on the other hand, this group of investors were at least fortunate enough to have at least met each other, giving them some potential to fight back.

Despite him missing twenty minutes of the call, Jag really hadn't missed much. His makeshift location had turned from Sainsbury's car park to a nearby side street. He just needed a quiet spot, away from residents and especially Balden.

He had left soon after that awkward conversation with Balden, ensuring he was out of sight as he left. They say out of sight is out of mind. Well, in this case, Balden was out of sight, but still banging on Jag's mind, and with that familiar smile on his plump face.

So, he found a side street, not too close to housing, before connecting. That didn't completely exempt him from the embarrassment of the situation he was in. He still felt unclean about the lies that had brought him to where he was but tried to somehow let the positive vibes of the others wash over him.

There was so much light pollution around England that his attempts to conceal himself in the darkness were made that much trickier. Fortunately, once again the condensation built up around his windows, hiding him inside his glass prison; the other inmates were waiting on the line.

'For the latecomers, welcome. I hope you are all well, wherever you are. I expect more people will join as we continue. I may have to keep checking in the online waiting room area to allow any of the other invited ones into the meeting.' It was Martin speaking, introducing those who had made it to the meeting.

It really helped, having Martin, with his business acumen and professionalism at the helm. At least it gave them some chance of progress. Of course, Martin had as much, if not more reason, to give this endeavour his all. He had lost a huge chunk of money.

'As this is our first meeting, it may well be a little slow, but well, we got to proceed the best we can. There is no easy way of dealing with this issue, we just got to keep the microphone open and invite ideas. None of us wanted to be in this position but we are here. Let's try to make it as positive as possible. I'm sure there are ways we can proceed to get our damn money back.'

It was somewhat straightforward from Martin, but it was the truth. One of those moments that broke up the atmosphere of meeting introductions. It made it real, real silent, ensuring that if not serious before, it certainly became so.

Jag, for one, let out a sigh of stress at that point, as if he had just realised, he needed to get his money back. His microphone was muted thankfully, as he released a stressed sigh. It was as though the feeling of this whole Zoom thing had diverted his emotions; glamorised the situation. Well, that had changed now. Talk of trying to get his money back jolted him back into an electrifying reality.

And he looked out of his glass house into the world outside. What was worse? The outside world of crime, delusion and lies, or the world he was inside now?

The world inside of his glass windows, windows of condensation that seemed to look at him in such a condescending way, slippery and wet.

Inside his car, he found himself in a world driven by the greed shown on the tiny screen in his hand. A tiny screen capable of even more deceit than that outside of these windows; windows Bill Gates would not even approve of. Windows concealing dark secrets, hidden secrets that Jag for sure, was not willing to divulge. Strategic voices, unknown soldiers, talking to each other, or against? It was just so hard to tell as it was the first meeting, for Jag at least. Where, at the end of the day, nothing was supposed to be private, yet everyone wanted to keep it so, as much out of shame as well as fear of the unknown.

At times he thought that those clowns at The Forex Group were spying on him right now. They had tricked him so easily, toyed with him, spying on him. Jag was now the one with the red nose, together with the jesters behind the window in his hand; a window of sunlight he hoped would rise in the future.

Inside his car, in a new age travelling so fast that even the passengers couldn't keep up, an age of artificial intelligence. The device in his hand, accelerating along the track at supersonic speeds, led by corporate greed and that desire to feed not so smart addicts.

Inside his car, inside his mind, motionless, hearts in need of a supercharge. Clinging onto something, but not knowing what, the superhighway of dreams, or the road to nowhere?

Inside his mind, his plexus of nerves, meandering arteries, there to guide. The channels of hope he saw on his screen, giving at least a moments pause until the turn to green. But his fear, well, that was clear, clearer than the expectation that these glass prison walls confined him to.

Jag felt that repetitive desperation. 'Get my money back!' he whispered to himself in a kind of yearning, looking at the screen. His dreams, they were held tenderly in the hands of a man he didn't even know; Martin O'Leary, whoever he was. The odds were against him inside those six glass walls and the outside world.

Lots of questions were offered and suggestions made in the Zoom meeting. Many things already acted upon, like raising incident tickets with the National Fraud Office. Pretty much everyone had done so already, but it had been good to clarify and ensure all attendees went down that route. A few attendees had already mentioned they had received responses back. It was a standard response confirming that the Fraud Office would investigate the situation. It gave dwellers behind the glass walls a slither of optimism.

Scouser, Dave Jackson, one of the attendees, brought up the issue of contacting banks. 'If we connect with our banks, then maybe, I dunno, maybe there's a small chance of maybe getting somein' back? Surely, they must have a network or somein'? I would expect it's worth it anyway least, to give a try?'

Dave's belief was that if payments were made to overseas bank accounts, then maybe they could be traced and identified. It was certainly a logical option, just that many of the investors had used credit card payments which had no chance of being reversed. Also, it was starting to look like a possibility that the devious tactics used by The Forex Group included opening and closing accounts quickly, thus avoiding future tracking and reversing of payments.

Dave recommended that each member should at least try whatever they could to put pressure on their banks. Of course, Jag had already been down that lonely road, resulting in nothing positive. In fact, in his case, as Jenny had opened the banks letter on that topic, it even made his little predicament a little bigger.

One of the attendees, Jiri, made probably the most lasting suggestion. It was a suggestion that most were thinking but reluctant to ask about. 'One option, err, we could ask a lawyer to maybe look into the issue?' His English was a little broken, but the point was clear, and it was on everyone's mind from the beginning.

There was a silence, then Martin broke in to release the unease. 'Tha... That's a great idea, Jiri. I must say, it is something I have toyed with myself as an idea, but I think the costs will be high. Maybe if err, we can get a law company that will work with us on a no win, no fee basis, then it may work. I'm sure others have at least considered the option. Are there any lawyers online?'

Then again, silence. 'Okay, well, we can make a note and I'll email the idea as a future possibility. It will be on the minutes of the meet...'

'I err, I'm a lawyer.' It was a voice, out of nowhere. 'I work in conveyancing law.' A voice of anonymity, at this stage. 'I know a few people around who can at least give us advice.' There was a little surprise from everyone, mainly at the delayed reply. But it was positive at least. More importantly, everyone's ears perked up. It was a lady, a lady without her video on. Most of the others had their Zoom cameras on either via mobile or PC, but the lawyer had neither. It was just a voice online... the voice of an angel?

'I lost quite a bit with these fraudsters also, maybe I can ask around. I feel very stupid with the lack of due diligence I took, but maybe I can find someone in the business willing to look. The only problem is that this type of internet crime is very specialised and sophisticated, maybe only large and niche companies will consider even looking at.' It was clear she had knowledge. To Jag, she sounded to be a person to keep in touch with; another straw to clutch to.

It was like the whole audience was now standing to attention. The lady had sure captured everyone's attention with her knowledge and background. Jag for one, had forgotten where he was. He could easily be in some large auditorium now, or business meeting, not in a cold BMW, surrounded by condensation and six walls of glass. It added a tension to the occasion, more importantly a strand of hope to cling to.

The glass prison walls he was sat in had become glass castle walls, fortifying any signs of emotional turbulence. For a moment he felt like the king of his castle, looking out into his kingdom. There was another sigh from Jag, this time an auspicious sigh, one he welcomed, but that still made his heart race. It was more like relief, hope built on the realms of possibility.

The whole mood of the meeting had changed. It wasn't necessarily a change based on anything concrete or assured. Moreover, this Zoom group of forsaken investors had seen a sunrise on the horizon; without hope you can't start the day.

This was what this meeting was all about, a steppingstone to step on and a chance to hold hands and move onto the next stone. The next stone maybe would not be easy to reach, or be a slippy one, but it was a step worth risking, when options were limited.

The Group, their Group, had been formed.

CHAPTER 23

Jag reached home. Finally.

It had been a long meeting in the end, longer than he had expected. A long meeting also meant it had been a long day, an even longer evening, and that wasn't even over yet.

Being late home meant it was going to be a long walk too, from the short distance of the driveway of his car to the door of his house. To top it all off, after such a long day, and with the notorious topic of the meeting, he was the one with the long face.

As it had been their first official meeting, it was expected to overrun a little. Also, delays at the beginning, due to late arrivals didn't help. Jag was conveniently overlooking the fact that he was one of the illustrious late ones.

There were a few avenues of investigation to work on. Following up with the fraud office, banks, and credit card companies all on the list of check boxes to tick off. It became clear that Mark Goldsmith was a busy and disgusting guy. He dealt with most of the investors. A Crafty Cockney full of bull.

It had transpired that Goldsmith was the Account Manager for around twenty of the attendees. Quite a gift he had, that of the gab. So many fake promises he had dealt out; a real David Blaine feeling no blame.

It was 10:30 pm, late in anyone's book, but it was what it was, and he shut the door politely behind himself. There was always going to be a tension, coming home at this time, but these were the cards that Jag had dealt himself. Then again, as per his message to Jenny, he was supposed to have been working late at the office, so perhaps there would be surprising compassion from her side?

'So late, Jag? What's going on? You never come this late. Is everything okay?' There went Jag's optimism. He half-expected the negativity. In theory, your husband’s been working for the last fourteen hours, and that's how you greet him? From the outside it did seem a bit odd, but, of course, Jag was no angel.

‘Yes, sorry, Jen, we're coming towards go-live for the project, so there's going to be long hours of testing and scripting ahead. There’ll be a few more late ones, even weekend work.’ It was like he spoke with alarm when he mentioned the weekend because he never was one to enjoy working at the weekend.

His deception had grown so good now that it was becoming natural, a part of his identity. And it was even reaching a point where he was almost articulating true lies. Scripting? It certainly seemed very scripted from Jag. A lot of scripting going on now, never mind in the future!

‘Anything left over?’ He spoke casually, as he headed into the kitchen. The warmth that used to be there between the two of them was now only there in fragments nowadays, more like an icicle. A bit like the food, it was cold.

Eye contact between the two was now rare and there was starting to become an uncomfortableness. They were the same eyes that used to look at each other fondly for so long. At times, Jenny still did… She still searched behind those eyelids for salvation and memories of the short but sweet years they initially had together. Bunny had been that glue that bonded them further together. But when Jenny looked into those eyes, she did not see the same man she fell for seven years ago in that multicultural night. But she searched… and she intended to go on searching for the man behind those glassy eyes.

There was a bitterness that was gaining traction. This was more a feeling Jag felt, inevitably accentuated by his financial shenanigans. Despite the way he was adapting to his situation, there were still tell-tale signs; indelible fingerprints emotionally prodding him in the face.

‘Of course, Jaggy. There's some biryani in the fridge. I'll get it out.’ It was another sign of how late he was. The food was already in bed for the night. Jaggy, Jaggy, Jaggy, he thought horribly to himself. He'd rather drink poison than be called that. Here it comes again... The deep voice of Shaggy singing

'Mr. Lover Lover,' argh. Looking the other way, 'Gimme a break,' he whispered to himself, as the terrible music reverberated in his ears.

And, as he walked into the kitchen, he stopped as he passed the wall clock; the same notorious wall clock; the disobedient wall clock. He raised his eyes to look closer. So, unfortunately, did his wife. It started with a shake of her head. Meanwhile, he again felt that familiar feeling you get when know you were meant to do something but realised too late.

What was he meant to do?

Fix the damn clock, of course.

Failed again!

Time after time, it was like the clock itself was laughing at him.

'*I've told you a million times to change my batteries.*'

It was the clock, ticking him off once again, like that unwelcome reminder you've heard a million times before.

And, as he looked up at the clock, it read a stagnant 6:03 pm. Well, at least it was pm, so maybe only stopped a few hours ago? That was Jag, scraping the barrel, searching for positives. That positive was negated by his next look, at his wife taking a quick look at the clock, then back towards him in disappointment.

'The clock stopped again, Jag. How many times you going make me look at that damn thing? Can't you just fix it?' It sometimes felt like she was talking to a five-year-old, and she kind of made that clear. That antagonised Jag even more, like a vicious spiral of hate between the two.

Why didn't Jag just change the batteries? Mainly procrastination intertwined with forgetfulness. He had other things on his mind and often found himself mentally absent.

Why didn't Jenny herself just change the batteries? It mainly came down to a vindictive streak she had developed. It was a streak she would never admit to herself. But it was there, and every now and then it simmered. The last thing she was going to do was change those batteries herself.

Reversing his steps, Jag then attended to the clock, but again only to give it a shake. He then took the three batteries out of the back and blew forcefully on them, then warmed them in his hands. It was like global warming on a minute scale. Or maybe it was pure stupidity, a ritual for the absent minded.

As if by magic, on replacing the batteries and putting the clock back onto its perch, it started to chirp once again, musical tick-tock, as it was again resurrected back into life. A sigh, as he continued back into the kitchen, in search of his stomach's batteries. It had been a long day, and Jag was in no mood to start farting around with clocks and batteries.

Chapter 24

Voila, dinner was served, courtesy of the multifunctional microwave Jag often used. Rather than 'Bon appetite,' it was more of a 'Have you finished yet?' but at that moment it did not bother Jag what it was.

Dinner provided the function it was supposed to, temporarily recharging his batteries. 'So, how was the meeting?' Jenny asked. Jag was surprised by her question as she normally never asked him anything about work. He immediately went to think about the Zoom meeting.

Did she know? Impossible. He had certainly not mentioned it; not given any clues. There was a sudden shocking jerk of his head back in her direction. A jerk of the head that he simply had no control over, as if remote controlled by a possessive wife. It was like she was pulling his strings, as each pull hurt a little more each time.

'Your meeting, at work? Was it okay?' Another mental phew as his clock clicked back online. He was a little confused because he had told her he was working late, but never mentioned any meeting. She had seemingly just put two ends of a string together to tie a knot. Well, it had turned into another sticky wicket for Jag to deal with.

'Oh, you mean at work, well yes, it was good. Was as expected, things going okay for this part of the project.'

'Is everything okay?' This time it wasn't the meeting she was asking about. It was the general wellbeing of her husband; a husband who hardly seemed to listen to her nowadays. She came over from the sofa to sit by him at the table, concerned. This was the real concern of a loving wife. There were times when she had a go at him, of course there were. But they were husband and wife after all, and the blood ran thicker.

She brushed her long straight brown hair away from her eyes as she knelt forward across the table. 'I mean, really. Are things at work and away from work, okay? This is not the first time you know, Jag. I've been noticing you don't seem with us, even when you are. You would tell me if there was anything wrong wouldn't you, Jaggy? Remember we used to discuss things together and... and talk!' it felt strange to Jenny that she was even uttering these words. Just to talk about things had become difficult and it was never in her nature to bottle things up.

She smiled as she spoke, part defensive, part in sympathy for how she felt about things and especially about her husband. There was also disbelief in her words too. Jag was the quieter type, she knew that. But the mute type? Jag was never like this, she thought to herself. For the second time, she brushed a long line of hair from her eyes, more out of habit than frustration.

There was a moment of pause. Maybe a time for reflection once again. A time for even more devastating thoughts to enter both of their minds. Then, out of the blue. 'I've been thinking, Jag, the garden is a real mess. Why don't you spend the weekend cleaning it up and planting some stuff? Might be good for your mind. Might help to give you a hobby? It'll give us a chance to get ready for the summer. Garden needs a bit of work also.' It was a little patronising, but that was where they were at. At least she was trying to look at options, solutions.

It was in her nature to look for solutions, not problems. She didn't have the project planning of Jag and his team, but she had the heart and determination to figure things out. Not for any bonus or recognition, but because it was the right thing to do. That was who Jag had met and married. Maybe that was why he found her?

Jag on the other hand, had become more quarrelsome, his problems antagonizing him. You don't think I'm busy enough, he thought to himself. That was the only thought that came to him. He was in no mood to either argue or make the situation worse. His mind was quickly weighing up the situation, her offer. Perhaps it was a kind of truce?

Jenny had always had that compassionate touch. Right from her early school days. Her dream was to be a nurse in her innocent years. It never worked out, got distracted with other things along with the sudden death of her father, but she would always be the one to help others out, especially her friends.

Her benevolence also guided her mother through the tough times. No doubt it had been a tough, terrible time. But she showed strength, she always did. That motherly figure that she had been bequeathed with ensured ironically a great undefeatable friendship with her own mother.

And now this. Jag, stunted by the complexities he now faced was not even willing to face up to things with the same woman by his side. He wanted to go alone into the darkness.

Her intention was clear. She wanted her old Jag back and was looking at options to achieve this. A counteroffer? Well, he couldn't think of one. On the other hand, simply accepting her offer would at least potentially put him back in her good books, or at least get him out of the way. Could give him more time to think his problems away?

Eventually Jag replied. 'I'll pick up some things from the garden centre. Maybe think of growing some roses and, I was thinking potatoes, maybe potatoes will grow? I think they will. What you think of potatoes?' He'd never grown potatoes so would have to do a little research but at the end of the day, she was right, without really knowing the full story. He did need a hobby, a hobby other than the one which involved staring at a laptop screen, whether home or away.

And potatoes. That was a different idea, suggested on the spot due to time of year they were in. Winter was coming to an end, and it seemed like the most suitable suggestion for the moment.

Most of all, it at least suggested a glimmer of hope for their dimming relationship.

CHAPTER 25

It was late, but almost a ritual that he must go and see his daughter before going to bed. Sleeping so soon after eating was not the greatest thing in the world, but Jag did sometimes succumb.

He quietly pushed on his daughter's partially open bedroom door. She turned as he entered, fitting snugly into her single bed, adorned with flowers and fairies and Frozen night lamp that warmed her dreams. He went to sit by her side.

As he began to tuck her in, he felt something under the bed sheets. Under closer inspection he found it to be her Tinkerbell doll. It was the same Tinkerbell doll that was missing its spinner. The spinner that gave life to an inanimate child's toy. The type of child's toy that was just another piece of plastic until you put it in its spinner, gave it a spin, and let it loose into the sky. Given its freedom, it would add magic to an otherwise dull child's life.

Despite being in the comforting and relaxed hands of its owner, Tinkerbell must still have felt so alone, unable to fly shouts of freedom, at least once divorced from its wings. A little instinctively, Jag went over to the box of toys in the corner of Bunny's room, toys, organised in a disorganised way. The plethora of toys certainly looked random, but that was to uneducated eyes. To those over the age of twelve the mix of toys must have looked a mess. To those below, the toys were mesmerising and exhilarating, not to mention, perfectly placed.

Jag was in search of Tinkerbell's other half; her partner in rhyme, but this time not Peter Pan, to build up the rhythm enough to spin around the room in peace and tranquillity. Poetry in motion.

It had been quite disconcerting to Jag, to see his only daughter, Bunny, hurt so much by Tinkerbell's missing spinner. He was determined to do his best to find that piece.

So, he rummaged around in the chaotic labyrinth that was her collection of toys. Set up like a network of plastic pieces, each one, a fingerprint into another world. It was another world of unfathomable imagination and dreams. It was a dead zone of fluffy and fancy, sometimes attractive objects, that was to unenlightened eyes.

To the inspired, informed, chosen few, it was an ecliptic glimpse into the corona; where nothing could really be explained, other than what was visible. To Bunny, it was a black hole of adventures, where no one outside would be invited to find out about. That was the world Bunny lived in. These toys were her reality.

Trying to make as little noise as possible, Jag fought ambitiously to find that spinner. His efforts to find the spinner and make minimal noise were both defeated, as, even with the light from the bedside lamp, he was unable to keep himself from pushing one toy against the other. Noises followed, as he worried about waking her up.

Even worse, in the semi-darkness, he found himself hurdle straight into one of the cabinet legs. An explosion of agony in the form of a prism of pain that seemed to pulverise his body. That inevitable explosion through his body, a corollary of such carelessness. It really wasn't that dark, and Jag should have evaded the protrusion, almost staring him in the face and blurting warning signs at him.

He squealed like a mouse, though felt like a rat. In his efforts to conceal the pain he almost let out tears of hurt. Then, a few seconds later, he did. It had simply been a trigger; a trigger that pulled at the piano strings that fed blood into his heart. Though the pulsing beat of the throbbing pain sang through his body, it had been a trigger that made him ask himself 'Why me? Why always me?' He'd been the one to suffer the ignominy that plagued his mind, so why now did he have to suffer more chords of mental and physical torture, heavy metal heartache.

For a few minutes he sobbed. He sobbed like a baby. It was a release caused by accident, but medicinal in outcome. Like most medicine, it did not taste good, but gave a glimpse into the future. Maybe there was a blessing in that act of pain and anguish…? Maybe. Nothing happens by accident. Wincing with pain though, Jag was not fully convinced.

Then he got on with his life. It was an emotional mission he was on. His love for Bunny was so strong that it meant so much more to him. Seeing his daughter sleeping, hands clenched to her favourite toy, added to the emotion. He was determined to at least try his hardest to find that toy's other half, maybe then doubling his daughter's pleasure.

Like his own life, it was something he, himself was looking for. Something missing in his own life. Something to help the cogs turn once again and return to normality. That spinner was symbolic of the missing piece he was looking for, as much for himself as for his lovely daughter. The half of his life he had left felt like the unwanted half. He was looking, searching, for the golden part, to put a spin back into. He wanted desperately to get that motion back into his world; let the world spin once again.

Keep spinning, Jag. Life is no good without that spin. Spin to win. Keep looking, Jag.

Unfortunately, the spinner seemed well and truly lost. It seemed only one of Tinkerbell's adventures could rediscover it. In his attempts to recover the spinner the noise he was making was a little loud. As he was still recovering from the smash on his toe, he was a little louder than was hoped, as his toe now started to throb. He caused Bunny to shuffle in her bed once again. By now, it was a miracle that she had not been awoken by her father's noises.

Naturally, Bunny moved around, almost waking up to the sight of, what to her would look like a toy thief. So, Jag stopped for a second, fearing he would fully wake his daughter. Then, getting used to the light, or lack thereof, he simply began to look for the spinner once again, this time, more cautiously.

Then, a whisper from his left side. It sounded unclear, but surely it was a whisper. An angelic whisper, as he started to lose interest in his mission. He found himself refocusing on his daughter, as dreamy whispers escaped her. Thoughts of finding that spinner were losing traction.

'Daddy... daddy... daaa...' It was Bunny whispering in loose tones. Her shifting around in bed had been replaced by a verbal shifting, uneasy. She was sleep-talking, but was it a coincidence she was sleep-talking to the person who was in the room?

Big coincidence. It immediately grabbed Jag's attention. What was she trying to say? Jag, for one, was certainly quizzical.

Don't wake her, Jag. No more noisy moves. Let her talk. Let her talk.

Jag was intent on just that. It was spying in on someone else's private conversation, and it had an attraction, an inevitable enticement. Jag moved closer, whispering 'Yes, Bunny...' Whispering so quietly, it was almost as if he was talking to her without wanting to wake her, an interesting paradox.

Talking to someone in a dream was quite a delicate challenge. Jag somehow wanted to coax out whatever was on Bunny's mind. And it seemed to be working.

'Tinkerbell wants her spinner, daddy. She's lonely. She's lone...' It was Bunny's voice, soft and innocent, almost dying out from lack of energy. She got her message across, that much was clear, but it was a fading request, as if she felt like she was losing the battle. The voice of a cancer victim vacant of hope, or that of a resident in a care home devoid of any reason to live. For so long now there had been that relentless desire to find that spinner. Bunny, herself seemed to be losing hope, accentuated by the tone of her voice, or was it simply her dream?

There was a sadness that overtook Jag, as if that spinner was more than just a spinner. A symbolic lifeline or a shambolic countdown? It meant more than simply a piece of plastic. Unlike what happens to most plastic, this was recyclable. It was recyclable like an emotional victory, to be cherished and celebrated time after time. It was a portent, a sign of hope. A reusable, environmental piece of plastic. An intangible gem of plastic, melted down into a diamond of hope, sparkling like the smile of his child that would renew itself over and over. In essence, it was hope.

Despite his financial problems there was always hope, the environmental recyclable friend of nature, that would always be there at the start of the day to shine down.

This was why he wanted that spinner.

'Daddy, mummy's not happy. She's sad. I can see in her eyes, she's sad. Just tell her, daddy, just tell her.' It was as if Bunny was drugged, the way she breathed out the words. They were almost whispers rather than words; air carefully and painfully being blown out. Daddy was shocked, surprised and a little speechless. It was as if Bunny knew his little secret. But how? And really? It was just a dream. She's just playing games with my mind. Kids can do that. Emotional pinball machines.

No, Daddy, this is no joke. No more clowning around, Jaggy. The cat's out of the bag.

Maybe Bunny just sensed the unease developing between her parents, her subconscious hoping for the best. Maybe that barrier between husband and wife illuminating their existence. Bunny must have noticed, thought Jag. It was still a little concerning though, that it had become so damn obvious.

'Stop giving money to those people, daddy. You got to stop, daddy. They are bad people. I know they are. You know they are.' Jag stopped breathing, not sure whether he really was hearing the words or his imagination. He stopped doing everything, like time stood still. Even the sound of the kiddies Tinkerbell purple wall clock seemed to tick louder and slower as if it too, was reprimanding him, coming ever so slowly to a stop. Echoing, painful reverberations like gongs smashing against his ears, pulverising his ear drums like Neil Peart. Then it seemed as if the clock itself stopped ticking; the drum-roll came to its end.

Silence. No thoughts. No movement. Nothing.

Well, we did warn you didn't we, Jag? You carry on spinning, Jag. Keep the spinner turning and the forex dream burning. Let it burn, Jag. Let it burn.

He was gobsmacked and felt himself shaking, all in a split second. It did not make any sense. Or, at least, he did not want it to. Either way, it was not what he had expected. How could she know about The Forex Group? Maybe she overheard him sometime, or saw some of his papers?

Or maybe she was psychic? Kids can be.

Or perhaps she was just mumbling randomly in her sleep. That theory rang better with Jag, already bordering mental paralysis. Just mumbling for sure. Jag thought to himself the number of times he had gone through dreams that had no head or tail, complete nonsensical dreams. Bunny likely was experiencing one of those. This explanation was easier to digest than the high fibre drivel his mind was making him consume.

More words escaped from his daughter's mouth, too vague for him to stomach or understand. To Jag, it had turned into verbal vomit... without the bag. She was clearly uneasy though, as she rambled on, though only for a few more seconds. They say dreams seem to last for hours to the dreamer, but only last a few seconds in reality. Time, exemplifying its abstract nature.

He turned his head away from his daughter's world, back into the old one of troubles and strife, away from his nightmare and into reality. His mind flicked back to the spinner, but only for a second, as he realised there was no chance he would be finding that tonight. Tinkerbell's long-lost spinner would have to wait another day.

Chapter 26

The weekend's auspicious arrival saw Jag pay a visit to the garden.

It had been planned, a peace pact with his wife. The past few months had been challenging and they both knew it, but Jag especially, was still mentally denying it. Still keeping it his little secret. As a workaround, Jenny had suggested he spend some time fixing the garden.

She had not been wrong in her assertion that the garden was a mess and spelt it out as such. It was her way of doing two things. Firstly, it would get Jag and his absent mind out of her hair. More importantly, it may give Jag a chance to dig deep enough to discover what it was that had changed his personality so much. Jenny had noticed a disinterest developing in Jag. Maybe a spell in the garden would plant some seeds of hope in their relationship.

Jag too, had no complaints. It would get him out of the house, and more importantly out of the sight of the woman he had got increasingly antagonised with. Also, it bought him time to come up with some solution to his financial vicissitudes. Even better, it was a lovely sunny day.

In the past he would spend those lovely sunny days with his lovely wife. But that was the past. They used to walk in Stanborough Park. Though not ones to participate in watersports, they loved the ducks, watching them feed and their mannerisms. Once Bunny got a little older, she got so excited for the ducks and swans.

Jenny remembered going to Brighton for weekends with mum and dad during those long summer days. Whenever her and Jag visited, those old vague memories with her parents would come flooding back. Those days, whether with parents or Jag, they seemed an age away now.

Those were the sunny days. The real, 'sunny' days. Today it was sunny, but the shine had all been used up. The shine today was Jag getting some time away from Jenny to avoid her doubting him.

The shine had all been used up.

It wasn't the first time that he had explored the garden. He was the one who planted most of the flowers in their homes. He liked the privacy, living in a detached house with a nice sized garden. To add to his privacy, he had got a local builder to put up some large wooden fencing. There were no noisy neighbours going to spoil his days in his garden. He had few ideas and a good size garden as his canvas.

Jag wanted to try to grow potatoes. A new project, untested.

It was not something he had tried before but thought he could give it a try.

He planned to dig deep to promote better growth, but was looking at raised beds, maybe three or four. This would give additional depth to ensure these potatoes had enough space to grow to their requirement. The fact that he had never tried this before gave him greater interest but did leave him asking questions about the whole project as he was not too knowledgeable.

Initially he spent some time planning, using the slope he had to section off the part he would dedicate to the potatoes, then popped over to his local garden centre for advice and to buy the planks of wood for the raised beds.

He found himself craning his neck upwards as he explored the expansive garden centre. B&Q always had a welcoming feel for Jag. Open and spacious, he enjoyed the sights and smells. It was certainly not going to be easy carting the bags of compost and planks of wood he had in mind. Jenny had taken Bunny to her mum's. It had been a few weeks and Jenny tried to go to her mum's weekly if she could. This visit was overdue, especially as her mother lived on her own. So, it wasn't ideal, but Jag would have to get the gardening demands on his own.

Aside from wondering how he was going to carry everything back home, he found himself spending the most time in the implements and tools section.

He would need a strong shovel for sure, for what he had in mind. It might have been an idea to look for some elbow grease as well, based on the amount of work that lay ahead. Picking and trying various types, he was looking for the one with the least hurt on the hands and arms.

He felt a bit silly, but to find the best set of shovels he would pick them and try them on the ground, picking up fictitious clumps of soil. It was a little comical, like he was playing charades with Lionel Blair. In the end, he plumped for two shovels to assist him. Why buy one when you can buy two?

Why potatoes? Well, why not? He'd tried other things like radish, lettuce, and spring onions, but found the idea of potatoes different, challenging, and most importantly, a little project that might just take his mind away from the distractions that preoccupied him.

Being early spring, it also felt like a good time to begin. Despite the cold, potatoes supposedly grew well from early spring planting.

That was the start of his gardening project. It was an honest project, at least to some degree, not like the gardening leave his old foe, Mark Goldsmith had concocted. In Jag's case, it was honest, though one of the very few things he had been honest about recently. His main priority had always been to take up Jenny's idea and in her eyes, appease her. From his point of view, he just wanted to get himself out of Jenny's sight for some time. Give himself more time to think about the only things he ever thought about.

Gardening leave, he thought to himself angrily. Mark Goldsmith, and gardening leave. That's all that dug into his mind. Where Mark's gardening leave had been like painful dirt in his eyes, maybe his own gardening leave could be the seed that would sprout roots of hope? Hope springs eternal.

It had been a hassle, a big hassle. Lugging bag after bag of compost into his back garden. But that was the challenge he set himself. He was also lugging the emotional baggage of his problems. They weighed pounds. Jenny and Bunny had made it back early, as some visitors had decided to drop by, unannounced at her mother's place. Despite friendly chords of help from his loving daughter, and a few loving strains of help from his wife, Jag had managed to drag enough compost based on his estimations, to fill four rectangular beds. These beds would be slightly raised off the ground and allow the potatoes to grow deep enough under the ground.

The work of making the potato beds in lines, was work for another day. He'd done enough hard work for one weekend.

'What's going on, Jag?' It was his wife, as she was watching his green fingers at work. She had been watching him bringing in many bags of compost, together with the wooden planks. Her idea of his gardening project was not so messy. The can of worms she had opened may now have begun digesting their garden.

Jenny thought to herself that it had been her own fault. She was the one who had rocked the boat, pressuring him to '... do something with the garden.' She never expected raised potato beds.

Jag had also decided on two apple trees, a pear tree, and a plum tree. He was going all out, didn't give a damn! It would perhaps make the garden look a little smaller, but would give more character to the place and eventually, more privacy. For Jag, this was quite an extravagant gardening experience he had concocted up. The line of additional roses and low-lying colourful crocuses and carnations should help to appease Jenny, he thought.

CHAPTER 27

Thud.

Definitely, a large thud.

Jag was not a particularly large man, around eighty kilos, but he made a very loud thud. I suppose anyone would do. Anyone, even a child would make a loud thud when dropped from a two feet high bed. Unsurprisingly, Jag's thud was an expected outcome if you fall out of your bed onto wooden floorboards.

'What happened?' moaned Jenny. 'You okay?' Jenny had been half-asleep, but not fully asleep, as Jag dropped like a sack of potatoes onto their bedroom floor. Whatever unwanted fire there were between the two of them had been extinguished, at least for that moment. There was irony though. Irony like one of those seldom moments when there was genuine care from his wife. A moment he was not even conscious enough to appreciate. That's life.

Jag groggily got back to his feet, slowly the steadiness coming back to him like an old, but loving friend. He checked himself, as if making sure all his body parts were still there. Yes, they were. Slowly, his senses were making a comeback; a boxer rising from the canvas before the count of ten, though thoughts of Jag being a boxer seemed far-fetched.

'What happened?' repeated Jenny. He had no idea.

'JJJen? I'm okay. Did I fall out of bed?'

I think that was pretty obvious, Jag.

'Yes, Jaggy, looks like you did. But you, okay?' It was that name she used again. He hated so much being called Jaggy, but at least this time tiredness was taking precedence over anger.

'Well, I feel fine, apart from the fact that I just fell out of bed.'

Did you push me?

That was the first thought that came to him. But he stopped himself from thinking out loud. That would not have been a good move. More pressing matters prodded his mind, like how did I fall, and why? Clearly Jenny would not have done that, would she?

Yes, apart from the grogginess he felt surprisingly okay. Considering that Jag had just fallen two feet from the bed onto the hard floorboards, it was not a bad result that he felt fine. Being asleep when it happened probably helped. Only being woken up by the impact helped even more. His numbness hid the reality, like the numbness that ruled their relationship as of late.

Amidst his drowsiness, trying to recover, his right thumb went over to the top of his t-shirt near his shoulder. He generally preferred to use t-shirts rather than traditional pyjamas. His thumb gestured three or four times as if to lift a strap or something at the top of his t-shirt. It was an impulsive movement that he only realised the meaning of some moments later. His odd actions made him look like he was a trying to hitch a ride. The only ride he was taking was back to his bed.

'I think I'm fine now, Jenny. I think I'm fine. Go back to sleep.' Jag headed to the bathroom, yawning, as much to relieve his senses as much as his bladder.

Yawning repeatedly, Jag looked like he was trying to do an impression of the MGM lion aka Leo, again an unlikely comparison. It wasn't Jag being grumpy or dismissive. Moreover, it was his mind starting to register where he was and the thoughts that preoccupied him.

Where was he? He was back in reality.

Throwing water onto his face in his bathroom helped the reality to become real. Looking into the mirror, glimpses of his recent dream and those reflections started to hit him. Echoing in the back of his mind was the sound of spectators, screaming, shouting, jeering...

... The muffled sounds, some cheering him on and others aggressively spurting expletives at him as he stood there, the centre of attention. The canvas he stood on was a little bouncy as he leant backwards, finding the elastic rope stretch behind him. His right thumb felt for the strap of his singlet, missing once or twice, then finding the strap. Now he felt more comfortable.

He was in a wrestling match.

His senses were just finding their place as he realised he was in some wrestling bout. Being in a wrestling match meant there had to be an opponent. He looked across to the other side, partly looking into jeers, as well as cheers. An overweight man; a big daddy. It was the familiar sight of an old foe. The one who often spurred on his envy. James Balden, who else, arms out, slightly stretched, looked smugly at him from across the stage.

Catching his breath, he looked around, appearing normal, from the outside at least. Of course, he was sweating profusely, the heat of the moment, mingling with the heat of the attention. But part of him liked that; his alter ego coming to the fore. They both walked around the ring, eyes focused on each other, peripheral sounds adding to their focus.

They drew close to each other, intensity increasing. Clearly Balden was a much bigger man, his weight advantage was obvious, but not his height. Nevertheless, Jag quickly jolted forward, grabbing his opponent between the shoulders and the neck, a kind of stranglehold. Balden did the same. Jag realised straight away that maybe that was not such a good idea as he felt vice-like fingers pierce into his shoulders like knives. The shoulder claw, like the two were playing the piano. Jag realised this was not music to his ears as piercing pain drilled through his body.

It was paralysing, not just the pain. Jag's eyes were paralysed by Balden's and vice-versa, not to mention their muscles that felt frozen solid. Balden had the advantage of size and strength and immediately Jag realised it was the wrong move. Worse still, Jag knew that Balden was a great project planner, experienced, well rounded, confident. Jag had none of that. He was young, more agile, fitter, but right now he needed a plan.

Balden grimaced with effort as he dug his fingers into the shoulders and neck of Jag. Painful piano chords causing squirms of concern. And they both looked like zombies fighting for their lives... or maybe a return to life?

It was all starting to look grim for Jag as he felt himself lowering onto his knees from the spasmodic cramps that were overtaking him. Balden knew he was close to finishing it, his battle with Jag. Then, with a smile to himself and Jag, he inadvertently loosened his grip. It was just for a split second. But that was all it took. In that split second Jag found that glimmer. Just a glimmer, but when you're surrounded by darkness all you wish for is a glimmer of light and hope.

As Balden tried to get his grip back, and practically strangle Jag, his fingers slipped on the sweat of both of their bodies. It gave Jag a few extra milliseconds. Smelling life, Jag released his hands from Balden's neck, shot up his arms as if making the 'Y' from YMCA, successfully removing that death grip of Balden. Almost, instinctively, Jag started punching Balden. It would have been nice for Jag if he had been given a few seconds to give an emotional thank you for the release from his pain, but there was no time for that.

Now, it was a different Balden. It was a tired, overweight Balden, not the controlled smiling Balden of only a few seconds ago. The smile had turned into a grimace. This was a different grimace; a grimace of fear and trepidation; numb.

This was a Balden worse for wear, age, and enthusiasm. No project planning had prepared him for this type of outcome. It wasn't the milestone he had mapped out on his chart. There was no professionalism nor the smug smile that normally accompanied. Just a shriek of anguish. That's all he could muster.

The crowd erupted now like a goal had been scored in an FA Cup Final. It felt like the roof was going to fall in or explode off. Such was the excitement. From nowhere, but unscripted, at least to Jag, it seemed that somehow, he had come back from the jaws of death. Out from the mouth of the fish to fight a second life.

Balden was now a blubbering mess; a wreck now ready to be shipped out. He was salivating and feeling increasingly less stable with each punch on the chin and face. He was too tired to fight back, lethargic, and drained. There wasn't even that look asking for mercy. Just an empty expectant look, like he had accepted the inevitable.

Jag now set off on a sprint, from one side of the ring to the other, gaining momentum as he ran. His energy was the inverse of how Balden felt. As he gained momentum, he sprung stronger and stronger from side to side on the rope, adding to Balden's imbroglio. It seemed like each time he bounced off the rope, he gave himself energy, a kid's toy string being pulled more and more, and more.

Then he lifted himself off the ground. The flying kick. Bam! Right into the chin of an already jaded Balden. Not what the doctor ordered, though the doctor may be needed after this. With the force of the kick, Balden rocked backwards; a tall building hit by an earthquake, unsure whether to fall or hold on and hope for the best. His human instinct and innate desire for life kept him in the game.

More running from Jag. Side to side, rope to rope, it seemed an alternative attempt to confuse Balden. It seemed to be working. Such were the frantic actions of Jag. Momentum again reached. Off the ground he leapt, Bam! Double-Bam. This was turning into the inevitable. They weren't twins in that ring, but one of the towers was looking fragile!

Balden could take no more. His shaking legs gave into another diving kick. He was the muscular equivalent of a stutterer. A feather could have toppled him at this stage.

Ring-a-ring-a-rosies,

A pocket full of posies,

A tissue, a tissue,

Balden fall down!

He lay flat on his back, breathing heavily. Conscious but confused, all he could see were the spotlights staring him down. Like a prisoner, the spotlight stare froze him to his spot. Balden, paralysed to his spot, dead centre of the ring, did at least, feel at ease.

There was a calm amidst the cacophony of jeers and cheers. Some were for him and some for his opponent. Unfortunately, all he heard were the cheers at this stage. Unfortunate, because those cheers were not for him, and he knew it.

The people were getting what they came for. Entertainment. Paradoxically, maybe the cheers were for him; him playing his part in this vicious parade. Win or lose, it didn't matter to these mindless onlookers. They just wanted entertainment. Blood would be a bonus.

The world just sounded so mixed up and vague to Balden, as he lay in wait on the surface. It seemed like a lifetime but was only a few seconds. For some of those seconds, the ones that seemed to last even longer than the other ones, he heard nothing.

There was a blankness to those seconds. As though he had been transported into another world of nothingness. It was a place he had no control of going to or existing in. It was a world that didn't care to help him, nor hinder him. Just a place of silence. An empty void; a dead Balden waiting in his grave for his day of judgement. It was no man's land, especially if your name was James Balden.

Balden, as he lay down on his canvas bed, at least felt some relief for those few pregnant seconds. A place where he felt no need to cry out like a baby or moan in pain. He just lay paralysed and deaf to the world.

Meanwhile, in his former world, the cheers belted out, the jeers whipped along, the chants cracked ahead. Jag was now in a much more positive mood than he was a few minutes ago. He was running around chanting the crowd on, milking the nutrients out of them. Whipping them up into a frenzy, it was his turn to shine.

Then he headed for one of the corners of the ring. He chose the corner screaming the loudest. Ironically, it was also the corner closest to the motionless James Balden. He felt magnificent. More magnificent than the great redwoods of Muir Woods.

They were chanting his name now. 'Jaggy, Jaggy, Jaggy.' Music to his ears as his grin widened. The pleasure got all that much greater as he cast valued glances at an almost motionless foe on the ground.

It was his turn to shine.

Stomping his feet on the ground to the tune of 'Jaggy, Jaggy, Jaggy.' Despite not being a fan of that name, now it felt right. It's two syllables, lengthened as 'Ja' and 'ggy'. It fed his adrenalin like an intravenous drip piercing his skin.

He knew it couldn't last forever, but there was no crime in wishing it would. A penny in the pond, as Jag took his chances with his wishes. Tingles through his body as the chanting grew into a crescendo. His bones were now tingling too, tuned like piano strings with perfect resonance and an arena with just the right amount of echo. His heart seemed like it was playing the keys of the bones in his body; a grand time he was having.

Finally, he reached the top of the corner. Jag's nickname was 'Jaggernaut.' There was good reason for this, and he was about the show packed arena exactly why. This was what they came to see. This was why the whole place was packed to the rafters and buzzing with anticipation.

Whenever someone was at the top of their game there became an expectation. Reaching that expectation got tougher and tougher each time. But that was what drew the crowds. Tonight, was no exception. Having fat guy Balden as the victim made it that much more rewarding.

The people liked to see the smaller guy pulverise the big guy in wrestling and this seemed about to happen. Added to this was the fact that Jag was about to smash his work colleague Balden, personal satisfaction to curb those nine-to-five blues.

Jag wasn't much of a swimmer, but his finishing move was the called 'The Diving Splash'. That's what all this fuss was about. That's why the crowd were crazy and getting crazier by the second. That final move, all that mattered. The rest was just a preamble, fluff in an otherwise sweaty affair.

This was the final song in a concert, extra time in that World Cup Final, the last and most talked about episode of a long running serial drama. Dramatic it was, sporty it clearly was, tuned music to a composed Jag, it most definitely was.

Jag was stood on top of the world. Well, actually, it was the top of the corner pole of the ring, but it felt like the top of the world to him. It was a familiar feeling now to him that had the added benefit of the view. He had reached the top of this greasy pole, greasy through sweat and tears. Not an easy journey, but a rewarding one. All that pain was now forgotten.

The view of the crowd was special, almost as special as the sounds coming from them. The panoramic view he had; the top of a mountain looking out into the distance, cool and conquering. Stood on the shoulder of giants, his view of the distance awe-inspiring. Below, was even more breath-taking to Jag. Breath-taking, yes, but a place Jag feared. It was the same place he had come from, with no plans to go back down to.

As he looked down, a long way down at Balden, he saw nothing more than humiliation. Humiliation in the form of a living heartbeat. It was a humbled, craven, helpless heartbeat, beaten. Not the posh voice of confidence and credence. More the timorous whimper of stupidity. All those office meetings flashed across the mind of Jag like a cinematic portrayal of embarrassment. Those memories were now distant. It was Jag's turn now to play the leading role, the hero.

The 'Jaggernaut' gave one last look around his panoramic empire, then down to the serf that lay below. An inevitable gesture that he was ready to dive and make a splash into the breathing but helpless Balden below. A tired Balden gazed up, eyes widening.

He crouched. He dived. He screamed. The 'Jaggernaut' was on his way...

Thud...

Chapter 28

Thud...

'You sure you're okay, Jaggy?' Jenny repeated, a little louder and more caring as Jag shook himself a little. This was not in any way a response to Jenny. Moreover, it was a response to deceiving his conscience that had seemed to play a nasty trick on him. And suddenly 'Jaggy' didn't sound so nice anymore. It wasn't the 'Jaggy, Jaggy, Jaggy,' aka 'Ja' and 'ggy'. Not the same rhythm or rhyme. More indecision and whine.

He was slowly coming back to his senses... unfortunately. These senses though, were not always sensible, as his past had proved. No more the champion wrestler that he thought he was, this was Jag, the loser of thousands of pounds of hard-earned money. The flop at work, or at home. One thing that he and his alter ego 'Jaggernaut' had in common? They both couldn't swim.

Sink or swim, his personal survival guide told him it had to be swim. He had no choice. 'Maybe I was tired from the gardening? Probably bit out of touch. It's been a long time since I got to work on the garden. I guess I was just still thinking about digging or something?' He was making vague guesses; didn't want to own up to the fact that a few minutes ago he was a world champion wrestler. That would've only made his wife think he was even more crazy.

'Maybe, yes, Jaggy. It's been a while.' She was sounding much more compassionate this time, pensive, and it was genuine. Despite whatever aloofness he had been showing, she still did love and need him. 'You've only just started, but maybe you need some gardening leave?' She spoke jokingly, though Jag didn't appreciate it. He was more concerned with her using that phrase... Gardening Leave. It was a little alarming to him. Etched into his mind like an indelible black spot was that email from Goldsmith.

Gardening Leave!

She laughed out loud, as she was quite chuffed with herself. It was mainly using the gardening cliché, and Jag was a little surprised she had it in her vocabulary. She also was sarcastically letting Jag know that even after one day, his gardening skills were tiring him out. Her way of belittling him.

In his surprise, he shot around, looking her straight in the eyes. Her hazel eyes were oblivious to any hidden code that Jag's dark brown eyes had decoded. The after-effects of his initial thud were now a distant, ever-decreasing echo in the back of his mind. Now, this new thud had entered his mind, an unwanted beating of a drum. Mental or physical, these thuds were bullets in his chest.

How could she know about gardening leave, he thought to himself? Did she know about Goldsmith? The scam? His secret? The Group? His bad luck? If she had some idea, he just wished she would have some ideas to reply to these dreaded thoughts.

It had not been the first time Jag had started to doubt his secret-hiding skills. Earlier, in her dream, Bunny also seemed to recollect some information. He was starting to wonder what was going on.

'Yeah, I mean, I don't know... maybe tired from work? Maybe just a bad dream?' Fumbling around for tired excuses, Jag had to offer something.

Yes, it was all just a bad dream, that's all. Get used to it. Maybe time to start putting a pillow on the floor next to the bed? Falling and feeling like a sack of potatoes. Dream on, Jaggy!

'Go back to sleep, Jen. I'll be fine in the morning. We better be fine tomorrow; we got that birthday to go to.'

CHAPTER 29

At least Jag woke up in his bed in the morning, rather than on the floor.

It was Bunny's friend's birthday party today. She had been looking forward to it for weeks. Her best friend was turning five, and, though Bunny was her best friend, she couldn't help feeling jealous of the fact that her friend would be five yet herself still only four. At that time of life, it mattered.

Jag had been getting increasingly fidgety over the past few weeks. It hadn't struck him just how bad things were, but they were getting worse. Times he would sit there biting his nails, even though the length of his nails was fine, or extra fine, as they were cut right down to the skin already. He would search through his fingers for something to bite on, his appetite for hope increasing all the time.

Spending longer days in the office helped but was only his way of hiding away his problems. It helped to mask his nervousness a little, simply by not being at home. There was no scientific calculation to his plans, just spontaneous and defensive acts. And he never could stomach up the courage to tell her the truth.

Often, he sat around, feet bouncing up and down frantically, as if he was continually trying to kill a cockroach on the floor. These frantic bouts would last a few minutes, then he would move onto another area of the floor, as if he had just spotted another insect to crush. The only thing getting crushed though, was his nervous mind, playing cantankerous games with himself.

The birthday party was a big deal, as much for Bunny as for her best friend, Hannah. Without it being Bunny's birthday, she still felt the day's importance, like everything had to be perfect.

Jenny had bought a beautiful long dress for Bunny. It was an amazing blue frock that had the potential to overshadow even the birthday girl, but Bunny didn't care. Some would say it was wasted being used as a dress to attend someone else's special day in. Of course, Tinkerbell went with her, without the spinner. That spinner had still not been found, despite Jag having searched high and low. However nice her dress was, it was just no compensation for the remorseful loss of her spinner.

Despite having nicer dolls, Bunny would always take that particular doll with her. It was her twin, her living doll. At times it had been forgotten at a friend's house, always to eventually find its way home. Those nervous times, Bunny awaiting the news of her long-lost friend; her soul. Thankfully, it always turned up, at least so far.

Bunny was the first to arrive, of course. This was Hannah, the best of her best friends. Bunny liked Hannah's dress but knew her own was nicer; subjective but true. There were even a few envious glances from Hannah to Bunny. Bunny deduced without question that Hannah was simply admiring her lovely dress.

'... Yeah, it's quite rampant now. It's just so easy, you know, to just log on to a PC and trade. You don't even need a PC. A mobile phone is just as easy, in fact easier. Even a child could buy shares or make a trade. There's very little to stop these problems getting out of control.' Jag couldn't help but overhear, especially as he had been so easily distracted lately.

He hadn't really paid much attention to his wife moaning about the fact that her shoes didn't match. In the end, an argument with Jenny, and she had refused to go with Jag to the birthday party. It was a little chaotic, and moody, but in the end Jag made up some excuse for his missing wife.

Some mumbling woman was chewing his ear off, nattering on about the time she first drove her new car. She was carefully explaining to Jag that she could not get used to the start-stop feature on her car. Jag couldn't give a damn and was clearly and understandably more attracted to the other adjacent conversation. The other conversation was much more relevant.

'It's all a little anonymous too. You can set up with a company to trade with and never even meet anyone from there. A bit like your just throwing money down some black hole, hoping you can bend down and find it. Well, you know if there's no light, you ain't gonna find it. And that's why there's so much corruption, because it's so easy and, like I said, almost anonymous.' It was Hannah's mum. She was talking to one of the parents. Jag was hooked.

'You know, this, and other cybercrime is in the trillions. The amount these guys are making. You really wouldn't believe it. It's like financial rape, or I suppose, suicide.'

Some of those trillions are mine, thought Jag, feeling more stressed, angered, and sweaty. I'm the one committing financial suicide here, DO YOU HEAR ME? He was clearly getting internally emotionally involved without saying a word, even without those having the conversation knowing about him. His heart was beating faster, even as a bystander.

He had to step in. And he did. 'Sorry, I'm, err, Bunny's father.' It was almost like a question. Like he was asking, '*Am I Bunny's father?*' Well, he just wanted to be invited into the conversation. It was relevant to him, needed to be a part of it. He was a stakeholder in a roundabout way. And if he hadn't bumped himself into the conversation, his day would not have been complete, even if two is company and three, a crowd. It mattered not one bit to him at that point. He was happy to be part of the crowd.

The two women looked at each other, a little embarrassed, awkward. Who was this guy? Why is he butting in? Well, he was Jaggy, and he was a stakeholder! Bunny, one of the women thought, is that the pet or something?

'Bunny... is my daughter. She and Hannah are best friends. The one over there next to Hannah, with the sequined blue dress?' Jag was desperately trying to prove himself and his prestige, and Bunny was his ticket. Otherwise, he was just another loser from the Indian subcontinent. Jag was pointing, hopeful but a little forlorn, almost doubting himself as being the father of Bunny. He was sweating a little.

He was fighting hard to be convincing, though struggling even to convince himself. Bunny was not his pet, though she was his little angel. She was also his ticket into the conversation.

It was starting to click now, with Hannah's mother, Olivia. She had met Bunny so many times, but never her father. It had always been her mother. And the first thing that struck her, off course, was that Jag was dark-skinned, but Bunny not. She knew Jenny from a few visits but had never realised that Bunny's father was Indian. It was no big deal, just an unmistakable observation. Not something Olivia was looking for, though on thinking about it, it did make Olivia feel a little guilty.

If you were not looking for it, why did you find it?

'Okay, you... you're Bunny's father.' It was like a question and answer in the same sentence, as Olivia spoke and thought at the same time. Also, it felt to Olivia a little like when something starts to click mid-sentence. Things were starting to fit together. Olivia simply didn't expect that Bunny's father would be Indian. 'Of course, you are Bunny's father. We've met her mother so many times, and never the father. Well, nice to meet you... So how is Jenny? Did she not come today?'

Olivia had only met Jenny a few times and she had never mentioned that her husband was Indian. But why would she?

My name is Jenny. Oh, and my husband is Indian.

'Oh, yes. Jenny was not feeling too good. I think a virus or allergy. She was unable to come, but she was very sad about not being able to come, especially for such a big day.' Jag just had to make something up to close the topic of his wife's absence.

Olivia was trying hard to hide her observation of the fact that he was Indian. It was mainly a guilt thing. The guilt thing had taken over from the awkwardness that introduced this parent into the conversation. She had almost forgotten that some parent in her daughter's birthday had just butted into their conversation about something or nothing.

'My name is Jag. Nice to meet you both.' Jag shook their hands. Finally, a degree of informality to break the odd introduction. Jag would probably never have bothered breaking their conversation had it not been for the topic under discussion. And he realised, or guessed, that they were looking at his skin colour, rather than who he was.

He had seen that a million times or imagined it. On the bright side, at least his awkward introduction had been somewhat tapered over. It was almost as if they had just created an even playing field. Jag's inappropriate, slightly intrusive hijacking of their conversation verses the clear reflection on Bunny's father being Indian.

As Jag spoke, he kept flicking his gaze over to Bunny, eyes of a loving guardian watching over her. 'Sorry, but I overheard your conversation about foreign exchange scams? It is something I am a little interested in. I hope you don't think I was prying? I've heard about this kind of thing before and seems to be on the rise. I've got a friend who suffered heavily from a scam like this, wondered as you seemed to know a bit about it?'

'No, no... it's fine. We were just having a general discussion. It's a very easy thing to fall for nowadays.' Olivia hid the fact that something felt strange to her. She had never mentioned anything about a foreign exchange scam to her friend Diane in their conversation. She was sure about that. That struck her as a little odd. She had mentioned share trading and cybercrime, but never specified mentioned what Jag spoke about.

A little suspicious, Olivia decided to ignore her observation. What was she going to do, confront Jag about his wrongly made assertions and add to the unease? She already felt like she couldn't get Jag's skin colour out of her mind, mainly because his daughter was so, so white-skinned. There it was again. That topic of skin colour taking over once again; hidden but always on the tip of her mind.

'Cybercrime really has ballooned tremendously over the past ten years, in-line with internet usage. There's no surprise in that, I know. It's like, as if we went into this web of technology blindfolded. Hindsight is certainly a lovely thing, but it could have saved a huge amount of people's money. Some of the people who've lost thousands on internet fraud and deception, makes the money gained on share trading seem like child's play. Whether it's options trading, foreign exchange, high frequency trading, or whatever. There's always someone at the other send we don't see or know where they are. Someone we don't see, but ironically has so many ways to see us!'

Olivia was speaking with what seemed the right experience, knowledge, and confidence. She seemed to know what she was talking about, and Jag found himself nodding in appreciation and acknowledgement. As well as that, but not overtly, Jag was also nodding with regret.

'You know it's funny, but not in a ha-ha way, how so many people fall for these scams.' Olivia was almost starting gloat now, like some *I told you so* policewoman. 'People can be so gullible, easy targets.' Jag's nodding had stopped. He was not enjoying or appreciating it now, like he was earlier.

A few seconds ago, Olivia was sympathising with how easy it was to fall for this type of scam. Now, she was practically condemning those gullible enough to get tricked by such fraudsters. Out of self-guilt, Jag had started to feel even greater remorse. Sadly, he knew all what she was saying was painfully true.

'You know, we deal with dozens of clients a week who have been down that ugly road of cyber-overindulgence. As they say, if it's too good to be true, it probably is.' That's what she called it, cyber-overindulgence, if such a word ever existed. She was affording herself her own self a little overindulgence it seemed.

‘Sorry, so how you know so much about this thing?’ Jag inquired. He really didn't know much about Olivia, other than that she was the mother of his daughter’s best friend.

‘Oh, sorry. Yes, I am a solicitor. I work in conveyancing, but our other department receive so many cybercrime related enquires. We are planning to expand that section, simply because we can't keep up with demand. Some people are just so gullible you know. Most of these victims don't even know the first thing about share and forex trading. They just think it's an easy way to get rich quick. Quite sad and pathetic really.’

As Olivia’s abuse continued, Jag felt worse and worse. As her flippancy grew, so did Jag’s anxiety. It didn't help that she was addressing him, eye to eye, blinding him with the truth, without even knowing it.

‘So, you mentioned you can deal with these cases, for clients? I mean, I can pass on your details to my friend who may need to discuss things with you? Or maybe he can contact you for more information?’ It was a desperate tone that Jag was trying to hide. His conscience was telling him he was not doing a great job, but was that his imagination talking? Maybe he was convincing, but not to himself?

‘Well, yes, you... they, can contact me and I'll pass the details over to our team.’ It was an apt slip on her tongue, addressing Jag rather than his notorious and fictitious friend. A large part of Jag believed that it was not actually a slip of the tongue. He was starting to believe that she had realised his true ambitions, that he was in fact his fictitious friend being referred to.

‘Yes, my friend might want to contact your company, thanks. I think he's looking at any way possible to get his life back to normal.’

And the autobiographical truth spoke. Very little role-play needed there, Jaggy.

Olivia had a little snigger to herself. A little smug, conceited act of overconfidence. Jag had surmised that she knew he was the other darker half of the story, but of course he was not letting on. Not much he could do about it, but it angered him tremendously.

Jag then looked around the room in envy; looking for suggestions of what to do next. Like an embarrassed child at a... a birthday party having just lost at pass-the-parcel, his anger and discomfiture possessed him to at least do something rather than look around the room for answers.

Olivia's home was a nice place, nicer than his, he felt. Such nice furniture and adornments legally bought. Legally bought often through the mangler unable to divorce itself from immoral funding. The life of a lawyer, poisoned pay cheques signed in blood; that of the victim. One man's freedom for another man's life; the positioning of power in the hands of the strong. The smug smile of success battering the honest frown of humbleness. Like a psychopath, compartmentalise your thoughts and responsibilities for the right occasion. It all riled Jag, now more than ever.

'I'm sorry, do you mind if I go to the bathroom?' It may have sounded at little out of place, but Jag needed some place. He needed some time to himself. He tried his best to speak as calmly as he could, though couldn't help feeling like he was impersonating tranquillity rather than being it. That awkward, out of the blue question, delivered in such a way that it seemed like he was not even listening to her words to start with. Quite rude!

A short silence. It had to be expected. Even Jag expected it. 'Oh, yes, of course, Jag. It's the, the room down the hall on the left.' Trying to sound polite and not too perturbed by Jag's timing, Olivia passed on the location, gesticulating instinctively.

Jag, she thought to herself. That's an odd name. It was her own way of showing hidden offence taken from Jag not really seeming to listen to what she had been saying. Truth was, he had been listening, just needed to get away from the truth he was expected to face. What kind of a name is Jag, she continued to herself, feeding her own negativity and pride?

The bathroom was a bit of a distance away so was well out of sight of Olivia and her friend, which he felt was a good thing. He shut the door behind him.

A sigh of relief.

Away from the action, for a while.

A chance to look at himself in the mirror. He was a mess. That was his conclusion.

When he looked at himself in the mirror, he did not simply see someone looking back. He saw the inner details that only he knew about. It wasn't the normality that others saw. He saw a depleted man.

He didn't see a successful IT Consultant, working his way up the ladder of professional progress. He just saw a path littered with snakes and slippery obstacles. That was his normality, an ever more depleted man.

Terrible thoughts stalked him. More challenging, the words and humiliation of Olivia burdened him. That smug cow, self-absorbed, self-opinionated. His pulse was building as he stared at himself in the mirror. The mirror stared back. His sweating forehead only intensified. Without yet even sitting down on the toilet, he flushed it, acting out his role. As he continued to look in the mirror he saw the conceited Miss Olivia, scolding him.

'How stupid you were, Jag. How many thousands of pounds did you say? Your so-called friend, messed up, Jaggy. Your so-called friend, called Jaggy, by any chance? Why the big secret, Jaggy? You worried Jenny would find out? Embarrassed? You're a big loser, Jaggy. Go back to your gardening, Jaggy. It's all you're good for. Take some gardening leave too!'

She was virtually screaming at him through the mirror now in his imagination, fingers piercing his cheek, prodding at his thoughts. She smirked at him.

Jag, now totally confused, started seeing images of himself digging and digging, and digging in his garden. How deep? Very deep. Digging uncontrollably, no end in sight.

Potatoes, he thought to himself, bloody potatoes! Deeper and deeper.

That familiar smell of soil, dampness, worms, grass... but paradoxically no oxygen! What an upside-down world he was in.

Digging in hope; hopeless hope, digging for hope!

No potatoes in sight, only a familiar cantankerous voice in his head grappling for attention... and winning.

His arms were tired, but he had no control over them. It was like they weren't his own arms, but were digging tirelessly. Robotic arms.

Fingers trembling through effort told him that they were in fact his. The tiredness spoke to him, through the pangs of pain. But still, he could not stop digging.

Keep digging, Jag. No gardening leave for you, my friend!

His hands were tied into submission. Forced to dig… dig… dig.

Fingers pressuring down on a rusty shovel. Splintered fingers to go with his splintered mind!

Blisters forming through hard digging, starting to sting his tired hands.

Dig, Jag, dig. Dig until your fingers burn! Gotta dig, Jag!

Fingernails black with effort and soil, now collecting on his fingers; soiled fingers and a soiled conscience!

Digging deeper and deeper in search of utopia, never-ending and suffocating! Only finding a dystopian disaster!

The frustration of digging but not knowing why. The same fingers that clicked away on the keys of his board, seemingly equally as pointless and unfortunate as his daily ambitions.

Digging in hope. Mining for glory, not a coin of consolation anywhere!

Realising he could not stop but not knowing how, he just went on digging; deeper, yet pointless.

Then he looked up from his tiring, bleeding fingers, straight into the present day; the mirror of Olivia stared back emotionless.

He was back in reality.

His muddied thoughts were climbing back into reality. Mirror, mirror, on the wall, who is the stupidest of them all? Jag did not wait for the answer... because he knew it.

Then he lost it; his limited control of the situation, as if falling deep into the hole he had just been digging.

Finding himself back in reality, he looked straight into the mirror, straight through it, and without a second thought, punched his fist into the mirror!

It was bizarre uncharted territory. No project planning went into it, no logic, no as is, to be mapping... just an uncalculated madness. Like the way in his mind, he was digging that hole, deeper and deeper, he had no control. He just thoughtlessly punched with no control. But this was not in his mind, it was real!

Then an explosion of pain to go with the explosion inside his mind. His hand jolted back, as he groaned in pain. It was physical pain, far greater than any psychological or mental pain from the words of Queen Olivia, at least on the surface. Her harsh conceited words, Jag could hardly remember now. What he was feeling now were sticks and stones.

A long crack formed on the mirror. Fortunately, it didn't shatter. Just a long crack from top to bottom. Yes, the noise was loud, but so too was the party, fortunately.

And his hand, his poor tender hand. Broken bones!

Can't dig with those hands, Jaggy!

That's all he could consider when he looked at those fragile knuckles. He could hardly move his fingers. Each time he tried, jolts reinforced the tattered nerves, evidently irreparable.

If it had been a boxing match it would have been a unanimous decision. Yes, the mirror had a long crack Jag had inflicted, but looking at Jag's hand and feeling the pain; there was only one loser... again.

Mirror... hand... mirror... hand. Take the mirror any day!

Mirror, mirror on the wall... who is the stupidest of them all?

His delicate fingers, and especially knuckles, the aftermath of pent-up frustration. The painful, lasting aftermath, real and irreparable.

Blood started to drop slowly from his knuckles, cut from the shards of the mirror, more evidence of his defeat. It had been an impulsive action. Once again, something he had little control over.

This was the same colour as the blood from his imaginary digging, but this time real... painfully real.

Instinctively, he grabbed the toilet roll with his left hand, the odd drop from the knuckles of his right hand falling into the sink and onto the tiled floor. The pain was bad, like he had a clenched fist of razor blades.

Each movement felt like he was squeezing those blades, a little harder each time. Before wiping the tissue onto his knuckles, he lowered his hand into the sink and turned on the tap. Making sure the tap opened slowly, he felt a mixture of relief and stinging burning as the initial seconds passed. Then, keeping the cold tap on, he turned up the pressure, intense torturous pain flooding through his hand.

Relief slowly started to take over. Jag was in no rush to raise his hand, the numbing cold water helping to alleviate the alarm he had been feeling, numbing his hand, and momentarily, also his mind.

He was in a bit of a pickle at his daughter's best friend’s birthday party, now like a prisoner in his cell. Only a mirror for company, and the face he saw inside that mirror was not too pleasing. It was either himself or Queen Olivia, the lawyer. This time, when he looked in the mirror, the relief and cooling on his hand made him at least see no one for a few seconds. He only saw relief.

Then reality hit back as he came to terms with where he was and what the hell he was doing. So, he turned off the tap and raised his hand; not a victorious raising of the hand, simply to halt the blood flow. Not a solution, more like patchwork.

He stood there thinking, looking like a schoolboy wanting to give the answer, even though he was an adult looking for solutions. He faced his mirror, knowing he had many consequences that would hit him. He faced that mirror, unable to find answers he hoped for.

It was all in segments of a second, but after gazing into the cracks in the mirror, Jag decided to wrap his hand up a little using bandages, also known as, toilet roll. As blood seeped through slowly, he had to keep patting it dry before the final application of roll. Rock’n’roll, he thought, though his hand was far from a rock now.

This was his permanent solution to his quarrelsome problem? Toilet roll? Quarrelsome, because it seemed each time he applied the bandage, blood started to seep through within a few seconds. In any case, he was in no major rush. He wanted to stay there as long as possible to avoid embarrassment.

Finally, despite the stinging pain, he reached a milestone in this little project. He kept his right hand on his head for as long as he could, stemming the open flow of blood. It was the only way he could figure out to reduce the blood pressure on his fingers and hand. Head, shoulders, knees, and toes...

Tidying himself up, and the bathroom, he used his left hand to clean as much of the blood from the floor that he could. To Jag, it felt like the stage set for a Halloween movie, but he was in the thick of things and looking for the minutest traces of blood, indelible evidence.

Hand still on his head, acting out part of YMCA, trying to control the blood flow, Jag scanned the room for abnormalities. Looking through abnormal eyes didn't help, but to him the bathroom looked as pure as it could do, given the circumstances.

His hand still throbbed, pulses of pain passing alongside intervals of quieter moments. Those quieter moments were what he longed for. Also, as it had been about fifteen minutes since he had punched the hell out of the mirror, he had started to get used to the palpitations drumming through his fingers.

As if taking his hand for a test drive, he lowered it from his head, steering his hand down to balance it in mid-air. Looking like a zombie, he had one arm outstretched. The zombie simile was further strengthened by the fact that he wore a white toilet roll glove; a perverted Michael Jackson... thrilling.

No diamonds decorated Jag's white glove, only dampness and the impending gloom of blood. His hand stuttered around chest height, shaking with its recent spontaneous collision with the mirror. And Jag possessed the physical equivalent of a stutterer, unsure of whether to move out of the bathroom and into the uninviting world on the other side. His legs now stuttered, reluctant to move forward, knowing there would be no birthday greeting to welcome him.

Eventually he decided to put his right hand into his trouser pocket. Fortunately, he was wearing blue chinos. That helped him in two ways. Firstly, they were loose fitting, and that was blessing. Loose fitting to go with the loose talking host, Queen Olivia. The loose chinos allowed him to at least put his hand comfortably into his pocket; painful, nonetheless. Also, being dark blue in colour, it meant that if any blood did ooze out onto his trousers, it would just look like any dark liquid, hopefully water-like.

It was painful as he settled his hand into his pocket, no idea if blood stains had begun to appear. He opened the lock, then door, of the toilet. It was still noisy outside, but he was hit by the surprise of four people waiting in line to use the toilet. Their impatience was as evident as their relief. 'Thank God,' was their resounding response in unison.

As the party was coming to an end soon, Jag went back over to Olivia who had a few other parents with her. She indicated to him, only to acknowledge his return rather continue where they left off. There was no burning desire to talk to him, just a polite gesture after he had left their conversation suddenly.

Despite looking for her, had no great yearning to meet Olivia. It was just he did want to at least get a contact number from her company that he may use at some point; a sliver of hope to ameliorate his financial misfortunes.

She did notice he looked a bit odd, one hand continually in his pocket to go with his sweating impatience.

If you'd just broken your knuckle, you probably would be sweating a little too!

Olivia did realise Jag was acting a little strange. She didn't want to get too occupied with him. 'You can use this card to contact me, but my mobile changed recently.' She handed over a professional looking business card. 'Do you have a pen?'

Jag did have a pen, but with only one workable hand he decided to say 'No, sorry, I left it in the car. Maybe you could just put your new mobile number on the back?' Again, it was clear he was hiding something in his right hand, especially as he kept gesturing only with the other hand, the one that had not punched the hell out of the mirror.

‘Come on, Bunny let's go,’ said one-hand Jag, using his head now as an extension to his right hand to motion her, not really caring how he looked.

‘My new mobile number is 07949205620. There you go, hope you can read my writing. So, if your friend needs any advice around what to do next after the crime suffered, they can contact me. I'll pass their details onto our relevant division. I'm sure things will get better for your friend. Stressful times I know, but every cloud has a silver lining, you know?’

‘Daddy, what happened to your hand?’ It was his telepathic daughter again. Last time she did that was when she was asleep, superpowers, Super Bunny. Last time she was sleep-talking about Jag’s problems like a concerned psychiatrist. Could she see through the cloth of his trouser pocket?

Jag had no other explanation for Bunny’s remarks. That was, until he looked down at his trouser pocket. It was already starting to get damp; damp with blood, but no one could figure that out... except of course, for Bunny. Super Bunny with superpowers.

Fortunately, they were on their way out when she asked him, Jag, thinking that he had done a good job hiding his bloodied hand, headed for the exit door. After a quick look down, then around the room, Jag realised a quick exit was the best option. But of course, if anyone did notice the dampness around his trousers, they would just assume he dropped a drink or something. Jag would take that.

The drive home was tricky, but Jag simply told his daughter that he got his hand caught in the bathroom door. Might be a little more complicated explaining to his better half.

CHAPTER 30

Home is where the heart is.

Well, it was, at one stage. Now it was where his wife was.

He entered his house, heart still intact, Bunny by his side, with his hand still glued to his trouser pocket. Knowing the dampness was still visible was a concern, especially the inevitable questions that his wife would spit at him.

He had managed to stem the flow of blood a little as he had a box of tissues in the car, so replaced the bloody toilet roll tissues with this new, upper-class tissue from the box, an upgrade from the toilet roll. But the blood stain was still there of course, leaving a dark uninviting colour behind.

Sleeping Bunny, in the back seat, allowed him to tend to his hand surreptitiously, painful, but out of sight. It turned into a tricky, but productive journey home from the birthday party.

'How was the party, Bunny dear?' An exclaimed scream of excitement from her mother met an equally excited daughter, still a little high but tired from the hyperactivity of her best friend's party. 'Was Hannah okay, and did she like your gift? Did she like your dress? I bet she did?' What was this, twenty questions? Jag's thoughts never held back.

'How you doing, Jenny? You been okay? Give Bunny a chance to sit down, won't you?' The invisible Jag invited himself into the conversation. He was still clearly in his wife's bad books after their argument before the party.

'Hey, Jaggy. How you been? Did she behave? What's that on your trousers? You spilt your drink again?' Round two of twenty questions, it seemed. And don't call me Jaggy!

'Yeah, that, err... dropped some Vimto. Was drinking then some excited child bumped into me.' It was a bit coincidental that he had makeshift dressing on the hand closest to the dark liquid mark. An investigator would have raised eyebrows, for sure.

Jag inadvertently took his hand out of his trouser pocket, adding to his unease, beginning to gesticulate his answer. Immediately, he realised it was the wrong thing to do. And the topic of the birthday party was history. The interest in whether Hannah liked Bunny's gift was irrelevant. The enamour surrounding Bunny's beautiful dress was now only a flickering inconsequence.

'And, what happened to your hand?' The inescapable question. Now, though, the initial scepticism, was giving way to the natural concern a family member has for another. Jag expected a negative tune but got care! She was emotional with long-lost care and fear for her husband.

'As I was closing the bathroom door at the party, well, the door shut on my hand. Not sure how exactly, but, well, it was painful at the time.' Bits of tissue drifted to the floor, the patch-up work on his hand clearly not been his best run project.

'Let me have a look, Jag. What you been doing?' They weren't really questions for answering, more of an observation on his antics. And then she did it again. 'What you been doing, Jag?' It wasn't just the immediate injury she was referring to. Moreover, it was his behaviour of late. She held his hand like it was a baby puppy, or a rare butterfly, reluctant to let slip away.

For the next five minutes she and Bunny cared for him as much as a mother does, her child. It was almost worth the punching of the mirror. After clenching his fist and feeling the pain he decided no, it was not worth punching the mirror for. But, no doubt, the attention and care he was getting was like a sweet-smelling breeze, refreshing.

In the back of Jag's mind was that mirror, and how Olivia and her husband were probably now wondering about, as he sat in the company of angels. They must be wondering how the crack came about. The mirror never lies. Maybe they had managed to put two and two together, whilst Jag was in his lap of luxury. The mirror may not lie, but Jag did, and more and more, with alarming nonchalance.

His five minutes of compassion were up...

'Oh, by the way, Jag, the clock stopped again.' Jenny motioned to the sedentary clock that silently smiled at Jag. The face of that clock never seemed to smile before, only when it wished to; hands not moving but acting like they were forcefully disciplining him at will. The ticks may not have been there, but the ticking off from his wife was enough.

That familiar observation. The damning clock! Now sleeping, maybe snoozing.

That damning clock. Maybe sleeping, but fully aware of the antics of Jagat Singh.

Time standing still at 06:30, or was it 18:30? Fortunately, not going forward, but unfortunately, not going back either. Despite having a bloody hand, he felt like punching that clock. Punching that clock with the same vengeance as the mirror. Objects of distraction becoming his objects of destruction.

A sigh from Jag. Damn clock. Damn the clock.

He felt like punching that clock like it was a punching bag, though truth be told, he was the punching bag. Clenching his fist, now back in his pocket he let the silence wash over them. It wasn't a refreshing wash though; didn't clean him. More like waterboarding than a waft of summer sun combined with quintessential drizzle. Concealing his anger, Jag went into cruise control.

Not for the first time, Jag took the hibernating clock from the cream-coloured wall, carefully raising it from the nail it was perched on. It was perched like a stuffed mute bird, nice to look at, but not functioning. It had turned more into a museum piece than a piece mechanical piece, a little like Jag. It had become a thing of derision and frustration since the battery had weakened, a little like Jag. Something supposed to be of use and good for planning, very much like Jag.

As if running on repeat, Jag turned the clock around, took out the battery, and blew into it like he was trying to start a campfire with a spark and dry grass. He seemed to be blowing a little magic and warmth into his hands, clutching the battery like straw. Maybe reciting some magical incantation or imparting pixie dust from the spirit of Tinkerbell. Then he replaced the same battery back into the clock. All this, whilst he could have easily simply replaced the battery with a new one.

It was clearly not Jag's style to do things the simple way. Simple minds hijacked by complex surroundings. 'Why don't you just change the battery? It's not rocket science, Jag. How many times you gonna do that? In a few hours it'll stop again, for sure.' He knew she was right, just didn't have the patience to change it right now. Jag, formerly known as the Jaggernaut, had become Jag the Procrastinator. Those were happier times.

'I'll change it in the morning, Jenny. Not in the mood to go up and look for batteries now.' He looked towards his hand, as if making a meagre excuse. Whether it was his hand or the hands of the clock, it mattered not, both were not functioning properly. Though, at least after giving the battery a warming, the ticking started, as time resumed once more.

Jag wasn't even at the top of the stairs before time stood still once again. The dying embers of the battery had faded, though he did not turn back to get the bad news. He had a one-way ticket. A ticket to his bedroom.

CHAPTER 31

It was a disturbed night for Jag.

Sleep tried to find him, but the days misadventures stained his memory and left him restless. Finally, he got to sleep but was awoken by the buzzing of his mobile.

It had been buzzing for a while. Jag had no idea how long, because he just found himself waking up to that quiet hum of the phone by his side. Quiet, from the perspective of a silent ring tone, but when surrounded by silence, not so quiet.

His first concern was Jenny. She normally complained when his phone went off at night, so he got used to leaving it on silent. Silent or not, that constant buzzing, had the potential to wake her. It was amazing to Jag that she was still deep asleep. Amazing and a huge relief.

His relief was short lived though.

Engulfed by drowsiness, Jag fumbled for his phone. Reaching it as carefully as possible, he looked at the screen, eyes squinting after getting hit by its brightness. He never did understand why the adaptive screen feature did not work like it should.

Moments later, his eyes were wide open. What seemed like over fifty Facebook messages stared at him, all from one user.

Mark Goldsmith!

The Gardener?

That really woke Jag up. Woke him up in a completely different way to the adaptive screen wake up. This was more like a wakeup call!

Fifty messages.

No missed calls.

Was it, THE Mark Goldsmith? Who else could it be? And the content was bizarre.

DO DUE DILIGENCE

That was the message text, repeated over and over.

Fifty times!

Like a message on a spool...

DO DUE DILIGENCE

DO DUE DILIGENCE

DO DUE DILIGENCE...

Fifty times!

Fifty times!

Mark Goldsmith, aka, The Gardener.

What was going on? Jag was utterly confused. Confused, with a tinge of hope, but realistically speaking, a very small flicker of hope. A tiny amount of hope from someone he never expected to hear from again.

Never sure what the meaning behind it was, but at least he had finally heard back from the notorious, Mark Goldsmith. A mixture of emotions to occupy his day. This time though, there was the potential for a very long day. A very long day of contemplation.

DO DUE DILIGENCE

Was Goldsmith drunk or something? Trying to help Jag? Trying to give some special code? Why would he help me now, thought Jag? And if he did want to help, he could just call. Whenever he's free from his damn Gardening Leave!

DO DUE DILIGENCE

Maybe it was Jag that was drunk? Blind drunk in a room with no lights, though as he stared at the adaptive screen, he begged to differ about the lights. Jag had clearly not been himself recently. As the message said, DILIGENCE. He clearly had not been living with diligence. A little too carefree, investing like the money he was using was Monopoly money; all a big game where he was taking too many chances.

DO DUE DILIGENCE

Sighs of retrospection, confusion, and tension, not only from the message, but also the number of times it was written. Perhaps it would not have been so striking if there had only been one message. But fifty?

Jag imagined Goldsmith physically typing the same message fifty times. Food for thought for Jag's already consumed mind.

DO DUE DILIGENCE

After no news from Goldsmith for over a month, this? Did not make sense. Maybe Goldsmith, himself had been hacked. That would be ironic. The master team of fraudsters, frauded themselves! That would be too much. Could be Goldsmith playing games, adding to his repertoire?

Eventually Jag took a partial hold of his senses. It was still very early, practically the middle of the night. He needed sleep for the day ahead, whether he liked it or not. This time, to be safe, he even turned off the vibration option on the phone. No need to alarm Jenny, especially as she had no idea who this Mark Goldsmith even was.

The morning would bring hope, a new sunrise, rays of optimism, potential, at least.

CHAPTER 32

Jag had tried to contact Mark Goldsmith over Facebook, phone, email, but of course, no response. Goldsmith probably from another metaverse. That's how it felt to Jag. He half expected it. Now he just put it all down to The Forex Group playing more games with him, this one an attempt at torture. From one group to the other, it was all getting bigger and bigger, worse, and worse.

It was all very random, Goldsmith messaging him out of the blue. He had delved as much as he could into the Facebook profile of Mark Goldsmith, finding nothing but closed doors, no windows.

Over the next few weeks more scammed victims emerged. From far and wide, The Group expanded. It seemed like a disease was spreading. Victims of fraud combined with the emotional turmoil that partnered the isolation that came with it.

Of these other scammed victims, most were simply late starters, slow movers, victims who had belatedly stumbled across the blogged posts from Martin and his new friends, trying to make some sense out of this tragedy.

Group chats continued, new introductions followed, hope, though dwindling, remained on the faces of newbies at least. Many of those affected did not even muster up the courage to contact The Group. Some, finding it intrusive, were left disgruntled but too afraid to click on the contact link. Some, worried it may even be another scam, landing them in more strife, steered clear. Others just wanted to forget the whole issue, hoping ignoring it would make it go away, from their minds at least.

Despite reduced hope, The Group's numbers were rising. To those members it was a carrot of hope, however small that carrot was. It at least meant a tiny ember could still burn from which a spark of hope could be rekindled. It was a long shot, they all knew that, especially as time passed. They all also suspected they would get nothing back, just had to keep that flickering alive, as much for their sanity as anything.

The Group had certainly toyed with the idea of legal support for their situation. It had always been there, in the backs of their minds. The National Fraud Office offered little or no help. Saying that they dealt with each case of fraud with the utmost care, the Fraud Office mentioned that they would need to pass on the dealings of this case to their London Police Department, though nothing more could be promised. After follow-up, Jag got nowhere. It was a similar set of disappointing responses from the others. The London Police Department suggested as the bank accounts were mainly overseas, reaching a successful conclusion was very difficult.

The banks from which transactions were made also gave no hope, despite requesting the logging of information into their black holes they called databases. Even credit card companies, bastions of financial crime, were unable to salvage any hope. So, the only way, agreed The Group, was to at least consider legal avenues.

That was where Jag introduced himself into one of those familiar Zoom meetings. An attempt to add oxygen to flickering hopes.

'... I know it has been mentioned before but has anyone explored legal options in detail. In a previous meeting it was mentioned, but, well, I also know a solicitor in the area who does have some knowledge of cybercrime. Maybe we could see what suggestions they have?'

There were a lot of nodding heads but not too many verbal commitments. Jag knew that was normal. All these group members would naturally be sceptical, having lost money the way they had.

'Look. Maybe I can have a word with this local company to see what they think? No harm in asking?' He was right. What else did they have to lose? Nothing could be lost in asking. There was agreement. Jag would find out what Olivia's company could offer to investigate The Forex Group. Jag could have simply gone direct to Olivia, just felt like he needed the confidence of the others.

What else could go wrong? Maybe only that Jag would have to bow to the pretentious sniggering that he felt from Olivia's attitude. Or was it Jag being oversensitive to what were normal reactions? From her point of view, Jag had already told her that it was a friend, not himself who had suffered the loss. So, her reactions were understandable. Jag never saw it that way though. He was going to have to bite his tongue when talking to her.

'No need to discuss, Mr Singh. I have already been in touch with a company called The Law plc. We are waiting to hear back, and it should be any day now regarding how to proceed with a plan to take legal action.' The Law plc, a specialist firm based in Brighton, worked in various areas of litigation. Cybercrime was one of their areas, growing at that.

An emoji was the voice of the words, no active camera, only an emoji. An emoji on Zoom. A female emoji to go with the female voice. It was the same lady who spoke up in a recent Zoom meeting they had. The lawyer.

It was a little anonymous. 'A few of us contacted this company some days ago on this very topic. We felt the only chance we may have of getting anything back would be to go the legal route. Sorry if this was not made clear before, but if you remember, it was touched upon in the last meeting?'

The emoji lady was right. It had been discussed in the last meeting, but no decision was made there, though it was noted. Despite Martin having reservations, he was okay with the discussion they seemingly had with this lawyer. At least it was a step in the right direction.

Initially, Jag was a little disappointed and surprised by the lack of transparency by these members who had simply gone along on their own path of investigation, without getting prior permission from the others. It made the whole effort seem a little disjointed.

Then it struck Jag. This was the same veiled lady who spoke up last time. The voice of an angel?

Jag then spoke up. 'A few weeks ago, I received these bizarre text messages. I'm not quite sure what was the intention, but I think maybe to confuse me even more. There were over fifty Facebook messages all saying the same thing. They all said DO DUE DILIGENCE. It was very confusing. They were all from Mark Goldsmith. I just assumed he was playing games because nothing came after, and all his contact lines were dead.'

'That's very strange, yes, Jag. You sure there is no way you can somehow contact him? Seems he may be playing games with you, and I suppose, us all,' Martin responded, a little confused.

'Would've been nice, but nothing. Nothing before, nothing after. All so cryptic and confusing,' replied Jag. The others, who had their cameras on, looked puzzled into their screens.

It seemed so far at least, Jag had been the only one with this special treatment.

Meanwhile, the emoji, the Lawyer, looked on with no change in her expression.

CHAPTER 33

The Group had at least saved Jag the uncomfortable burden of having to contact Olivia. Hopefully, the 'Angel' of The Group would rescue them. Maybe she could help to fight for their money the legal way?

Jag considered Olivia extremely unprofessional and almost spiteful, with her lack of compassion. At least that conversation need not happen, though even the thought of Queen Olivia made him grind his teeth in frustration.

Sat in his usual space in Sainsbury's car park, Jag looked down towards his fist, still showing signs of healing wounds and still a little painful on exertion. It looked like the best option of getting something back from The Forex Group was this legal route. The biggest hope seemed to be the voice of the angel from Zoom. She went by the name of Elizabeth. There was room for optimism, he concluded.

Jag had to get back home soon. He had invited his old foe, James Balden over for dinner. Ironic that he thought of him as a foe, and then was planning to have him over for dinner!

It just happened. Jag never thought to plan a dinner for Balden, but it had really been Balden's own idea that had set the thought of a dinner into motion.

Knowing Jag had Indian heritage, Balden had often talked about traditional Indian food. It was clear he couldn't get enough of it. And that made Jag feel a little more valuable to James.

Similarly, there had been many times when Jag had needed the professional help of Balden at the workplace. Jag just felt he needed to protect his investment, despite the cons that came with it. Pros and cons, he thought to himself.

Yes, Balden had that British stiff upper lip. He also had a dry, comical sense of humour, though usually he was the only one laughing. It was clear his comments and mannerisms portrayed him as a higher beast. That was just the aura that came with James Balden.

Sometimes it was clear he was exaggerating, accentuating his Britishness. But it never dissuaded him in any way. It added to that allure in many ways. Moreover, in some cases it added to the attraction that was James Balden and even won him contractor roles on projects. Confidence was his second name, he exhaled it like oxygen.

Where Jag had concern, was when on occasion James made fun of him. When he did it in front of others it was a little embarrassing for Jag. Most times, Jag laughed it off, without holding any grudge. But there were times, when it did offend Jag, though he was too timorous to kick up a fuss. Those times simmered inside. The biggest issue though, was that sometimes it felt to Jag that, because he was of Asian Subcontinent origin, he was picked on. Call it the race card, or his own shortcomings, Jag often felt belittled when around Balden.

Making it back from his Zoom meeting, late but at least before Balden, Jag made it to his house. There had been at least some progress in terms of a plan to investigate the possibility of legal action.

"Good evening, Sir.' Balden had arrived. 'How are you doing, Jagat?' It was the usual beaming smile that accompanied Balden into Jag's detached, yet humble home. Humble, for sure, in comparison to Balden's wonderful country home. Humble, also since it was hugely mortgaged.

'Hi, James. How are you doing? Good you found the place. Here, let me take your coat.' It was a heavy trench coat that James passed across to Jag, thanking him. Being early spring, the South of England, though warmer than the North, was still only in the teens, still chilly.

'The WhatsApp locator worked a treat, door to door. Took me on roads I never knew existed. Wonderful technology. Nice place you have, isn't it?' It was more of a comment than a question, though Jag wasn't quite sure. Balden's perennial grin was there.

Jenny was stood just behind, smiling in a nervous but welcoming way, ready to usher her guest into their house. 'Hello, I'm Jenny. You must be James. Welcome, and hope your trip here wasn't too bad?'

'Oh, no, not at all. Used to it. I've probably driven all around the world if you add up my miles. Driving doesn't bother me in the slightest. I used to work in Hatfield, you know. Not far from here. Not a bad drive at all.' The smile of James Balden grew for a second. 'If they had air miles for car drivers, I'd be platinum by now. They'd have to introduce a new level for me!'

They settled down, broke the thick ice that was initially apparent, then ate. James loved Indian food. He was impressed how well Jenny had adapted and developed her culinary skills, especially as she was not Indian herself.

Chicken korma welcomed the mouth-watering eyes of James Balden. Homemade chapatti and sauces and salads helped to keep that smile on his face. Kulfi and Indian sweets added to his already bloated stomach. Jenny, having spent some time with Jag's mum, had learned the art of Indian cooking. With her natural born interest in multicultural Britain, she had experimented enough to more than get by.

'I hope you like the food. I'm not an expert at Indian food, but I keep trying,' Jenny smiled, looking in Jag's direction as if to say, *'I'm learning this for you, my love.'*

Balden looked down, utterly impressed by the spread. 'Wow, looks amazing! I'm sure Jag gave you moral support? How much of this was your planning, Mr. Singh?' No words from Jag, just an embarrassed look around the room, bemused.

They ate and it was a wonderful dinner. Jag knew Jenny was great at cooking. She was a natural and loved making new things. Jag had no idea where to start with regards to cooking, only how to do the eating!

'So, Jaggy, you going to show me around your house, or is that not allowed?' James was being comical, highlighting that it was perhaps normal to show guests around, especially ones that have known each other a while now. Truth be told, Jag was always a little unprepared when it came to guests. They never had that many guests around, so when they did, Jag was always a little uninspiring. It was never his intention but was a little out of his hands until he got more practiced and experienced.

Jag was also a little taken back by another thing. Balden called him 'Jaggy' rather than simply, Jag. Jag was pretty sure he hadn't called him that before but couldn't be sure. Things like that stuck in his mind, especially as he hated being called Jaggy. 'James, how did you know to called me Jaggy?' It was a bit spontaneous, but Jag just came out with it, unrehearsed and a little unexpected. This time there was no preparation needed from Jag. It was, odd and somewhat inquisitive, demanding, and almost aggressive.

James, a little taken aback, gave a polite grin, as if being challenged. Their eyes met, as if looking for clues. Jag was staring pensive, thoughtful, trying to figure out whether it had been a coincidence, or hidden knowledge Balden possessed. From Balden's point of view, he just stood there, repaying the stare, not giving anything away. Jag's dark brown eyes met James's light brown ones. And Jag felt the piercing nature of James's stare, powerful.

One out of place blink could be one too many. Like their alter egos, wrestlers in a ring, they looked deep into each other's eyes, marbles glazing over. The 'Jaggernaut' delved deep inside for answers, his elder opponent giving no clue behind his smiling demeanour.

'Just seemed a natural nickname, you know, Jag becomes Jaggy, like Mick becomes Mickey. Something odd about it, Jaggy?' he smiled. The stare-down continued, or was it Balden taking the mickey? It was that part of Balden that vexed Jag. 'Are we good, Jag? Promise I won't call you Jaggy again.' Balden detected Jag had become a little more fidgety so decided to put an end to it.

Their eyes departed but it left another impression imprinted in Jag's mind. More layers for his subconscious to tussle with.

Some time passed, as Jag talked to James about his past and then the present mortgage set up he had been burdened with. Maybe a little personal, but Jag was starting to confess.

'I used to contract for this great, small investment and mortgage company. Let me check once home and get back to you with their details. I remember they're a small set up, but they give great rates for first time buyers.' Jag had earlier mentioned the heavy mortgage they were under at the moment, flexible, but high rate. Balden was offering some possible ideas to improve repayments.

'Okay thanks, James, yeah, might come in handy, though not sure how easy it would be to change now. These banks have so many clauses and exit fines, not sure if I'll be able to escape from their clutches. Fees are so high nowadays, hard to avoid debts. Banks, I have had enough of, to be honest. Only there to take your money and give no service in return. I once had this financial dilemma, but they had no offers of help or hope.' Jag knew the kind of thing he was referring to, but didn't want to open his box of confessions, so held back at that point.

'Agreed, Jag. But see if you can get out of this mortgage without these exit fines. Not easy keeping up with the Joneses. But keep working hard, keep learning, Jag. That's the best advice I can give you. Keep thinking of ways to improve your financial situation whilst your young. Gets harder as you get older. Working all the hours of the day, not for the golden oldies, Jaggy... I mean, Jag.'

James was offering his words of wisdom, then picked up on what seemed to be Jag's odd plea for help. 'You mentioned a financial difficulty or situation? Something you want to talk about?' Balden had that maturity of age in his voice, style, persona. It gave a calmness, as if, *everything will be alright.* A little like how a psychiatrist gives that comfort and consolation, James, despite being burdened with arrogance at times, also had a warm confidence, irresistible. Never boring around him.

Balden's various personalities were what enticed Jag to him. He couldn't help feeling safe at times in the office, with Balden's confidence and control of a situation.

As they were both in the same team at work, there were clear advantages, and Jag often hid behind that living beam of confidence; Balden. This was one of those situations, but this time, at home. 'Yes, well, did have a situation. Bit of a financial difficulty. In fact, big financial difficulty. Don't want to go into detail but had lost a bit of money, hoped the bank would help, but they were useless. Like I said, can't go into too much detail, but hopefully we have a plan to figure it out, with, or without the banks help.' Jag looked around to make sure Jenny was not around, but still spoke quietly to avoid being overheard by the walls.

'We?' James questioned Jag.

'What?' returned Jag, not fully understanding.

'You said, We. I thought it was your difficulty, dilemma?' Balden seemed concerned, was clearly starting to take an interest.

'No, it's just there are a few of us in the same situation, financial mess. We're looking at solutions though. Sure, we'll figure something out.'

'You said the banks couldn't help? Why could they not do anything? Don't they have audit trails, connections... I mean nowadays you can't even take money out of the cash machine without a camera taking your picture. I'm surprised they can't help.' Balden made a good point Jag couldn't argue against.

'Yeah, you're right you know, James. I thought it strange too, how they couldn't trace payments and accounts. You know, bit disappointing but, like I said, all they want is your money.'

'True, Jag, true. That's all they want. Listen to me, Jag. You need any help or need to contact anyone let me know. I've been around a bit. You never know, I might be able to help.' It was all very positive, and Jag felt a warmth he had never felt before from James. Even his smile, that smile that was once an arrogant grin, had turned into one you would more often see from Santa Clause.

'Thanks, James. Let me show you the house.' It was clear he didn't want to divulge too much, despite the comfort from Balden. Jag arose, then waited a second until James followed.

As he got up, Jag noticed the light glisten slightly on the top of Balden's head, bald from years back. Bald from way back when he was in his twenties. It ran in the family but, even then, his case of early male baldness was a bit extreme. Now, aged sixty, baldness was the last thing he would even think or care about. Almost in unison, James's eyes also shone, like glass marbles in moonlight. If you mistook them for crystal balls, you could be forgiven.

'It's certainly a nice place you've got here, Jag. Forget the huge mortgage, keep working and investing, and I'm sure you'll have it paid off in no time.' Jag wasn't so sure, financial success seemed a way off.

'Four bedrooms up here, pretty standard but obviously more than enough for us.' Jag was doing his tour guide thing.

'You're going to have to get to work, Jag. Four bedrooms and only one child? Talking of children, where's that wonderful daughter you always go on about? How come she didn't come down for dinner?'

'Bunny should be in here,' replied Jag, opening the door of Bunny's room in coordination with his words. 'She was in a bit of a mood earlier, ate early and came up to her room. She often likes her own company, and her toys of course.'

And there she was, sat on the rug in her bedroom, surrounded by a plethora of her favourite toys. Dolls, of course, like a shop window of mannequins, parading in a Miss Doll Championships. There was, of course, only one winner; Tinkerbell, less her spinner, closely followed by Elsa. That additional part, the spinner, to the Tinkerbell doll had been missing for so long now, it had become a saga without a happy ending.

Cherished like a precious gem, Tinkerbell always took centre stage. But each time Jag's eyes met with Tinkerbell's, he couldn't help but mentally look for the spinner, as if his mind had the answer.

The day she lost that spinner a piece of his daughter went with it; lost in space. The only thing missing was the burial. But at what point do you bury something that in your eyes is only misplaced?

Determined to find that spinner, each time he saw Tinkerbell it would trigger fresh vigour inside him to look for that other half, until his mind got distracted once again. At times it became easy to forget about. Then, the trigger. Anytime he saw Bunny with Tinkerbell, it would hit him like malevolent pixie dust.

Now, as he had got more and more distracted with the complexities of life, it somehow became even more important for him to find that spinner. His quest continued.

'Hi. How are you doing, Bunny? Are you feeling better?' There was excitement in his voice as he found his daughter. There was an uncontrollable love that he had for her. 'What are you doing down there?' It was clear what she was doing, but it was common parental chatter.

'Hi, daddy. I'm good. Just playing.' She never even looked up, just responded, autopilot, engrossed in her everyday duties and the requirements of her dolls. 'How you doing, daddy? You want to play with my dolls, daddy?'

Then she looked up. She saw the two of them. Stopped in her tracks. Stopped what she was doing. Almost stopped breathing. Even the trail of snot progressing down her nostril seemed to stop. The clock downstairs, well that probably had already stopped. Time stood still.

Then, 'Who's that, daddy?' And it wasn't a *'Who's this nice man, daddy?'* It was like, 'Who on earth is that man, daddy!?' Then, before Jag even had the chance to consider his answer, she grabbed as many of her doll's as possible, ensuring Tinkerbell was part of that grab, and ran under her bed.

It was certainly odd behaviour. Was the type of behaviour an animal would make at the start of a night of fireworks on the fifth of November, or an allergy sufferer on Diwali. She was running for cover. True, many visitors did not come into Bunny's bedroom, but one could clearly see it as odd behaviour.

'What's wrong, Bunny? Where are you going?' Jag was clearly more than a little embarrassed, bending down now, whilst also looking towards Balden awkwardly. 'Come out, Bunny. Why have you gone under the bed? That's not nice, is it?' Jag was trying to be polite and harsh at the same time, knowing both were listening.

Then, bending on his knees, he took turns at addressing her, then Balden. 'What's the problem, Bunny?' a bit harsher. Then, 'Sorry, James, I think she's got a bit protective of her dolls lately. She's been a bit overprotective, cause a few of her toys got misplaced.' It was true that Jag was unable to forget the lost spinner but was also looking for a way out of this embarrassing scenario. Truths or untruths, it didn't matter. It was damage limitation.

With equal awkwardness, James Balden stood, overlooking the shenanigans, his perennial grin on display like that of a Cheshire cat. It was always difficult to understand what was behind that grin because it was his default pose. 'Don't worry about it, Jag. I get that so much of the time. Glad my own offspring are older now. Even they run away from me now!' It broke the ice well, bringing welcome informality to the delicate atmosphere.

By now, Jag was still on the ground like a dog on all fours, not salivating, but feeling a bit embarrassed with his awkward child. His only saviour was that Balden didn't appear disgruntled. It made his task a little easier.

'Tell him to go, daddy. Get him to go!' Bunny was crying now, almost screaming. She was clearly distraught by Balden's presence. Neither Jag, nor Balden could figure out why, but there was clearly a problem.

'I'll just pop downstairs, Jag. I think I've seen as much of the house as I needed. Lovely house by the way.' Balden was already out of the room and heading back downstairs. He just surmised that Bunny had been alone so long and not used to guests.

On his way down and a little embarrassed, he passed a quizzical Jenny stood at the foot of the stairs, preparing to ask Jag what the hell was going on? As he continued down, she continued up.

A minute later Jag was back down, musical stairs had come to an end, and with that, the charade that was Bunny's rather erratic mood. Jenny was upstairs picking up the pieces with her daughter. Putting them back together, a little tricky.

Balden, with the minute he had alone downstairs, noticed the garden from the window. 'Nice garden, Jag. Nice size at least. Some construction going on at the back?' Balden was referring to the many bags of compost and the area where the potatoes had been planted. There were also many loose planks of wood dotted around the back. 'Now, all you need are some tombstones for those graves out there.' Balden pointed at the four rectangular potato plots aligned nicely. And James was right, they did look like graves.

It hadn't struck Jag before, but on Balden's observation, it clicked that his alternate view on Jag's farming was interesting. Lined up, symmetrical, Jag seemed to have his own personal cemetery in his garden. Wow, he thought.

A little uneasily, Jag replied, 'Yeah, funny, never thought of it like that. Those are potato plots. I've decided to grow potatoes for a change. We've never tried anything like that before and fancied a challenge. After what you've just said I half expect zombies to dig their way out tonight.' It added to the laughter that Balden had just given birth to. Even better, it took all their minds away from Bunny's erratic behaviour.

'We used to have a greenhouse, grew tomatoes, cucumbers, that kind of thing. Turned into a real mess, so we got rid of it. Provided us with a lot more space in the garden. I still wanted to keep up the gardening thing, so thought why not try potatoes? More of a hobby, you know?'

James nodded, more in awe than understanding, 'Looks like hard work to me. We have a gardener who comes once a week to take care of ours. Otherwise, it would turn into a real tip.'

'That reminds me, James, why did you not bring Mrs. Balden with you tonight? We were looking forward to meeting her?' As Jag spoke, Jenny was making her way back down, herself a little uncomfortable after Bunny's tantrum. Looking in Jag's direction she shrugged her shoulders as Balden was looking the other way.

'Yes, sorry about that. She already had a night out planned with her friends. It was either cancel that or this. I lost. Never mind. Next time. Next time when we come for potato soup, with an Indian touch, of course.' James gestured over to the potatoes as he referred to the potato soup.

'Oh, Jag, I almost forgot. Give me a second, just let me pop to the car.' Without waiting for an acknowledgement, James was off to his car. His Jaguar X-Type sat confidently waiting, gleaming like a showroom piece. He came back with a huge square box. The box sat on his bloated stomach as he made his way back to their house. He was like Mr. Blobby without the costume.

Jag and Jenny just looked at each other for answers, partly excited as it was clear they were receiving a gift. But the other part wondering how to react. They had expected some kind of gift, but normally at the start of the evening. As nothing had been forthcoming, they just imagined he had forgot, or couldn't be bothered. Either way, how wrong they both were.

It certainly was well wrapped. Even more certain was that it was not wrapped by Balden. Too well wrapped, Jag surmised. 'Got something for your little angel. I hope she likes it, took me a while to find. I hope she likes cats. If I'd known she liked dolls so much I may have got something different, but I think she will like this.'

'Well... err... thanks so much, James. There really was no need,' Jag said, looking as much at Jenny, as at James. He felt a little embarrassed and surprised, clutching on to this large, wrapped box, the words *It's a Gift!* plastered all over it. Party poppers and fireworks glittered the wrapping paper. The party had just begun.

Husband and wife were very surprised. Jag had talked a lot about Bunny in the office to Balden, but still, Jag was totally taken aback. And Jenny was completely dumbfounded. Jag expected some flowers or chocolates at best, never a gift for Bunny. And, that big!

Finally, Jenny came to her senses, 'Wow, this is nice of you, James. I hope she likes it and feels bad for the way she hid away before. I still feel so bad about the way she behaved. She really doesn't deserve this, especially now.' Jenny searchingly looked upstairs, 'She really doesn't deserve this,' now looking at the box again.

'Of course, she does. All children deserve the gifts they get. It goes with the territory of being a child. One of the benefits of being a child. If I knew she was so cute I would've bought two!' That was Balden again, his grin as perpetual as his bloated stomach. 'Jag had spoken so lovingly about Bunny over the past few months that I felt like I knew her well. She is a lovely child.' It did sound a little contrived after the evening's antics, but had to be said, especially after investing in such a gift.

'Okay, James, that's too kind, really. Thanks again. Bunny, come down and look at this! And you can start by saying thanks!' This time Jenny practically screamed her voice upstairs to get the attention of Bunny. Her daughter was not forthcoming, she was happier sat alone in her own room.

'Pass on my best wishes to Bunny. Food was great, mouth still burning, but wonderful taste. See you in the office, Jag. You all have a wonderful evening.'

'Thanks again, James,' Jag returned.

Then, old foe, James Balden left in his executive Jaguar X-Type. And a lot of the negativity that surrounded Balden had started to evaporate from Jag's subconscious thoughts. That emotional condensation though, would take time to dissipate. Sometimes, a dose of interaction can help things along.

Bunny came down soon after James had left. The coast was now clear. She heard the noise about the gift that had arrived and wanted to find out more. But not until James had gone.

There was intrigue in the family response to that gift. Jag was surprised, especially as James passed it over, half-forgetting about it. Jenny thought a more appropriate gift would have been some cake or something for the house. She had not expected something for Bunny.

Bunny had mixed feelings. A child would never turn down a gift, whether from Santa or Satan. But this time she was a bit in the middle. She was tentative despite seeing that it looked good from looking at the cover, and she was starting to judge it that way. She had a good supply of toys, dolls, and the rest, but a child can never have enough toys. Bit like a champion, they can never win enough times. Or a millionaire, they can never make enough millions. Similarly, Bunny could not say 'No'.

Jenny broke the exciting silence, 'Well, go on, open it.' She nodded, as if providing parental guidance. To be honest, Bunny didn't need any approval, she knew exactly what she had to do.

She was just being a little more careful this time. Handle with care, Jack jumping out wouldn't be nice. It was a large gift, that was for sure, as Jenny helped to find the most suitable place to begin opening from. What difference does it make where I open it from, thought an impatient little Bunny, her anticipation was brimming? She could make out at least a letter 'M' as she worked her way through the wrapping. It certainly was well wrapped.

'Magic Mittens,' said Jenny, proving she could read. The mystery was over, solved by a few mounting moments of marvellous mystique; childish acts of aggression. It was a cat, a big cat.

CHAPTER 34

It was a cat. Motionless. Big.

A Big Cat.

Not a Big Cat in the tiger or cheetah sense, just big in size. Larger than life.

Jag was impressed and shocked at the same time. He had never expected such a gift; must have cost a fortune. Cost a fortune, not simply because of its size but more so from the kit that came with it. Looked like an artificially intelligent cat. That was from looking at the box and the advertised features. Looked impressive to Jag, but Bunny was more interested to get inside.

It was a Russian Blue cat, grey in colour and it came with a remote control. It also had batteries already included. There appeared to be an app to download to control it from your phone or PC.

To start with, Bunny was enchanted by her new gift. It was so real looking, so soft and fluffy, like a hand-held carpet. Jag was engrossed too, the smart phone app catching his attention. He had already started downloading it via the QR code on the side of the box.

Bunny was already talking to the cat, Magic Mittens happily sat in her arms. Then it moved, or she thought it did! It moved in her arms, like a real cat! When something that is not real appears to be real, it becomes more than real; unreal! Ironic for sure, but it seemed to add a new dimension to reality.

Larger than life!

Bunny let go of it. It, because there was no knowing what it was. Unbeknown to Bunny was the fact that Jag had installed the app and the cat was alive, albeit artificially.

Just before Bunny dropped the cat, she noticed a few things. First, the cat seemed to feel warm. Second, as she noticed its movements, it seemed to come to life as she turned it to face her.

It stared at her!

What faced her was the cat, the Big Cat. But what was alarming to her was the look of the cat's eyes. Not necessarily what you would call evil, but there was, or seemed to be, familiarity she couldn't put her finger on; Deja vu.

There was something spooky that she felt as she looked eye to eye with that Russian Blue.

The eye of the... Cat!

There was something, for sure.

Uncanny!

A resemblance that she could not figure it out. It was that which made her release the cat; the gift she had been so thrilled about a few seconds before. But she could not pinpoint the reason for the change.

It was probably the cat seemingly coming to life that made it feel like it was getting warmer. A lifelike aura that passed some hidden energy into the cat, that was then passed into the mind of Bunny. A corollary or blessing of life?

Life after death!

Bunny dropped the cat, shocked by how real it was... had become. It was real, wasn't it? Had to be. Or were the eyes and mind playing tricks on her? But whose eyes?

The eyes of the... Cat!

Bring back Tinkerbell!

Bring back Tinkerbell!

Life was less complicated, then at least. Old friendships are hard to break, reassuring to keep.

Even on dropping, it made a soft screeching noise as if in shock itself. It scampered across the floor, tail wagging anxiously. Jag assumed it was anxiously, but could easily also have been happily. Turning instinctively, the Russian Blue searched for somewhere to escape to, like a cockroach searching for some camouflage.

Jag continued to experiment with the app and the cat continued to respond, though its movements continued to seem so natural. Even though Jag had an IT background, he had never felt such realistic, smooth, accurate movements. He wasn't even sure he was the one controlling those feline actions and gestures!

He quickly shutdown the app. Bunny was a little panicky too. It was partly his own disconcertion, but especially Bunny's, that made him hasten to close that app. To be sure, he even chose the option to close all apps on the phone!

The cat sat there, now stagnant, not even a whimper.

Dead again!

Hopefully!

Heavy breathing, not from the cat, but from the humans. Eyes searching around the room, surprised, and dilated. Eyes of a stranger looked back, dead and now motionless, life after death no more!

Resting now... Sleeping... Tired... Batteries recharging?

'Wow, that's some gift,' laughed a sweating Jag, now starting to adapt to situation. 'I wonder where James got that thing from. So realistic looking. Amazing technology to produce such a thing. AI technology for sure, but never knew things were so advanced. Must be Chinese.'

The three of them continued to look at the cat, unable to keep their eyes away from it for long, half-expecting rigor mortis or something.

The Russian Blue had added a chill to the Singh household!

'Yes, certainly different. Never seen such a real looking toy before.' Maybe it was a real animal acting dead, thought Jenny. 'Will need to get used to that cat but certainly very lifelike.' Jenny spoke in a confused, questioning way, as if her mind was poking a stick at the cat. Her head twitched for a better view with each word, like she was examining a dead corpse for the first time.

'I don't like it, daddy. Can't I get a doll, a normal doll?' There was confusion all around, not least from Bunny. She was clearly perturbed, had never seen a toy like this before.

Eyes wide open, the cat looked on.

And so, they all sat there in contemplation, eyes hypnotised by a silly Russian Blue cat, that ironically, was grey!

CHAPTER 35

And the adults and the child contemplated the events of the day.

Enjoyable and eye opening in the large part, especially for the adults. But the child, she was traumatised. Traumatised into sleeping with the light on, though neither father nor mother really understood just how affected their daughter was by the 'moving' cat; the zombie that could have been a Russian spy.

It was strange that all the while they had the cat in the room, the eyes, the cat's eyes, they seemed to follow their own eyes, wherever they looked. Glass eyes, dead eyes, yet appearing all too powerful and fully aware.

Finally, daughter got tired. Fed up with thinking about the cat as much, as tiredness took over. She went off to sleep, though with the help of her mother, clearly aware of her daughter's fear, partly because it was mutual.

Mother and daughter ended up sleeping together for part of the night, only awoken by the father. He only came in to drop off their guest's passing gift to its owner. Daughter was not aware, but father had placed the cat in her room, near her other toys. In the process, mother was awoken, naturally getting up to move to her own room.

Why had her father put the cat in her room? To start with, it was her toy, however initially fearful she was of it. Secondly, he wanted to get his daughter's fear out of her. Maybe this would help? Get the cat used to the room, and daughter used to the cat. Also, he had to do something with the Russian Blue. It seemed logical to put it where it would reside for its future. And to live happily ever after. That was the plan at least.

So, the cat lay there, eyes shining, reflecting off the side lamp still on for safety reasons. A lamp of security, illuminating eyes of danger; multipurpose, though of course, not on purpose. Two opposites maybe, but with the hope of causing some attraction. Glass eyes, looking into the future, knowing the future like two glistening crystal balls.

The daughter slept oblivious, breathing deeply, rapid eyes moving all around. Constant shuffles hampered the innocent breathing, hopeful breathing, auspicious potential, hidden behind the closed lids and welcoming the darkness.

CHAPTER 36

In the maze.

They were in the maze.

Bunny with her favourite toy. It was her Tinkerbell. Literally in the middle of nowhere. It was a lovely sunny day and perfect for a trip to the maze. A puzzle from above, puzzling for those below. She was in a human Rubik's Cube but all in green. That was how the maze would look from a drone.

But there was a tension. The more corners turned, the worse it felt. And with every turn it felt like you were somehow getting more and more lost, though that was not necessarily the case. Bunny's trepidation rose with every wave of the corn leaves, as if they were waving goodbye to mum and dad. This was a maze, a maze cultivated with corn.

Queues had, of course, been long. Sun in the English summer meant queues, guaranteed. Today was no exception. The smell of vegetation met an inquisitive Bunny who had come with her parents. It was more for the grown-ups, but they were hopeful Bunny would enjoy too. Their logic was not uncommon. Many other families and kids had arrived also. Anywhere to make the most of those solar rays.

Now, despite the queues, there were not that many people inside. This maze was simply that big. The Great Maize of Borehamwood, a local attraction, had been on the shopping list for Jag and family for some time. They had just been waiting for the right day. Today was that day, and they hoped it would stay dry.

With the safari park next door, Jag had planned for both activities in one day, sure that Bunny would at least love the safari park, if she still had any energy left after the walk to escape this maze.

The safari park boasted some of the most varied animals in England, including elephant, cheetah and even Rhinoceros, horn intact. In the open, that would mean a drive-thru safari, always a favourite with the kids, second, of course, to the McDonalds drive-thru.

To Bunny, so deep in the countryside it literally felt like the middle of nowhere. This was accentuated by being surrounded by greenery, and once inside the maze, huge cornfields. The high, wall-like corn stalks blew in the occasional gusts of wind, heavy rustling sounds being produced. But while the weather was nice it was more refreshing than daunting.

These were cornfields without any corn, genetically modified. It added to the paradox; the genetically modified maize had become a maze.

The entrance looked welcoming enough. The Great Maize of Borehamwood, written historically over the entrance arch, gothic font used to increase authenticity.

Large squirrels carved from stone welcomed guests into the maze, as if challenging humans to see if they could take on the great twists and turns like these vermin so easily could.

And that's where the welcoming came to an end, false promises perhaps? Once inside, the atmosphere changed.

For Jag and Jenny there was a buzz, excitement, anticipation. Bunny though, she was not so sure, right from the beginning. A fear of what was around the corner, or how long this would take?

Bunny was still young, a four-year-old, who had not adapted to the idea of this type of puzzle. She had been more looking forward to the safari anyway.

Bunny hid behind the safety of her guardians. She was more than happy that way. The thought of being lost here, not knowing where to go, how to get out? It filled her with terror. She had no plans of spending even a second here on her own.

The corn stalks whistled in the wind. Not a cold wind. It was a nice wind, refreshing, pleasant. But there was a loudness that came with it, like those stalks had a microphone, trying to take centre stage. Like they were trying to say something. To Bunny it was as though they were trying to give a warning. They sounded angry.

'Stay with us, Bunny. Last thing we want is to lose you in here. We'll never find you, and you, us.' It wasn't the nicest thing Jag could have said to his daughter, but he was being blunt to get attention. Sometimes that was necessary. 'Seriously, make sure you stay close. Jenny, keep an eye on her, all the time, please.'

All Bunny could think about was finishing this maze with her family and being able to see the animals, as if that was her prize. She was trying to keep as calm as possible, holding onto Tinkerbell like her life depended on it. Sweaty palms and fingertips occasionally slipped in the midday sun as Bunny tensed with time.

It was a very large maze, made to feel bigger by the sheer size of the corn plants, strong and sturdy, even in this powerful breeze. The ground was just soil, hardened over time and use, no path or paving.

Around the entrance though, was stony gravel, no expense spared. It was quite simply an event for a lovely summer's day. That same open ground, once the rain started, would take on another mood. Not as welcoming.

Huge walls of corn stalks, green overlapping on green, blades of stalks running over each other. Their height must have been at least ten feet, well fertilised and healthy. To Bunny, these stalks were like beanstalks, reaching up into the sky. Except, she was not Jack, nor had any lofty ambitions.

The stalks were, at times mesmerising, the verdure that surrounded them all. Overwhelming too, as this huge maze hypnotised and hurried travellers from far and wide. The moving stalks disorientated victims, confusing some and befuddling others. That was part of the challenge. It was part of the reason why it was not just The Maize of Borehamwood, but in fact, The Great Maize of Borehamwood!

As the three of them made their way through this magnificent maze, they could hear the happy screams of other kids and chatter of elders nearby; nearby but far, far away from the point of view of this game.

They certainly sounded like happy screams. Certainly, sounded nearby. 'Okay, kids, let's try to beat this maze, eh?' Jag enjoyed this kind of thing, even if the others were not so over the moon. 'Keep close!' Jag was being clear. Getting lost in a maze could take a lifetime to be found.

Bunny, despite listening and not particularly enjoying this experience, was, as usual, in her own world with Tinkerbell. She preferred her conversations with her little friend rather than any human, even parental, having her own worries, let alone the fictitious one her father had brought her to.

They worked their way through the maze, finding the inevitable complexities. In the words of Yogi Berra, 'When you come to the fork in the road, take it!' Jag and family encountered many. So, they took their chances and were in the maze for a while.

Bunny, for a second, stared into the corn stalks; the wall of corn stalks; the never-ending corn stalks. She was mesmerised. So thick with growth. So tall. So strong. Suddenly, she felt a little trapped inside. Suddenly, she felt the wind on her skin as if generated by these energising green stalks, solar powered green stalks, or was it wind powered?

Suddenly, Bunny looked around.

She felt a claustrophobia that she had never felt before. It was something her father knew well about, having suffered with this for most of his life. Most of his life he had hidden it away, and it only came out very seldom these days. But Bunny, she felt the energy of these corn fields sapping her own. It was as if they were feeding off her trepidation to gain their own fervour; a fervour to puzzle others.

Bunny looked around. Her only company was the little doll in her hand. Tinkerbell would need some of her pixie dust. The hard soil ground below her, and the wall of green on all sides, were their only companions now.

The parents? She could certainly hear them, or something sounding like them. But it was so confusing as voices were all over, all around. Muffled voice, combining with the whooshing of the wind between the stalks.

A puzzling claustrophobia held onto her throat, making even screaming a challenge. She stared into the mesmerising stalks, whistling in the wind now. All around now, nothing but green stalks, like green knives defending their territory.

The sun was now well passed its zenith, and the temperature had clearly dipped. This was common in England. Once the sun's power began to fade, chillier weather would generally prevail.

The first signs of thicker cloud started to appear above. Bunny could not see far to her side because of the high walls of the corn stalks. But she could make out that clouds were forming. So much so, that, at times, shadows stopped forming, as the smiles of the sun began to hide behind clouds, forming frowns to shade out the sun.

She continued, hypnotised by the swaying stalks of thick green. The maze of greatness, surrounding her now, alone with her doll. A doll that would not guide any tours out of this place. More like a mannequin now, lifeless. How long had she been staring into the green? No one knew, especially herself. Gripped by the green, Bunny hardly blinked as she felt time stand still.

The stalks swayed, stalking her now, stalking without talking. As if they were not taking their eyes off her. The eyes of the corn to go with their ears, watching and listening. Shapes came and went with the blowing of the wind, gaps forming then closing in the declining sun. And clouds formed above.

Clouds, now more solid increased, the early signs of a changing day. Shadows had now given way, conceded to stronger forces; now all one huge, dark shadow. The sun had begun to capitulate. Gusts of wind from the same origin took on a different guise. The same stalks separated then reformed, but with a different intention, as the gusts of wind whipped up into a greater frenzy.

Now so loud, the crashing knots began to fight with the stalks of corn as the first few pats of rain collided with anything in its path. Fat blotches of water spitting onto surfaces, then slowly dripping where they hit the green.

It had been advertised that the Great Maize would be closed during rain, based on management discretion. Bunny, stuck out here in the middle of nowhere, could not benefit from that concession now. She, and her guardian, Tinkerbell, not Jag, stood alone to face their fears.

Bunny thought to hide in the giant stalks, in her attempts to evade the intensifying approaching storm, though that would mean mingling with the 'mesmerisers'. That's the last place she would feel safe. Her pretty dress was getting soaked, yet still, she tried her hardest to ensure Tinkerbell remained dry. Like Jag to her, she was responsible for her child, and doing a better job than her parent, it seemed.

Waking up, finding her senses, she realised she needed to move. The rain was battering down now though, the ground and soil was already starting to get messy and muddy. Now it became clear why the management of the Great Maize closed this place down during rain. It all became painfully clear.

Her clothes were a complete mess. Shoes had turned from grey to brown, thick with mud, as the heavens opened up. From environmental green to soiled brown, her clothes messy, showing signs of hard work; hard work passed and harder work to come.

The mesmerising stalks, asking the questions, forcing the answers, would have to prey on someone else, though she couldn't refrain from continuous looks over her shoulder to make sure those long leaves were not creeping up on her.

But which way to go? The first problem, being inside a maze, that had to be the question. Lost inside this huge Rubik's Cube, where more questions than answers ensued.

More chances finding Tinkerbell's spinner than your way out, young girl!

Still, she tried, the panic of being lost topped up by the pouring rain and deteriorating surface. Could things get worse? How could they possibly get worse? Whispering to herself was the only way she felt to comfort herself. Talking to herself to keep her mind off those corn stalks. She would never eat corn ever again, even popcorn, she thought. The whispering was more of a sob than a whisper, begging for help and a way out of the situation.

'MUMMY! DADDY!' Screams now reverberated from within her, bouncing of ever-encroaching walls of green. Not the verdure she wanted to see right now. The sounds just bounced back.

There seemed to be no one listening, except of course, the stalks. They moved around, whistling, their form of communication, shapeshifting. They were shiny now with the relief of rainfall refreshing their wings, letting them fly free in the wind.

Torrential weather in Borehamwood. Localised flooding in the town. Not just in the town though. This Great Maize was starting to swell, mud piles dotted around this puzzle. It was more like a snakes n' ladders game with all the hazards in play. And Bunny continued to fight, and of course, figure out this puzzle. A ladder would have been useful, for a better view.

Yells for hope and freedom, though expectations narrowing by the second. Corner after corner she turned, random movements, not calculated. How could a four-year-old be expected to solve this labyrinth?

But you have Tinkerbell with you. Surely, she can help? NO!!!

Tinkerbell was silent and motionless, like a fake god, idolised but useless! Idle!

Then a sound nearby.

It was an odd sound; a sound not fully recognisable to her but somehow vaguely familiar. She turned the corner with impatience, in the direction of the sound. Then the deep sound again. She got closer. It was a deep, heavy sound, not human, that was clear. A deep and low kind of resonating, shaking noise.

There was at least something around the corner though she was a little tentative because it was not a normal sound. Meaning, it was not something she normally heard. But it was a sound. With sound came hope... maybe.

Bunny looked at Tinkerbell. Tinkerbell looked back, unable to help in any way. More puzzling looks at each other. It even looked as if Tinkerbell had put on a quizzical face, somehow reacting, but it was all in her mind.

Maybe it was the direction of the finishing flag, or possibly, the last straw? Bunny had to go forward into the unknown, into this abyss of mud. Deeper and dirtier she went, no idea what lay around the corner. No time to even think what the deep noise could be.

Rain, pelleting down like angry slaps on the face, reminding Bunny of her mother in a bad mood. Utterly drenched and feeling beaten and battered, another maternal bout of anger, this time, mother nature!

If only she could step out now and see the reality of two parents crying their hearts out for a helpless, fragile daughter, on the edge of hope and sanity.

Then, the noise, in metaphorical touching distance, a final turn away. The whistling wind between the stalks combined with this deep powerful noise. Which one was more powerful, dominant, most daunting? In collaboration, the cacophony, like distorted buildings being demolished at intervals.

She turned the corner, to see them. Three huge elephants in the distance. Their trunks flapping in unison with their big ears, shaped like Africa and crashing in panic against now fragile looking stalks of corn. Many stalks had been crushed by these powerful beasts.

Humbling, these creatures handed out a dose of reality to these once beanstalk-like corn fields. A thing of awe replaced by something of greater awe. What does that do to the thing that used to be feared and dominant? It humiliates them, degrades them, shows that every dog may have his day. But when night comes, they become like tame puppies.

The ground shook. At least, it seemed to. The elephants were on the rampage, crushing any part of this maze that was in their path. This Great Maize was now not so great, reality biting. It was one way to reach the finishing line!

The problem was that Bunny was also in the maze. She simply froze in shock and didn't know what to do. She had become a statue, now herself, twinned with her other half, Tinkerbell. They really were best friends now, both becoming still and lifeless, twins, not so towering.

Coming back to reality, Bunny turned and started running the other way, any way! There was very little thought that went into the process. Just a case of turn and run... like hell. It wasn't helped by the rain though, hampering her efforts.

The elephants were still heading in her direction, though taking alternate routes as opposed to the now very muddy soil. Trampling on nearby vegetation, they were simply crushing whatever was in their way. The vegetation did though, make the elephants stumble a little, as they trumpeted their way through, a clear sign of distress.

Somehow, Bunny, in taking one jagged turn after another, seemed to get out of sight, as the noise from the elephants grew fainter and fainter.

As she took a moment to breath, she looked down to give Tinkerbell a congratulatory shake, as if they had just come first and second in the London Marathon.

There was at least a moment to relax as she forgot where she was. Then she remembered. Bunny thought back to her parents. Then, 'MUMMY! DADDY, DADDY, DADDY!'

This time she screamed, not holding back. There was no point holding back. Who was there to complain? Certainly not her parents. They seemed long gone now, no sight or sound from them for ages.

A squawk from above. It was a different sound but must have either been very close or very loud. It was both. Just above her head, high in some undamaged corn stalks were a few parrots. Very odd, she thought. Of course, they were wet, drenched from the incessant rain. But they seemed calm considering the circumstances. Droplets of water fell from their beaks and feathers, wonderfully coloured red, green, blue, and violet. They were like living rainbows in a place with a disappeared sun.

A moment of tranquillity. A moment of pause. A moment of beauty as Bunny looked from Tinkerbell to parrot, as if expecting amazement from her doll. Nothing was forthcoming. Tinkerbell looked from Bunny to parrot. For a second it seemed like the human had become the parrot, copying uncontrollably.

And, for another few seconds, time again stood still. This time, time stood still in beautiful enchantment. Tropical birds on corn leaves, panoramic and aesthetic.

Their ears pricked up, always on the lookout, always on the perimeter of potential danger. Nature had given them such wonderful hearing, good enough to detect the perils of nature and beyond. A bit of rain was no harm to them, only evil predators.

Bunny carefully arose, wonder written across her forehead. She was bewitched, not for the first time today. First, the whistling, waving, mesmerising shards of the corn leaves. Then the sounds and magnificence of the elephants. Now, the visual audacity of parrots, oblivious to the rigours of this Great Maize. The Great Maize, with its obstacles of all types.

For that moment, that short space of time, nothing affected her. Not the rain, the wind, the stalks, the mud, or even this deceitful maze. But that was only short lived.

The heads of the parrots bobbed up and down, this time more suddenly and rushed. Some rustling in the corn stalks. The parrots were not waiting around. Effortless lifting of wings, and they were off. So easy to escape the maze. So easy for some, impossible for others.

The rustling continued, closer this time, causing concern for Bunny. She stepped back. Then she heard shrieks. The shrieks were followed by the appearance of more creatures, this time monkeys. Monkeys, many of them. What is going on, thought Bunny? What is this place?

Again Bunny, feeling like a captured animal, stepped back, away from the monkeys whose numbers were growing by the second. They had their eyes on her, waiting for a false move.

Encroaching slowly, tricky, and intelligent, they tried to encircle her. The walls of the corn stalks seemed to be closing in on her and Tinkerbell. She felt it, the claustrophobia that was trying to devour her.

As if communicating with each other, these primates chattered in unrecognisable tones. Strategic planning it seemed, casual glances to each other in a planned way. One of the monkeys had taken a liking to a long corn stalk. He was holding it like a spear, inquiring with the others as to how he could use this particular stalk. Others, cantankerous in nature, seemed to be arguing with each other. It was organised chaos.

Disorder was the name of the game, at least from Bunny's perspective, not knowing where to look or give most attention. Another monkey was picking his nose and admiring the results, disinterested in the main event. The encroachment continued as pressure built on Bunny and her hopes.

In the distance, she could hear a paraphernalia of sounds as if she was in the jungle. She heard all sorts of calling. Peacock screams, bear growls, even lion roars. That deep drum-like roar of lions and tigers, unmistakable and earth shattering.

Then it struck her, what had happened. In this stormy wind and rain, somehow these animals must have escaped from the zoo next door. How it happened, she had no idea, but that was the only explanation she could give. What had happened was now not that important. She needed a plan to handle what was happening now.

Looking to Tinkerbell as usual for ideas she tried to remain as calm as possible. The situation had started to mature her at an intense speed. Then, just as the monkeys were ready to pounce, they turned and were gone as fast as they appeared.

Now, Bunny just heard thuds on the ground. Occasional screams from animals trying to escape as fast as they could. Being so small and stuck in this heavy rain, she had no idea what it could be but it was getting louder. Whatever it was, it had saved her from those ravenous monkeys, and that could only be a good thing, couldn't it?

The ground was moving, shuddering.

Bunny knew it was not an earthquake, but more likely caused by the thing behind the layers of cornfields. The thuds continued, sounding like dinosaur steps. How do you run from these thuds? She held so strongly onto her soulmate, only hope keeping her alive. Her fingers were red with the pressure with which she held Tinkerbell.

The thuds were literally bouncing against her eardrums, so close and so loud now. Stalks of corn bounced to, confused by the wind, rain and now this heavy bombardment.

Bunny, being so small, could not make out what it was. Until that was, a nearby batch of corn stalks was crushed by a huge, huge paw. Not a lion, or tiger, or bear.

This was a huge cat!

It was about ten times larger than the largest lion you had ever seen. This was mythological. No words could explain or try to understand what this was, other than the fact that it was a huge cat! Terrifying too, in a way cats normally are not.

It stopped as it got closer to Bunny, licked its huge lips and released warm air as it took a long breath. The cat looked straight into Bunny's eyes. Bunny was transfixed, hypnotised. Then it looked up to the sky and back down again. It stretched its body and moved into a position, making it easy to pounce on its hind legs.

She turned and tried to run, but her shoes got stuck in the heavy mud. It was like she was sinking in this mud; sinking sand to match her sinking heart. There were no friends here, here in this Great Maize. The mud was dragging her down as if it had its own mind and desire to control. This maze had its sights set on Bunny. Tears drained from her, mixing with the sweat and rain, and mud. Screams acted as evidence that she was losing hope.

There was desperation. No hope, only desperation as again, Bunny looked into the eyes of the huge cat, water dripping from all angles.

She looked in the cat's eyes. Deep into those eyes. There was a familiarity. Something she could not figure.

Those eyes. Glass eyes.

Eyes like crystal balls, looking into the past, not the future. Eyes reflecting eyes.

Deep, deep inside those eyes there was something.

Then it hit her.

Her eyes widened in realisation. The eyes she saw, recognised. Wider and wider her own eyes opened, pupils dominant.

The eyes of James Balden.

... Then, the eyes of the cat as she woke up. She was in her bedroom, sweating buckets. Her own eyes wide open, staring into the eyes of the artificially intelligent cat that James Balden had gifted her last night.

CHAPTER 37

She wanted to scream but only paralysed air escaped like someone was strangling her. Eyes as wide as could be imagined, Bunny could not even find it inside her to blink, as, in her bedroom, over, besides the other toys, was the Russian Blue cat. Squashed air did manage to creep out of her lungs... eventually.

She had so many questions. Even more confusion. The Great Maize? The rain? These zoo animals? And... and that huge cat. Images beyond her comprehension. The fact that she had just had a nightmare about the very cat staring at her now, that didn't help things. It made it all that much more real.

Somehow, she felt too scared to scream. As if, if she did, perhaps that cat would wake up and attack her. Maybe it was voice or sound activated? A real nightmare, she thought. She was only a small child but had never felt such reality before in a dream.

So, she remained lying down, eyes focused on the cat, unable to intentionally close her own eyes. Finally, tiredness overtook her, and heavy eyelids closed her eyes shut.

The morning would bring new questions and challenges, but for the rest of the night, she slept peacefully.

CHAPTER 38

It was the start of the weekend again the following day. At least a day to rest a little. Despite finally getting her rest, the start to the night had been a little disturbing for Bunny. Jag and Jenny also had confused thoughts about the cat. They were sure it had a mind of its own.

The three of them were a little unsure how to handle that gift from James. It really was an amazing gift, and Jag was the first to acknowledge that. He spent some time trying to figure it out but each time he started the app, the cat seemed to get a life of its own.

So, it sat there, alone most days amongst the other toys. Bunny never got used to it. She never trusted it, or herself enough, to be comfortable around it. There were times she was sure she could hear it purring in the corner. Each time she looked at that cat, she couldn't help but see the eyes of James Balden, glassy and watery. Truth be told, on many occasion, Jag too, had that feeling of the cat's eyes bearing resemblance to James's, always watching him. He surmised it was simply because it was James who gave the gift. A simple and rational explanation.

In the morning, Jag tended to his potatoes. He needed news from The Group, badly. His email and zoom group of fellow losers, somehow hoping for a miracle. Impatience for some new lines of hope was even starting to wane, amongst the former jagged red and green lines of the currency exchange market. But his financial frustrations hadn't wavered, they just remained. How could I have lost so much money, he thought, dwelling, and punishing himself repeatedly? Was there really no solution?

Well, a little sliver of hope perhaps? A possible hint of auspicious belief that the group's idea may just pay off. The idea to go legal had been their only real place of hope. With no positivity from the crime police or banks, this had to be their best bet. Or just another gamble on the stock market?

The voice of that angel, Elizabeth, had turned out to be The Group's joker card, at least if they were willing to play. Not just Jag, but all the others unanimously voted that it would be the best course of action given the circumstances.

Plan had been, following Elizabeth's analysis, to discuss options with The Law plc, based in Brighton, who had experience of dealing with cybercrime and had supposedly won some cases through tracking down these internet thugs.

Jag had his contact Olivia, and did mention it to the others, but they felt Elizabeth's option seemed the most convincing route. Perhaps this was because they were all more convinced that a Group member would be more committed to helping. It wasn't helped by Jag himself. Because of Olivia's smug attitude to victims of cybercrime, Jag himself was reluctant, so when he offered his thoughts to the others, he was almost cowardly in his assertions.

Martin O'Leary called from The Group. It was a voice message into The Group's WhatsApp group chat. Unimaginatively, they had named their WhatsApp group, 'The Group'. With a bit more thought, they could've at least called it 'Hope'.

Messages into the group chat were few and far between, so when one came, it gave Jag the tingles. To avoid attention from Jenny, Jag had put his notifications on silent, but his eyes reacted where his ears didn't, seeing the pop-up on his screen in real time.

Sneaking back out to the garden was the best idea he could think of. That garden had become like a haven for him lately; a place where he could feel the open air and be free from the eyes and ears of his family, and of course, his own fears. He needed that privacy to take care of this matter.

It had been the first post on their group for about five days, so Jag wanted to give it the attention it deserved. Picking up a gardening fork seemed the best policy, because it meant he could go into the shed and be out of sight for at least a short while, as if tending to his plants.

He had built up a nice set of gardening tools. From pruners, saws, trowels, a wheelbarrow, lawn mower and even a peculiar looking sickle he had hardly ever used. The lawn mower was the oldest. He had bought it second-hand from eBay, and it had started to really show signs of age. Old, but cheap, and that was his main motivation for buying. His shed was full of all sorts of things, some useful for gardening, but mostly things that were not.

So, the shed it was, where he would devour the contents of Martin's soundbite. Tingles continued as he looked at the message in anticipation. A miracle perhaps? That's what he was hoping for. A miracle in a shed! Had a nice ring to it. A halo of hope in a shed.

A miracle in a shed!

He prepared himself for this moment, expectation now becoming the lead. Shiftily looking around, he placed the fork down on an already full and jumbled desk, where a plethora of old tools gathered dust. Then, he pressed play on the message.

'Hi, folks. Hope everyone is well. Just a quick message to let you all know that we got some progress on the plan to take legal action on the Forex Group. We must thank Elizabeth for her efforts, and we'll be sending everyone an email soon with regards to possible proposals for next steps.

'There's good and bad news. Good news is that there is a chance that we can move forward and investigate further to potentially track down these thieves. I feel without this hope we really have no options. Not so good news though, that our No Win, No Fee suggestion was not acceptable. The Law plc, the company we contacted, are saying they will need payment regardless, and up front.

'Seems like they want to cover themselves. I know it's not ideal but it's what we got, and we all got to think and decide what's best for ourselves.

'Further details will be in the letter addressed to you all in the next few days. Having contacted many law firms, the standard response from them all is that it is a very risky case to take on, from their point of view, of course. The international nature and use of safe haven accounts and offshore locations make the investigation untenable for many of them and not worth their time.

'Stay well, and all the best, Martin.'

The message ended. A big, big sigh from Jag, in unison with the thirty other members of the unfortunate group as they also pressed play on the voice message. He listened to the message there in that shed three more times without any side-tracked thoughts. There was deep concentration as Jag placed himself into the world of potential hypothetical outcomes whilst in his physical world of the shed.

At least he had options. That was some comfort. That's one way he could've looked at things. The other way, of course, was that to take a step forward into a chance of some recompense, he would need to leap into another unknown. A tricky situation yes, but did he really have a choice?

Carry on as you are or try to fix things. It was as simple as that, to be honest. It was the same tricky situation for the others in The Group.

DO DUE DILIGENCE.

DO DUE DILIGENCE.

These three words came to his mind, again. Where had he heard that before? There was a familiar tone to those words, and he knew they had a ring to them.

DO DUE DILIGENCE.

DO DUE DILIGENCE.

Then the hated tone of Mark Goldsmith. Mark, the Cockney. The Cockney that had shafted Jag then gone on gardening leave. He remembered Mark's repeated advice, mocking him on Facebook. It was, Jag assumed, just taunting. He remembered the fifty or so Facebook messages that Goldsmith had randomly left on his phone one morning, out of the blue. The messages that made no sense at the time, and still now. Jag just put it down to taunting of the most diseased type; heartless.

DO DUE DILIGENCE.

It came to his ears like a warning. Again, and again. And then, the eyes of that cat, huge eyes, and whiskers. The toy Russian Blue cat with a mind of its own. All these images spat at Jag's conscience like heavy drops of rain on bare skin.

But why take heed of a warning from the very man who put him in this situation to start with? It all made no sense to Jag. It felt more and more like there was some game being played, where he was one of the pieces; one of the pieces being moved at will. A puppet with strings, controlled by his master. Jag was simply moving his hands and feet on command.

Now he could do one of two things. Either cut his losses and get on with the remnants of his life, or cling on and fight for what was his.

One thing was sure. Whatever he chose he really would need to do it with DUE DILIGENCE.

CHAPTER 39

Two days later the email with letter attachment did come to the members of The Group. Since Jag had joined, a few more users had registered onto the online blog and confessed their losses to the others. It had become like a modern-day version of Alcoholics Anonymous.

The email attachment, letter headed by The Law plc, had been addressed '*To whom it may concern*'. It detailed an extension to what Martin had introduced in his short voice chat, and it was becoming increasingly clear that there were two options. Either take the fork in the road, or the known dead end.

The other members had the same dilemma. To cut losses or plough on. As always with Jag, whenever there were two possibilities, he would struggle to choose.

Jag wondered to himself what options Olivia's company would have had. Part of him was glad he had not needed to call her and her company's cybercrime section. Glad, because of her snide nature and cold, cold emotions for those who had suffered these financial losses. It angered him each time he thought about her. Pretentious cow, he thought to himself.

Still, the option that Olivia's company could offer would never be known, and that irked him somewhat. Maybe they would offer their services on a No Win, No Fee basis? That open question added to his woes. Each time he thought about it his frustration would boil. More things to blow his mind amidst this hurricane of anxiety.

The details of the offer from The Law plc became clear in the letter attached to the email. It turned out that the requirement was to contribute twelve thousand pounds in advance for their services.

From their side they had to cover themselves, and it could take months to get any evidence, or to follow these breadcrumbs of hope to trace the whereabouts of The Forex Group. The whole case was looking to recover over two million pounds for the victims.

It would not be easy, for sure. Having banks set up in Bratislava and other business in The Marshall Islands, it would take a while and expense to search for those breadcrumbs. Breadcrumbs that may eventually lead them to Jag's dough. Well, that was the hope.

So, decisions loomed large for the investors who had been left in the lurch. For Jag there was really only one choice: the choice of more pain. The choice to give his consent and agree to push ahead with legal action.

The discussions took place for him to reach his decision, but only in his head. How could he just close the door on over sixty thousand pounds? How could anyone? These were the emotional footballs that bounced around in his mind. He had to have a goal, ambition, moreover, a shot at turning defeat into victory.

After a couple of days, he and the others got back to Martin. Some agreed to push for legal action, whilst others cut their losses. They would remain in The Group, but more as silent members holding onto that emotional umbilical cord of hope; most unwilling to simply acknowledge that they would never see their money again.

The ones who agreed to pay The Law ended up at about fifty percent of the members, those who had invested large sums. They all acknowledged the risk but had too much to lose.

Martin took the next steps.

CHAPTER 40

The potatoes were getting along well. Tiny green leaves had started to show signs of life and hope. It always enriched Jag's mind, gardening. Even as a child he used to love going into his mother's greenhouse. He loved everything about it. The smell, the soil, the heat. Even the bugs and flies gave him a sense of the nature he thrived.

The arrival of early spring and the thawing of life's depression. It melted away the sadness of whatever may have happened the day before.

Many a day he would find creatures to keep himself amused. Small frogs were his favourite. They would often hide somewhere in the corners of the greenhouse, in shaded areas, or behind leaves. As tomatoes were the family favourite, little frogs would often hide in the humidity of the watered green leaves.

One time he caught a frog, small as usual and careful as ever. He always felt the vulnerability of these little amphibians and in this case didn't want to kill or accidentally wound it. He never actually figured out whether he was dealing with frogs or toads; didn't really care, to be honest.

On this one specific occasion, he carried the creature like a priceless butterfly, scared to disturb it. Hands of a child upon the tiny creature like he was holding a large snowball, or something even more immature than a child itself. This time he was going to show his sister. By show, it was more intended to scare her. Debatable though, whether a snowball or a frog would be scarier to a younger sister.

Curling his tongue above his top lip, it seemed his facial gestures were somehow controlling his handling of this tiny thing. A snowball, huge and practically in-your-face, versus the subtlety of a soft, nonchalant frog, harmless. Harmless, yet possessing that wow factor or some would call it, a fear factor, especially for little girls.

Jag knew that. That was his whole intention. He knew how to get to the core of his little sister's fear. On rare trips to their greenhouse, his sister was often heard blurting a phobic yell. Maybe she did have a phobia of frogs? Jag certainly hoped so. And that fed Jag's frog frenzy so much more. Anything to give him the upper hand.

Of course, the whole thing antagonised his parents, especially his mother, who knew getting rid of those damn frogs was an impossibility. There were times when she even considered converting that greenhouse into a shed. *'At least it be the end of all these bugs and pests!'* Procrastination, thankfully for Jag and his craze, got the better of his parents, and the greenhouse remained, despite showing increasing signs of old age.

Long live the greenhouse!

The greenhouse outlived his parents, however old it looked. It always had life to Jag. A land for the living, whether on two, four, six or eight legs. And then of course, these one-legged ones, called plants. The greenhouse was the favourite part of the house to Jag. That greenhouse gave so much life to Jag's youth.

Curling his lip once again, in unison with the movement of the baby frog in his feather-like hands, he headed indoors in search of his sister. He knew he risked the wrath of his irascible father, but that was part of the excitement.

His father hated pets in general. Animals inside the house was even worse. And a frog! Well, that was off the scale. His mother would often laugh at his father's detesting of animals, but on this occasion, a frog, that was out of bounds in her book too.

It was a risk young Jagat was willing to take. It was a risk, to be honest, he never even considered the consequences for. Does a thief really consider the thought of spending years behind bars before the heinous crime? Neither did a young, mischievous Jag.

Young Jag knew it was going to be tricky, but just needed to get used to handling the frog securely and with confidence. Each movement of the baby frog tickled a little, putting him back to square one. But as the minutes passed, he got more and more comfortable and slightly more in command.

To avoid creating a commotion, just yet, he planned to go upstairs, make up a story, then scare his sister with the spotty amphibian. It didn't quite go that way.

On entering the house from the back door, he found himself in the kitchen as normal. He planned to get upstairs as quick as possible, but his trip was cut short. As he tried to exit the kitchen, he heard the approach of footsteps, so he quickly turned and hid in the utility room, closing the door with his little finger, his loose hand holding the frog.

Inside the utility room he was filled with darkness. It felt like emptiness too, even though he was surrounded by equipment, shoes and general bits and pieces. As he heard the noise of footsteps outside, he couldn't come out, not with a handful of frog!

It was just him and the frog, now equal. Equal, because now they were both in darkness, rather than simply the terrified frog, blinded by the closed hands of Jag.

And then Jag started to panic. He found it hard to breath as claustrophobia hit. Times like this you don't forget. It had been around the time his own terrifying phobia found its foundations. He was in the little utility room in what seemed total darkness.

Total darkness!

And that total darkness made the room feel smaller.

Whenever he moved one way, he hit into something. When he moved the other way, he hit something else. It all added to the congestion of the room.

Long live the utility room!

The house itself, was not that large, so this utility room, in tandem, was proportionally smaller. Not much to utilise in this room, more so when in darkness.

He scratched around for the light switch above, almost succeeding in dropping the little animal. But for some reason he couldn't find the switch. And in that darkness his claustrophobia engulfed him; engulfed him like the smothering of a pillow pressed hard and firmly over nose and mouth. A suffocating darkness that squeezed the oxygen out of the air. It was as if oxygen could not exist without light.

It was all even more confusing to him as he was so young, having to go through this. Going through something as a child that he didn't understand at all.

To most, claustrophobia began with a 'c'. To Jag, it began with a capital 'D'. Darkness was half of his fear here, as if the walls were closing in on him in some kind of crazy Hunger Game or Squid Game of death.

Escape the walls of death before your oxygen runs out!

Squid or frog, what difference did it make?!

And the sweat had started to form, now multi-layered on his brow, especially around his hands as they still held onto the blinded frog. Ironically, the frog had already been blinded from before, from Jag's hands of control and domination. Now, as per natures law, the power of the frog and karma had evened things out. With a strange justice, Jag was now the blinded one, claustrophobia adding to the scales of justice that caved in on him.

He was crying now, sobbing quietly with small jerks. But he felt stuck to the place he was. He felt small and helpless, totally confused.

His slippery hands still tried to grip the frog as he still heard footsteps and chatter behind the door; what had become his prison door. Worst still, he was in a prison where he was not allowed to make noise, or risk getting caught out. What had started out as a tame prank on his sister, to pluck at her phobia, had revolved into a battering of his own mind and fears, burdening him well beyond any feasible expectations.

All the while he had tried to multitask, despite the tears. After closing the door of the utility room, he must have closed it shut too strongly. Now, he found himself unable to even open it again. Hence, his phobia's grip strengthened. The knot of fear blinding his eyes and squeezing his throat.

Trying to open the door, of course proved even trickier with frog in hand. It had become hard coded now that he was not going to let go of that frog. Yet the panic grew with the tears. The frog lived on. Jag felt it would outlive him.

Long live the frog!

Using his fingers in a hampered way to try and get out of this solitary confinement was proving a graft, his incarceration feeling like a life sentence. And the frog lived on like a parrot down a mine, breathing in all the air.

The panic was rising, the walls were closing, the air was thinning.

If Jag had a watch, the alarm would be ringing now. But alas, the only ringing he heard was the sound of his heart, beating like it was going to rip a hole through this darkness.

With no real time to think or plan, Jag fought hard with the door now. Little care or regard for the visitors on the outside. Outside, where another world lived and enjoyed the bounties of that world. Bounties like light and oxygen lived on the other side. Only congestion and cramped confinement for those in the darkness.

It wasn't a time for planning or strategy, now survival was the need, the function. Yet still, as if programmed into him, he retained his hold on the frog, despite risking losing the hold on his sanity.

Long live the frog! Long live the frog!

The utility room. That felt more like a cave now, seemed soundproofed to the outside world, as he harshly fought for his freedom and a better life. This utility room had become its antithesis. The grass is always greener on the other side.

On his side, even if there was grass, he would not be able to see it anyway! Anything must better than this clogged up existence; blocked from all angles, with not even a vein of hope to look forward to. A room of zero utilisation.

Perspiration and tears dripped freely now, from his head and hands. His grip on the amphibian now stronger than ever, as his grip on reality loosened with every second. It was now or never as he felt his heart shooting bullets of anxiety into no man's land. Like a wounded animal he couldn't even feel his hands. Those that once gripped the frog so tenderly, were now closing, intractable and harsh.

His hands didn't seem to be his. As he increased the pressure with his hands, they seemed to get numb, more so with every painful second, cramp setting in. They did not even seem to emanate from his body, especially in the darkness; this darkness that turned dreams into nightmares and hope into despair.

Painful groans escaped from his lungs, smothered by his intention to keep things secret. Lungs closing more with the passage of time as the claustrophobia closed in on him. He just wanted to get out but felt paralysed and glued with the weight and curse of the frog, or the prank he had initiated.

Long live the frog! Long live the frog!

Saliva now fell from his mouth, teeth grinding together like they were chewing on too well-done steak. Saliva dripped from mouth to hands, combining with the sweat and frog juices. An unsavoury cocktail from hell. Roll out the cauldron, alchemists united.

His hands, once controlling mechanisms, feather-like, innocent, and gentle, had become the human equivalent of a pestle and mortar. Slime juice had started to drip and hang below his hands, though thankfully now the darkness would come to rescue onlookers from that abomination.

The darkness!

The same darkness now under a different guise.

Nothing but darkness!

The darkness that had welcomed Jag in the form of rescue, had become a web of rage and indignation. That same darkness, once tamed and functional, had become a cauldron, a raging beast of painful emotions.

The claustrophobia seemed to have passed, or maybe had become embracing, as no thoughts gripped Jag's mind like before. He was growing up quick. Or maybe he had just become so preoccupied.

Now that the frog had become slime juice, there was no more the need to prank. The pranker had become the pranked in this visceral game of retribution whose only intention was to turn stomachs.

It was like a weight off his shoulder, or maybe his hands. The release of the little, harmless amphibian into a world of freedom. From the world of darkness into the world of light, whilst he still stood there, wounded, and guilty in abject darkness.

But he understood none of this. His little mind could not make any sense out of it.

No more tickling movements from the mess that was once a frog. Only a mix of cuisses de grenouille from a blind chef with no taste buds. His palms felt glued together. That, or maybe he just didn't have the guts to separate them. A superglue of puss and sweat, bones and slime, a green cocktail.

His little mind was working overtime now wondering what on earth to do now. He couldn't just stand there forever, even though he hoped to not have to meet those on the other side of this darkness.

It was too late now though. What was done was done. He would have to face the wise, maybe himself having learned a little wisdom in the process.

The silence now.

He could hear it. Feel it.

The calm, after the storm. He could see it.

Even in this darkness. Shapes, and even shadows in this tiny, unforgiving utility room. A utility room where lessons where taught. Lessons learned... the hard way. A room well utilised!

The utility room had a baptism.

Holy water!

Holy slime!

He would have to make a move. Couldn't stay there forever. But the reluctance to release his hands from themselves. At least if he did so, in this darkness, he wouldn't have to see the blood on his hands.

Childhood's end.

Then, whilst in mid-thought, a loud noise and the door was flung open. It was his mother. Amidst a pause in the chatter and outside noise, she did finally hear those calls for help in the form of attempts to open, what in fact was a faulty door. Being old, it had jammed from the inside and pretty much locked Jag in. It clearly didn't help that his hands were handicapped from the frog, but he still would have struggled.

'Oh dear, Jagat... Oh dear. You okay in there, son?' It was his mother, and Jag potentially had a get out of jail card. Jail, for real! The faulty door was the reason, nothing more.

A lifeline! 'Is it hot in there? Doesn't seem that hot, but you're sweating so much. You, okay? Jag?'

Jag was clearly not okay. Partly because his prank had backfired, but also because of the ordeal of darkness he had to suffer. 'It's… It's fine, mum. I… I only went in to get some shoes but… but couldn't open the door. Got stuck in, felt hot…' Jag continued to hold his hands together like some game show host trying to hold his hands together to be polite. 'Can… can you tell dad to see if he can fix the handle? It was so dark in there…'

'That'll be the Darkness, son. That'll be the Darkness!'

It was like an imaginary voice inside his head, portrayed onto the face of his mother. He thought he saw his mum uttering those words, without it sounding like her voice.

'Yes, I've already told him a dozen times to fix that door. Sorry, Jagat. You sure you're, okay?' Her attention was straight away drifting to Jag's father, who was sure to get a mouthful of vengeance.

Jag, meanwhile, was not hanging about. His game show persona still intact, slime residue still dripping occasionally onto the carpet. He rushed up into the toilet, finally released his hands from the frog handcuffs.

It smelt terrible for a long time, and it seemed weeks before he could get that smell to go away.

The psychological memory though, lasted much longer. Darkness, claustrophobia, confinement, and farming.

It had been an emotionally expensive experience.

Into the darkness and beyond.

Long live the Darkness!

CHAPTER 41

Yes, the arrival of spring and the potato leaves, and thankfully, no greenhouse.

He continued to reminisce. For Jag, he loved his garden, and gardening. His experience as a child had dented his fondness with frogs, but he still enjoyed growing and eating whatever he could. Any chance to get out after a day or week in the office was welcomed. For him though, a greenhouse would be too intensive.

His parents still had that greenhouse, now even more dilapidated. The frogs still visited, and so did he on occasion. Very little grew in that greenhouse now though. His parents were too old to look after it but kept it partly because of the effort and cost in replacing it, and for old times' sake. It had been part of the family and removing it would be like losing a family member.

At the same time, for Jag, whenever he went over to his parents, he would often reflect on those greenhouse memories.

The place now was a bit run down, to say the least. Moss grew around the stone on the ground and walls and even partly on the windows. It was beyond salvation. Now it really lived up to the name, greenhouse!

Cracks in the windows, not for air conditioning, but a result of years of poor maintenance. Soil, old and infertile, dry, and dusty in summer. Not the same frog paradise it once was. But occasionally, Jag's old amphibian friends did still visit, maybe missing him! This time they would die of natural causes.

However old and bedraggled the greenhouse was, it was satisfying to Jag, still harboured sentimental value to him. It was like an old shoe worn a thousand times before; hard to take off.

No other place ever gave Jag the feeling he got when he went into that greenhouse. That's why, despite how decrepit it had become, he would never be the one in the family to say, 'Shouldn't we convert that worse for wear greenhouse into a shed?' Maybe his sister, but not him.

Back in the present, Jag picked at some weeds near the potato leaves in his own house, his mind still preoccupied with thoughts of the greenhouse. For a few minutes, reflecting on his past, the memories were so vivid, and it made it all that much more emotional. He felt his eyes getting watery with reflection. Jag sniffed, trying to rid himself of the emotion he was feeling, a teardrop falling down onto the earth. Sentimental feelings had overtaken him for a few minutes, and part of him enjoyed it, the reflection to a time of innocence.

Not having to think about The Forex Group, at least for a short while, was great. But, when that sobering thought returned, it did so more powerfully and without remorse.

As he knelt to pick the weeds, he noticed a small frog out of the corner of his eye. It was so innocent. Jag, now older than when last handled a frog, moved his hand closer. A stupid notion that this baby frog could be the offspring of the one that a long, long time ago became slime in the hands of a young boy. This time, Jag simply slowly stroked the top of the frog. Then it jumped, off to live another day.

Long live the frog!

It wasn't long before his thought waves returned to The Forex Group. After spending some time away, thinking about his former life, it was like another twist of the knife, sprinkled with salt. His problems were not going to go away as easily as the baby frog in his garden.

CHAPTER 42

More pain followed.

Jag transferred the additional twelve thousand pounds to The Law plc.

He begged himself that this would be the last and hopefully the most successful transfer. A transfer of money and hopefully, luck. His dreams of profits to pay off his mortgage had been replaced by simply a humble plea to get his initial amount back. That was now all he wanted. Humbled and humiliated, fragile, and broken. Many of the others too, paid the lawyers, hoping for a change.

Transfer made. Now, a little patience. The patience of a gardener, Jag thought to himself. He wished all those years of growing tomatoes, cucumbers, sweetcorn and now potatoes would have put him in good stead. He wished now for blessed patience as he stared down at the motionless leaves of the sprouting potatoes.

Maybe there was some wisdom here, he thought. Some sagacity for him to acknowledge. He had often lacked this patience in life. Maybe this was the reason for all these problems? To teach a fortitude and add calmness to his personality.

To make him a better gardener! He needed some way of reaping something from what he sowed, a harvest from his efforts.

CHAPTER 43

A few weeks passed.

Time was dragging. It was like standing there, in his garden, watching the potato leaves grow.

The potatoes had grown over the past few weeks, progressing nicely. Jag was in his second home, his garden, working on his extracurricular activity. Some hobbies come and go, but for Jag, his gardening enthusiasm never waned.

'Hey, Jaggy, the clock stopped again,' Jenny screamed from indoors. She was just about to repeat it, but Jag turned in slow motion as her mouth opened for a second time. She saved her air, but a desperate look had formed on her face. It was as if her face was saying, '*Really! After all these weeks had passed, and still you've not fixed the damn clock! What kind of a husband are you?'*

There was a degree of truth in that though. He even often asked himself that same question. What kind of a husband am I? What kind of a fool have I been? He didn't want to face the answer, and was not prepared to, either. Both of their lives could have been made easier had she simply changed the batteries herself, but it had become personal now.

Procrastination ruled in Jag's house. 'Okay, Jenny, got it.' He gave the thumbs up as if to suggest everything was just fine. Once upon a time things were just fine.

Any day now, he expected to get an email from Martin or the group chat regarding an update from the lawyers on their request to track down Goldsmith and his cronies.

Not really interested, Jag wandered in from, what was slowly becoming his first home, the garden, into what he had decided was now his second home, the actual home. He simply existed now at home, without much enjoyment, being on tenterhooks waiting for an update. He had hoped that his gardening would teach him the patience needed to get through his financial crisis.

Performing his usual magic trick to warm up the batteries, he got the clock working again. He knew it would only be a matter of time again before it went, but he didn't care. Besides, this time, Jenny was not there to goad him, so he got of lightly.

As Jenny had gone to toilet, he even performed a little bow in her direction as if taunting her as the assumed boss of the house. After completing the bow in a sycophantic way, he arose, only to give the middle finger to her. It was childish, but his way of releasing his pent-up emotions. He could not give a damn about the clock. They both realised that by now, and he was in no mood to concede.

Jag headed upstairs. He popped into Bunny's room. She was playing with her dolls as usual. Tinkerbell lay on the ground, wings closed in an inoperable, almost paralysed way.

Jag noticed a change.

The big cat that James had given Bunny was out in the open! In the middle of the room!

Bunny seemed to be playing with it!

That was a first! Even to Jag, a disconcerting first!

It was the first time Jag had seen this. For weeks, that cat had simply been sat there, in the corner, facing the other way, to not have look into those shiny eyes. Facing the other way like child punished for bad behaviour. Now, somehow, Bunny had invited the cat into her life. It seemed that way at least; penance paid.

That cat had been a castaway item since arriving. Strangely now, it was there, amongst the dolls. Its time in the pound was complete.

Because of its size it was clearly prominent. And it seemed to have a gleaming smile on its face now. Like Bunny, a gleaming smile. It was noticeable too, that Bunny very rarely had such a beaming smile.

Jag could not recall that the Russian Blue had a smiling face before. 'Hey, Bunny, you turned the cat on.' It wasn't really a question or a statement. Jag, himself, was not quite sure what his comment was.

'Hey, daddy. We're friends now, me and Ruskie. He's nice now. Just took a little time to get used to his new home. Now he loves living here. Just needed time, that's all, daddy.'

Ruskie? She... He... It... whatever, has a name now? Since when? More questions than answers as Jag thought to himself. He felt a little uncomfortable opening up on those questions to his daughter though. It felt awkward probably because Jag himself didn't like the look of that cat. They all didn't to be honest. But now? Somehow Bunny seemed all at ease. No doubt it was a good thing, wasn't it? Had to be.

Finally, his daughter was playing with toys other than those dolls, and especially of course, Tinkerbell. It may at least take their minds away from that long-lost spinner, impossible to find. It gave hope, he ironically thought. If she could change and find solutions to problems, maybe he could too?

A few weeks ago, that cat, the big cat, was the thing of nightmares, for all the family. Now, She... He... It... was part of the family! Time to reflect, thought Jag, considering things deeply. Could be a good sign?

Yet he was still not sure. Firstly, a gift from Balden, someone who he had not fully made up his mind about yet. And more importantly, the eyes of an awkward stranger, not even a living stranger! It was uneasy, a little emotionally cumbersome. Familiar eyes of that cat, yet those of a stranger; a portent or a paradox?

‘Oh, okay, Bunny. That's... that's good isn't it.’ Again, not really a question or statement, but he was trying to at least sound like he was talking to a child. Jag was clearly surprised by the change in setup in Bunny’s room. It was like he had walked into his neighbour’s house. His lack of decisiveness was accentuated by those eyes.

The cat’s eyes never left Jag’s, like they had string linking the cat’s eyes to his eyes. David Copperfield wouldn't have been able to do any better. A dead animal performing hypnosis, impressive! An animal that was never even alive to start with! Even more impressive!

‘It’s good that... that you've starting to play with that gift, Bunny. You turned it on?’ There was a complete lack of confidence in his words.

‘Ruskie, daddy. He’s called, Ruskie. And he loves it here, don't you, Ruskie?’ Ruskie wagged his tail, as if responding. Jag did find that impressive too. Did the cat recognise that he was being called? How on earth could he?

Where Bunny saw Ruskie, the wonderful friendly cat, Jag saw a huge Russian Blue, wickedness, sinister eyes, and deception. Technology, he confessed to himself, despite being an area he worked in, sometimes got the better of him.

Bunny was clearly enamoured by that cat. It had taken centre stage, dangerously central, and a challenger to the unthinkable, Tinkerbell. Just a fad, Jag concluded, as he watched Tinkerbell lying on the floor, almost strewn on the ground. Jag even thought he saw sadness in Tinkerbell’s eyes, that he had never seen before.

And the cat smiled on. No, it was a grin, contentment. Top dog, or more specifically, top cat, in this world of cat and mouse. ‘See how soft Ruskie is, daddy. See how real his paws and whiskers are? Just feel him, daddy, he's so soft.’ Bunny, almost mesmerised, softly stroked the furry animal like she was moving a feather over a ball of dandelion seeds without wanting to disturb them. It was a physical example of poetry, tender and thoughtful.

Jag was tentative, but in a different way. He hadn't been close to the animal since the day it arrived. There was hesitation, but he knew it was stupid to act withdrawn. Pull yourself together, Jag, he thought to himself. So, Jag went closer, in an act of defiance against the voice in his head.

Feel the soft, soft fur. Soft and fragile like a meniscus on the top of a glass of water. Do it, Jaggy... DO IT!

The tail still wagged. Often a cat wagging its tail is a sign of annoyance, but sometimes it can be a sign it is asking for affection. It seemed to wag at intervals, random intervals. So real. And that caused him to hesitate. The cat seemed so real. The eyes, they seemed to move, in line with the face, as if following you around the room. Maybe it had even been following Jag around the house? Maybe it even knew about his financial endeavour?

Come on now, Jag. Pull yourself together!

He stretched out his hand, as if doing a dare, his daughters dare. Trick or treat? His daughters smile, encouraging, welcoming, hypnotising, warm. Why was he hesitant? Why was he making such a big deal out of it?

You know it makes sense, Jaggy.

But did it? Why the hell did it not, the other half of his brain interrupted? It's a toy! Nothing more, nothing less.

What's it going to do, attack you, kill you, curse you? Things are bad enough already, Jag. What more could a toy cat do?

That last suggestion resonated a little with Jag. A curse? Possible but highly improbable. So, he continued to stretch out, still ensuring his arm was fully stretched out, as if making sure he had his insurance policy in place. He still didn't want to get too close.

Then contact was made, and yes, the fur was unbelievably soft and even warm. Or was he becoming too emotional? Breathing became normal as Jag stroked the cat, though the cat continued to eye him, maybe even control him. All this, despite the irony that Jag was supposed to control the cat via app or remote control.

There, I did it, thought Jag. No big deal. He had stroked the cat!

'Yes, it's... soft, Bunny. It's... soft.' Dare over, Jag reversed, eyes not leaving the eyes of the cat throughout.

'See, daddy. I told you once you get used to Ruskie, he the best, right?'

'Right... right. You're right, darling.' This was Bunny's toy; she must be right. 'His fur is very soft... and warm, quite warm, Bunny. Funny how the skin seems warm?' Again, an unsure Jag spoke.

Fortunately for Jag, Bunny was so hypnotised throughout, that she never even stopped to consider how odd Jag's behaviour was.

'Isn't it cool, daddy?'

'It is, dear, it is.' Jag though, was not fully convinced, or convincing.

One thing that he was convinced with though, was that Bunny was happy. He had never seen her this happy since the time before she lost Tinkerbell's spinner.

It was a positive tone to end his day on. Maybe things were going to take a turn in the right direction for a change?

As he stared into the cat's eyes, he thought he saw hope, and the potential for change in his life, the way he saw a huge transformation in his daughter's.

CHAPTER 44

Jag turned on his laptop. It was the same one he used for his IT Integration work as a contractor. He used the same laptop for checking his fictitious forex balance that he once thought was real. It meant not having to worry about using a company laptop and the security issues that came with that.

He should really have felt blessed to have such a nice role in the project, but as with human nature he had grown to take things a little for granted. That, coupled with his recent forex complications, he found himself with little to be thankful about.

That was just the way things had turned out. In another episode of his life, he may well have felt blessed, and James Balden may not have turned into the antagonist that he had become in Jag's eyes.

The laptop was booting up. As he had been using the same laptop for a few years now, it was starting to get slow, and to start up it took a while. Finally, the Dell logo disappeared, and the screensaver appeared. A dessert island and a solitary palm tree, the default screen displayed. Jag wondered if that was the island where the thieves of The Forex Group hung out, with his money.

Is that what the Marshall Islands looked like? He really had no idea. What he did know was that at every opportunity he found himself dwelling on his problems. And if there was no problem there, he would try his best to find one.

He logged in, username and password.

And then...

... Then he thought he had typed something in wrong, or maybe the keys were sticking? It took a few seconds to register in his mind what was happening.

The cursor was moving around on its own!

He started to hit keys, ESC button, then again... and again, trying to take control.

But nothing, nothing! No response to his keystrokes!

Then any key! All the keys! What was going on?

The mouse pointer continued to move around on its own, insane! And not just move around but move around like it was on drugs! He had never seen a mouse pointer move around on the screen as fast as this. If a bot ever typed on a keyboard, this is how you would imagine it should move. Totally random.

He looked around the screen and keyboard for solutions, still pressing buttons madly. No response. It was only responding to its own desires!

The cursor seemed to be moving on its own! The mouse, wired and normally logical, though still, and motionless on the table, was moving on the screen. So, whilst it was completely stationary on the table, the cursor was moving frantically. Bizarre!

Jag held his hands up for a few seconds, as if to prove it was not him moving the mouse at breakneck speed. He knew it wasn't him. The computer knew it wasn't him. Who was it then?

Many things had not made sense to Jag over the past few months, but this was on a visual level. And Jag had become so unstable of late, that the slightest thing seemed capable of tipping him over.

He continued to shake his head but had to try to take control. He could see various files opening and closing. Word files that he briefly recognised offered glimpses. Then Excel opened, right-clicking, highlighting sections, typing gibberish. Oh, wow, sweat now forming on Jag, mouse, as cool as ever.

Looking around, now worried about losing important data, he tried to take control of the mouse. But that was just the start...

Excel closed; task complete. Word opened again. Jag's eyes followed the mouse pointer movements around the screen. The cursor highlighted an area then clicked away, pure random clicking. Then... pause... then...

On its own, the laptop started typing...

`Gardening Leave... Gardening Leave... Gardening Leave...`

`... For Those Who leave the garden... Don't leave the garden... Tend to the garden.... Your garden needs you!`

`DO DUE DILIGENCE`

`DO DUE DILIGENCE`

`DO DUE DILIGENCE...`

And that was it. Silence...

Silence, from the point of view of the laptop cursor. No more movements. Even from Jag!

There was silence on and off the screen as the only sound was the start-up of the laptop fan. For once, that was a normality that had been missing, the only normality thus far.

Breathless confusion. All Jag could do, for the first few seconds was stare at the screen. Like an infant, addiction growing to cartoons on a tablet, he just stared at the screen, glued.

He could do nothing but stare, dumbfounded. And part of him stared with even more perturbation, at the cursor bopping up and down on the spot. Rhythmic beats, up and down, on and off. The sound of silence. The cursor waited, or had it finished? A curse or a cursor?

What had happened? Jag had no idea, but to him it was still going on. He had to take some action rather than sitting there like a puppet in a show, awaiting strings to help him move. He felt and looked paralysed. He had just witnessed invisible digits typing words from another realm.

Jag's paralysis left him waiting for its next move. From an artificially intelligent cat to an artificially intelligent computer, he was surrounded by the cast from a different world, dimension, metaverse. A prisoner in a box; solitary confinement of his mind as much as body. And the cursor continued to bop, period.

The words. The typed words. Sharp, like a knife with jagged edges. They meant too much and dug so deep. Was it all a big prank? Had he been hacked? Once he came to his senses it seemed the only plausible solution. A solution in a life littered only with questions and confusion.

... For Those Who leave the garden... Don't leave the garden... Tend to the garden.... Your garden needs you!

DO DUE DILIGENCE...

Jag read the words again and again, without touching a thing. He read everything over and over as if it would result in an answer. Wishful thinking. As if it all was untouchable evidence in a high-profile court case.

What did it all mean? And was this impossibility possible? He hadn't been sleeping well recently, maybe his eyes playing tricks?

He had already tried all the keys with no luck. Whether keys on the keyboard or keys for the doors and windows of his life, they all had been locked recently.

Yet, he had to keep trying to win back control of his own laptop, his old friend, his former friend.

Fortunately, and finally, Ctrl+Alt+Delete seemed to work. The Word document went black, deleted, gone? He hoped so. If only it was all that easy. Blanking out the past with a simple Ctrl+Alt+Delete! Resetting life back to a more suitable point.

He slammed the laptop shut, believing that the harder he slammed it, the more likely that the bad news on the other side would have been deleted.

Then, he opened the laptop again, dreading the inevitability of turning on the power once more. Power, ostensibly not always a good thing.

Tentatively, Jag hit the start button once again, unsure what to expect next.

It was normal. Wow! Phew!

The fact that it worked normally made no sense to Jag. Ironically, even when the laptop turned on like it should, it did not make any sense. Normality in a world of abnormalities, making the sweet taste sour.

Deleted, gone... but only from the screen. Not from his memory. His own human RAM could not remove the history, nor overwrite the dreaded news he had been going through. Saved forever into his human cabinet of files to be unfortunately explored later.

The glitch, at least, appeared to have gone. The glitch of a permanent marker on a whiteboard. So, whilst the glitch did not appear after restarting the laptop, its indelible ink remained.

For a second time, Jag restarted the laptop, indecision still his only decisive emotion. Again, it was fine. Phew!

The laptop was fixed.

Long live the laptop!

CHAPTER 45

The vibration hit his phone.

A WhatsApp message had arrived. So close was the mobile to his sleeping head, that it woke him like an alarm. The vibration alarm, a new type of alarm!

It was a group message... and from Martin, group admin for their Forex Group related issues. Volcanic tremors this time as Jag was expecting an update from The Law plc, his last vestige of hope.

It took his eyes a few seconds to wake up, but once he saw it was a message from Martin, and about the legal proposal, he woke in a jiffy. 2:00 am or 5:00 am, it didn't really matter. When it came to The Forex Group, he would be awake in milliseconds.

The red and green lines of the forex trading platform had become like the lines of a cardiograph depicting the reaction of his fractured heart. Any murmurs about The Forex Group, and his heart would start to pound.

The message was short.

Dear Friends,

Please check your email in the morning. There has been an update we need to inform you about. Sorry, cannot explain over short chat.

Regards,

Martin

Intrigue, as Jag read, eyes wide open, but burning with the light of the phone against the darkness around him. Jenny was breathing deeply next to him, so he knew she had not awoken.

He was pretty sure he wouldn't sleep now, the anticipation of what might be, flooding his mind. Whether he would sink or swim now, it all depended on what Martin had to say.

So, he headed down. Even though summer was on the horizon, nights in the UK were still ruled by the realms of chilly temperatures. Jag headed outside. As the self-typing laptop had said, '*Your garden needs you!*'

So, that's where he was heading, unplanned and unaware of what he would do there. He put his jacket on, slid the patio door open quietly and headed out, closing the door behind him.

It was May, but a windy night as he wrapped up by zipping up his jacket. Phone in hand, trying to read between the lines was impossible. It would be a long night of contemplation and a short night of sleep.

The potato leaves were holding up well in the wind. Being short helped as they wafted left then right in the cool late spring breeze. Early chutes on nearby trees and flowers were splitting their way into the world. Their story on the complexities of growing up paled into insignificance to the turbulence Jag found himself in.

He looked around at nature. How innocent it all was. A simple and perfect existence. It almost made Jag envious as he yearned for a humble life.

He often wished he could be whisked off to some remote village in India. A place where mobiles, laptops and even satellite television didn't work. A place where you could spend a whole day searching for the days food or building a new thatch roof for your shelter. Sometimes he wished he did not have to think about checking his mobile for notifications and instead check his hand made fish trap for signs of real life.

Jag sat there, in his garden, overwhelmed by the vicissitudes of his life. Jacket on, a little chilly, dreaming about an alternative life beyond the one he had been given. And, if not a life given to him, then at least one he had set up for himself. He sat there; winter slippers still being used for the cool evening weather.

Whilst his family slept above, he fretted below, unaware of the outcome from his lawyers. His hopes hung from that perennial thread that kept him in existence.

Back to the jungle he went, thoughts of a life less complicated. Like a bird that wakes up in the morning, not knowing whether there would be food that day, living day to day. Jag's life was far less treacherous, but far more complicated. Yes, there would be food. There would always be food on the table, a year's supply. But more than that, too much food for thought, to gorge into his mind.

A life of simplicity was the one he wanted now. Not a life with too many options; too much food to choose from. Give me simplicity, he thought to himself. Take away my distractions. Take away thoughts and ideas of the extra things I can do. Take away the complexities. The fluff that ruled his mind. That didn't really have any value.

Sat there, on this chilly night, in his winter slippers, Jag wished for a simple life. He knew his wish was not coming true, but he could at least wish. It made him feel better; brought tears of regret and poignancy to his face.

The strong, fresh breeze helped dry those wounds as quickly as they would come. And in that vein, Jag still retained the dream of a return to happier times.

He sat there, watching the frantic moths sporadically circling a nearby lamp that he had set up at the end of his garden. Their battle for light was like his battle to retain his sanity. Anything to illuminate that bulb of hope before his light was extinguished.

The moths fought like mad creatures, an attack on light and time. Light was their heroin. For Jag, his greed had fed his appetite for more and more. But give him a mountain of money and what would he want? No doubt, a second mountain.

An easy buck, it had seemed. An easy way to make a quick buck. As they say, if it sounds too good to be true, it probably is. In Jag's case, it definitely was. Duped into feeding off his own light bulb, spinning around his light bulb like a kamikaze pilot. Only down from here. Thinking that the light bulb was his source of energy, life? How wrong. It was the light that fed his greedy mind into serial addiction.

A sigh from Jag. Realising what he already knew. The light was not his goal, it never was, nor ever would be. He was not a moth. Never was. Never should have ever thought he was. Just an addict, taking his fill. Thinking he was filling his boots until they were full, then getting kicked in his face by them.

The light had turned into his darkness, his claustrophobia. However frenetically he encircled his bulb, he would only end up more and more discombobulated. Law of common sense, result of greed. But when your blinded by the light, you only see the darkness.

Jag shook his head in disbelief, even though he had not yet found what the update from Martin was. He didn't know whether to feel positive or fearful of Martin's message. There was always a glimmer of hope, but fear was always waiting to pounce. A poisoned light to cataract-operated eyes. He had been forced to become a negative force amongst the rest of the crowd. A black moth in an eclipse of white moths?

He continued to watch the moths, mad, stupid, brainless, addicted to that lamp. When he looked closely at that lamp, he thought he saw the green and the red lines that fed his enslavement and ultimately, his weakness. At the end of the day, he sat there, jacket and winter slippers on. And, at the end of that metaphorical day he was beginning to realise, it was HIS weakness!

Turn the light off, take away that dependency on this attractive light, adorned with all sorts of temptations.

Jag was sat there. Instead of wondering what that message from Martin could be, he was having his own ironic light bulb moment. Starting to see his weakness amidst the blinding lights.

He got up, sighed again, then turned the light off. With that, turning off those moths at the same time.

CHAPTER 46

A small amount of sleep did welcome Jag after he had gone back up to bed, a pleasant and unexpected surprise. It took time, but once he had drifted off to sleep it felt like he had only been asleep about five minutes when his alarm for work jolted him up.

For the first few seconds he had forgotten about the message from Martin; a welcome oversight. Then, with a pulse of adrenalin right through his body, the memory came back, rippling through him.

He quickly checked his emails. Nothing from Martin yet. Martin had said to check for his email in the morning. Maybe that meant after some time in the morning? Emails came automatically, so he would keep checking after reaching work.

He had very little recollection of his thirty-minute drive into work that morning as he wasn't concentrating much on the driving. He recalled the time when his mind referred back to the image of those moths from the night before, and how he, himself, was like a human version of those insects.

Thankfully there were no meetings today for him, just more project planning to keep him busy. Today though, it felt like that project planning was more of a distraction. His personal email inbox was more of a milestone to him today.

As soon as he got into office, he checked his phone. Unopened emails had arrived. The tingles began again as he decided to go to the toilet to read the emails in peace. He hoped in peace, but wasn't sure there would be peace, internal at least, especially after reading them.

A toilet flush to his left side as he unlocked his phone. Jag tried to relax as his neighbouring visitor left their cubicle. Tingles continued as he felt nervous, unable to know what lay behind the unopened emails, but optimistic. He unlocked his phone.

There it was. An email from Moleary@igniteme.com, aka Martin O'Leary. *Ignite me? Yes, blow me up with a nuclear bomb if the email doesn't read well!*

It was the inevitable email, the dreaded email, the feared email. Jag read it. He read it very slowly. If it was a YouTube video it would have been playing it at 0.5x speed.

Jag finally lost the power in his phone-holding hand, as his hand started to shake. He nearly dropped his phone. He gulped and could not even move his head due to the numbness that had overtaken him. He looked around the sides of his cubicle for answers, still not really knowing the questions he should be thinking about now.

Martin's email:

Dear Friends,

This email is a follow-up to the very short group chat a few hours earlier.

I don't really know how to say this. I suppose I should just say it. We contacted The Law plc recently, and they agreed to begin work on our investigation of The Forex Group. It seemed to be the best option in terms of trying to get a successful resolution for our problems. As you know, we all contributed £12,000 each.

Well, we made the transfers about 7 days ago. Since then, there has been no communication from The Law. We have not been able to contact them for any confirmation, and their phones are all diverting to voicemail.

Even more disturbing, their email addresses are getting undeliverable responses and their website is not opening.

I think we are all fearing the worst but let's just hope one of us can get a response. Let’s keep our fingers crossed.

I hope to set up a Zoom meeting in the next few days so we can discuss further and consider our next actions.

Regards, and I'm as sorry as any one of you about this latest development.

Martin O’Leary

***

More sighs and gulps and looks around, the feeling of nausea already starting to well up inside his stomach. How is this possible? It can't be possible. Not again? Jag was left in disbelief.

Gardening Leave... Gardening Leave... BLOODY GARDENING LEAVE!!!

DO DUE DILIGENCE...

All these thoughts just naturally came to Jag, as if triggered by stressful news. They just echoed from one ear to the next, deafening his conscience.

He sat there, in the toilet and leant back on the seat, a sad, sorrowful figure. Then he started to cry. There was no one else around as he cried in silence. This was as low as he had felt, ever. It was the lowest he could ever remember he had been, desperate. And he just couldn't imagine things could get any worse.

He banged the sides of the toilet cubicle a few times, raging with regret. ‘No… No… No…’ he screamed to himself. Tears dripped to the floor flowing freely and naturally.

Teeth grinding, vengeance somehow still occupying his mind. Anger and tears mixed up into a cocktail of violent spirits, his mind now completely inebriated with confusion.

This toilet visit he would never forget, sat there, trousers down. An emotional wreck of a man. He was not even the shell of the man he once was. Things simply could not get worse.

A sad figure, he had half been expecting bad news. That was all he ever got nowadays, so expected more of the same. Despite that, there was always that glimmer of hope that he kept hold of. Even expecting bad news did not make the bad news less damaging.

Eyes red and devastated, he dried them with the inside of the cuffs of his shirt. Snot was mixed in with the tears. There was intense anger one second, remorse the next. Wave after wave of whipped up emotion smacked at his face, a tsunami erupting and baptising, then polluting each breath regretfully.

Starting to realise where he was, he stood up, put the phone back into his pocket, and tried his best to straighten himself out before going back into the wild. The other world, the one with foreign exchanges, Zoom meetings, corruption, Goldsmith, and the others.

He'd been here before. Felt this many times. But each time, it took a little more out of him. Like a failing boxer, he kept getting up, knowing the next punch would put him back down again. That's what his life had started to feel like. Even Bunny, his only light, had started to confuse him, following her allegiance to that huge cat. Even Bunny!

Jag felt so alone in a world of deceit and injustice. So, what do you do? You carry on and carry on… or at least you can try. That final nail practically visible in front of him. The number of times he had told himself to keep strong and positive. Those times seemed a distant memory to the one holding that white flag.

Jag went back to the office, his extended self-imposed toilet break over, like that of a man with constipation. He was about as vacant as the toilet cubicle he had just been in, a zombie project planning. He spoke to no one for the rest of the day, sat in his room spending most of the rest of the day with the door closed, focusing on the lines on the wall or the stitches of the carpet.

CHAPTER 47

'You still hiding in here?' The smiling face and shiny bald head of James Balden peered around the corner of Jag's office door. 'It's getting kinda late, you know?' Balden touched his watch as he informed him. Jag just had this reluctance to do anything or speak to anyone. The last thing he wanted was a smug Balden to wind him up.

'Oh, hi, James. I didn't realise the time. I suppose I should be heading off.' Jag had no real desire to go home. Go home and probably get nagged about the clock. The morning had put him in this deep, deep rut, and he didn't have the patience or energy to even try to get home. He was only in the mood to do nothing, just exist, and that, at a stretch. It was clear to James that Jag was not his usual self.

'You okay, mate? You seem a little off, not yourself?'

'No, things are fine. Maybe a little too involved in this project plan. You know, they expect to complete integration testing in one week. I think they need at least three, but, well, they are insistent.'

'Yes, Jag. These are the wonderful challenges. Be honest with them. The business are our customers, got to keep them happy. At least give your opinion strongly so they don't complain later,' said James. He knew there was something deeper though. A little thing like system testing never got Jag looking so stressed before.

'So, what's really wrong?' James was good at reading people. It was clear to him that Jag had a bigger problem than integration testing. He also felt as though he knew Jag fairly well by now. They'd had dinner together, spent hours at work together. From James's perspective, despite sometimes making fun of Jag, he felt like they were good friends.

The mickey-taking, arrogance and clear feeling given out by James gave the impression that he was much better than Jag. Then of course that gift, the cat. There was something not right about that either. Jag had never quite felt the same about James as James had for him. But today, Jag was rock bottom.

'Well, some months ago, I don't know, about eight months ago I think it was. Yeah, well, I did this investment, and, well, it went wrong. Well, in short, I'm in a bit of a mess and got more bad news today about it. So bloody frustrating.' Jag banged his hands on the table like a disobedient schoolboy demanding his dinner.

It was a little embarrassing for James, who took a step back, completely surprised by the random aggression from Jag. Then Jag, too, felt embarrassed after banging the table, showing a lack of self-control of the situation. James realised then that Jag's frustrations had nothing to do with any integration testing.

James did remember that Jag was also loaded up with a heavy mortgage as well. Can't be any fun, he thought to himself. 'Look, Jag, if you are really struggling badly, I may be able to lend you some money to get you through these difficult times? Just let me know.'

'No, no. Things will get better. Thanks, but no need, really.' It was an awkward moment. Jag wished he had never mentioned the problems, just to avoid that heavy awkwardness.

Then the tears fell again. He crunched up his face, unable to speak, head down. Eyes closed, seeing only darkness, Jag tried to hide his crying. There was just a quiet squealing that came from him. Part of him wanted to cry his heart out, but the other more powerful side kept him from screaming out his devastation. Drops fell onto his laptop keyboard, but he didn't care enough to wipe them. His office role meant nothing to him now.

James, clearly embarrassed, walked closer to Jag. 'Oh… Jag, I had no idea things were so bad. What's… what's going on? Let's go home. I'll take you home.'

James clearly realised he did not know half of what was going on with Jag. It was clearly more complicated that Jag let on. 'It's… fine, James. I'll be okay… you go, James. See you tomorrow. I… would rather figure it out myself. Thanks, James, but I'm good.' It was awkward for Jag, trying to talk and clean up sniffles at the same time.

They both shuffled around, Jag especially. He knew he would never take up James's offer. It all made him feel even more ashamed and sorry for himself. He wished the last fifteen minutes had never happened or could be blocked out of world history.

'Well, better get off,' said Jag, clearing his throat, needing fresh air. He was closing his laptop as he spoke, practically getting up to leave at the same time. The atmosphere had become so tense, awkward, and uneasy for both. 'Thanks for trying to help, James. I've got a few ideas and will figure this situation out soon, I'm sure.' Jag even managed a fake smile.

James, despite being reluctant, understood that giving Jag space may be the best thing to do. It was a problem Jag had set up himself and he would conclude himself. 'Okay, well, be careful, and call me as soon as you need anything, seriously, Jag. You understand?' James spoke and Jag just nodded.

Getting home that evening was a bind. Every few seconds his conscience would remind him of the morning's email, as if it was getting some sadistic pleasure. There had to be a plan, just Jag hadn't figured that out yet.

During his car journey back home, Jag punched the vacant passenger seat numerous times. He must have looked like a real looney tune to anyone outside who may have caught a glimpse.

Madman goes crazy attacking car seat. The driver has driven himself around the bend!

And there were many more tears as Jag could not figure out what to do next. The burden of a huge mortgage, twinned with losing money he did not have, it all forced painful tears; tears of the clown he had become. His only hope, however minute, had to be that maybe those lawyers would respond and not be a part of this fraud.

Maybe, he thought to himself. It was still soon. Maybe, yes hopefully, they will get back to us and begin the investigation.

CHAPTER 48

It was a punishing drive home, question after question prodding at his conscience. Whilst he knew he had to go home, he also knew that he had no desire to go home.

Each second at home was like the prolongation of a lie. It was the lie of him spending his family life, concealing the truth about his addiction. There, he said it. It was an addiction, pretty much a gambling addiction. But he just couldn't bring himself to tell his wife about it all. He'd tried many times but backed out each time.

That guilt made his home life like an alien one. Guilt beyond the depths of his imagination. It was embarrassing at times, living separate lives. One life in his own world of Mark Goldsmith and the torturous dreams that kept him going through the mangler. The other life, a husband and father of those who didn't really know him.

It was a painful existence that would come to a head at some point. The double life he was living was what had moved him so far apart from his wife. His preoccupation with outside matters had turned his inside world into an obsession.

The thought alone made him, already one feeling rock bottom, go even lower, down into the earth's core. A psychological visit to the lowest depths possible that a human being could go. Accepting these truths though, was like a weight being lifted from his shoulders. The realisation of what he really was. The next question was whether he was big enough to own up and admit these same weaknesses to his family. That would be the golden question.

He shut his car door and headed inside his home, his heavily mortgaged home. At the same time, he shut away the brave thoughts his mind had considered. The home where he went at night physically, though mentally never sought.

As usual, Bunny came running to greet him. She was the ember that kept him going. How could he express himself to her? How could he tell these things to the little girl who treated him like a hero? How could he sit Bunny down and tell her he was a gambling addict?

Each time Bunny seemed to greet him, with even more vigour and excitement. And each time the weight upon him got heavier and heavier. The world that he held on his shoulders was starting to make his knees wobble. For how much longer?

A big hug for his daughter followed by an acknowledgement for his wife. This was the first evening back since finding out the likely scenario that he had been scammed for the second time. Messages were flying on their WhatsApp group. He was a wreck at this stage, yet still trying to keep things together as he got home.

Lots of confusion and little hope. And no response from The Forex Group or The Law plc. Lots of noise and lots of silence, and inevitable regret.

Jenny could figure Jag was a little more subdued today. 'How was work, Jaggy?'

'Not the best, Jen. Not the best. Too much going on. Too many complaints and demands from the team. But well, hope things sort themselves out. They just need to realise that projects can't be done in a day.' Jag was being partially honest, obviously omitting the real reasons. He could not look her in the eyes.

He didn't plan on sticking around too long. The depression of his situation was making him fall in love with his own company, or at least out of love with anyone else. He just saw no solutions now as he sat down to flick through some satellite channels.

The evening passed, slowly, but eventually. He chose to take Bunny up to put her to sleep. It would get him out of sight. Of course, he also felt safer with

Bunny, less aggravation and fewer probing questions. That was much more conducive to a less stressful evening.

'I'll take Bunny up, Jen. Tell her some stories.'

'Yay. Daddy, yay.' What joy. What innocent joy. It would touch anyone, such simple happiness. Poignancy personified for Jag, who couldn't contrast his own situation more. Living in the same house yet worlds apart. It certainly gave him a breath of hope amidst his collapsing lungs. A canister of oxygen for his depleted heart.

It brought a tear to his eye as he considered himself and the pressure he had put himself under. So, he headed upstairs to escape any glares. Bunny, who had set off after him, was already overtaking him on the stairs as a sluggish Jag dragged himself up.

When Jag made it to her room, he found her already hugging her huge cat, the Russian Blue, aka Ruskie. That helped to slow his sluggish movements a little more as he stared into the cat's eyes with caution. By now, he too had grown more familiar with Ruskie, but knew he would never, ever, see eye to eye with that beast.

It felt more normal with the lights off as Jag looked up at the ceiling, an excited child by his side. He retold the story his daughter had heard a million times before. The story of Tinkerbell and an adventure only she could have where she saves Bunny and the family from disaster. Despite already knowing the words verbatim, her excitement with every word Jag uttered was like she was hearing it for the first time. This time though, as Jag told the story, tears were streaming down his face. Bunny did not even notice in the dark, as she was simply too engrossed with the story.

Jag then reflected to himself. It doesn't matter what kind of a day you've had, however bad things are and however you feel, once you lay in that bed and tell your daughter stories, it's like you enter a different world. These stories even take the storyteller into a different dimension.

And for Jag, any chance to take himself out of his real world of tortuous depression and betrayal was worth taking. He would be the first man on the sheet. On a storyteller's night one loses himself into a heavenly realm with only happy endings. That was why he loved story nights with his daughter.

After he was sure she had fallen asleep, Jag stayed in the bed, moods shifting. He'd held himself together so far since getting home, but again the tears of sadness and regret burst through.

He felt useless, pointless, wondering when the turmoil would end. And, despite Jenny being a wonderful wife of compassion, Jag was blind to all that now.

CHAPTER 49

So, yawning, and twitchy, Jag finally headed back down.

He was broken.

Down he went, from that heavenly world, Bunny's world, into the pit they called planet earth. The place where sighing was a more popular pastime and Tinkerbell only existed as a dream. Checking his mobile, just on the off chance that maybe The Group would have posted something of hope.

No notifications. No hope. Damn.

More frequent now, a strange feeling of helplessness that just kept coming back to him more and more often. And he felt like he had no control. That was the worst part of it. He could just not think straight.

He headed into the main room to find Jenny watching Coronation Street. Who needed Coronation Street when you've got the real thing? Jag was living his own dirty soap opera. His very own perennial show. Welcome to Jag's own drama, a serial liar but with execrable acting. No stunt actors needed. The only stunts where to Jag's chances of getting out alive; a life of stunted growth and a chance to act the fool.

The sight of his wife didn't make things any better. It only made him feel worse inside, like acid had replaced blood in his body.

'She asleep, Jag? She took a long time tonight?'

Well, actually she didn't. That was just me spending a bit of time away from the hell they call earth!

It was just that Jag was reluctant to leave the ethereal world upstairs to enter this world of toil below. He had just ended up daydreaming, or night dreaming in this case. Dreaming of more prosperous times. Fairy tales to keep him sane.

Back down in the insane world Jag found himself looking into Jenny's eyes with contempt, wishing she wasn't there. Then he spat some words of anger at her. 'Why do you watch this drivel? You know what's gonna happen next. They just keep regurgitating the same stories over and over!' Ironically, that was exactly what Jag had been doing with Bunny. The same story, time after time, after time. When he did it, it seemed fine, but when Jenny did, it was drivel.

There was an aggression in his voice. It had been the first time he'd spoken to his wife all day, and when he did, he did so with such a harsh tone. He had become unpredictable lately, but today, with the heavy, tortuous news from the morning, Jag had reached a point he could not make sense of.

'Whose having an affair this week? Whose fighting who? Whose dog died this time?' continued Jag, clearly antagonised by the television programme. The programme that the programmed watched to become dumb and dumber. That's how Jag saw it, mass programming of the mind and sense.

Instead of sitting down to join in and watch this mass visual suicide, he switched on the garden light and went out onto the garden. The high fences he had put up had helped his privacy, though one could see if in a nearby house from the upstairs. It would be possible that a neighbour could see into his garden from their upstairs, but only if they really sought to do so. None of the neighbours, though, could see from their garden, into his. That's the way he liked it.

It wasn't that he had gotten more love for his gardening. It was just to get away. He didn't even feel like doing gardening now, if being honest. He had lost interest in everything.

Jenny looked over her left shoulder to check the time. Time stood still… again. More specifically, once again the clock had stopped. It had stopped once again. A countless number of times. A painful groan escaped her as she turned back in anger and disgruntlement. Her natural response, to look for the clock keeper. That would be her lovely Jag!

Oh dear, Jaggy, here it comes!

‘Jag!’ she screamed out, the whole chair lifting as she shouted. To her, the sound of the television clouded out the noise, so it didn't sound that loud. From the outside though, Jag heard loud and clear. Too loud and too clear as she turned to look towards the noise in equal anger. Anger was building up as she turned back, ignoring her clamour.

As usual, Jag wasn’t in the mood. Jag, The Great Procrastinator. He just ignored her barking. At the same time, he knew the barking would come back louder. He wasn't wrong.

‘JAG!’ Wow.

If the last one was a scream, then this was a roar. She was the king of this jungle. She knew that Jag was keeping something secret, but by now had got a little fed up with his attitude shifts and lack of interest in anything.

Jag knew it could only be a delaying tactic. He would have to go in eventually to face the music, however out of tune it may be to his ears. Eventually, he casually turned away from the potato beds and headed back inside.

‘Jag, could you not hear me? I was calling you about the clock again. Won't you just fix it? Just change the damn battery, won’t you? I guess that's all it needs. Or get a new clock!’ There was much more calmness now in her voice, but a lot of force to her words. She had just about had enough. Turning back around to enjoy her soap opera, Jag approached the clock.

She was engrossed in her show, and the addictive nature by which soap operas played out. He could just see the back of her head now as she faced the television in front of him, giving out the orders. It made him mad, uncontrollably so.

Why can't you do it yourself if you’re so damn bothered?

Jag looked long and hard at his wife. There was real anger he felt towards her, even though she had done nothing wrong. He could almost feel himself getting more and more worked up, his heart beating faster, even finding it difficult to breath properly. It felt like his chest was going to explode. Working his hardest, he managed to keep himself relatively calm.

Then, instinctively, almost without a second thought he went to pick the clock off the wall in front of him. The corners of the clock were square and the face round. This time, he went to the clock, as normal, turning it around to see the back of the clock where the batteries sat.

His fingers went to the batteries, planning to inspect them as usual. Then he stopped.

His fingers stopped in mid-air.

As if a force had stopped him going further forward. His hand hung there.

Then he looked at the back of Jenny, then Coronation Street on the television, then back to Jenny's head.

He had become fed up with warming up the batteries, extending their life. A time had come.

A time to take a stand. A time to make his point.

And his fingers just hovered over the batteries still in their position, but of course, not working.

The pregnant pause ended, giving birth to a new feeling in Jag's mind, a new swing. The grip he had with his left hand in the square clock tightened, as his right hand moved from mid-air to the other corner of the clock. Then he released his right hand and, with clock now sideways in his left hand like a kind of saucer, brought his hand back like holding a Frisbee and hurled it.

He hurled it like his life depended on it!

With a small groan he threw the clock, horizontal like a plate, in the direction of his beloved wife!

Jag was good at sports, so from such a short distance it would be no problem hitting his mark. He once won the school cricket ball throwing competition. That was his most memorable achievement as a child. He won comfortably, and there was no need for arguments or disputes about his cricketing exploits.

It not only won him the school competition and the ability to represent his school in the district cricket ball throwing competition, but more importantly, it gave him prestige. Prestige and respect from the other boys as well as a cheeky admiration from the girls.

That cricketing honour made hurling the clock a piece of cake, especially over such a short distance.

So, the clock ripped through the air, a very short distance, maybe three feet. It was so quick that Jenny didn't even turn or react. It smashed straight into her temple, or just behind. He could not have chosen a better spot to hit her.

It must have hit just perfectly, a distant groan escaped from her. More like a low moan as the impact registered. Then silence, from her at least. The only follow-up sound was of the inanimate clock, bouncing from head, to sofa, to floor.

What a throw!

What had he done!

What have you done!?

There was no further damage to the clock. In fact, the clock landed on its back, face upwards, then began ticking once again! No need to warm the battery this time!

Jenny fell slowly onto her right side, as if tired and deciding to take a rest. This was no rest though, she was out. 'Wow. Oh... shoot.' Jag was stunned himself, and even though he was not one hit, he was hit by shock.

What have you done!!!?

What have you done!!!?

He looked up to his right, to the wall, the place where the clock normally resided. Then he looked at where it was now. He was in shock, and he felt like he was at a crime scene. His hand came up to his own head, wiping sweat from his brow. Wiping the spot on his own head where he struck his wife, on her head.

For some strange reason he let out a quick breath of air and a hissing sound left his mouth.

'Is this for real?' he whispered to himself. It felt surreal to him at least. And he just stood there, it seemed for hours, just blanked out. It was only seconds though. Finally, he timidly called out, 'JJJJenny?' Then again, 'JJJJenny?' As expected, there was no response. He lifted his heavy feet from the floor and walked over to the two victims. One was Jenny, the other, the clock.

Jag sat down on the sofa where his wife lay. There was peace and quiet, except for Coronation Street on the television. He switched that off. Then there was real silence as he tried to collect his thoughts and ideas.

Looking over to his right, over at his motionless wife at peace on the sofa, there was one big question? Was she dead? That's what Jag was thinking. That's all he could think. He'd never seen a dead body so was hesitant to check, preferring just to look, as if peering into some zoo animal's cage. On closer inspection, he could just make out her body was raising slightly, then lowering. That meant she was still alive.

Phew!

He picked the clock up off the floor.

The ticking clock!

Long live the clock!

It was fine now. It was as if life had been sucked out of the human and into the clock!

Time to face life.

As the clock was working, he just picked it up, checked the place that had come into contact with his beloved wife, then dusted it down. Then he headed over to his left and hung it back up on its place.

Then, he noticed a line of blood making its way down the face of the clock, distorting time. A third hand on the clock, but red! He went back to his wife. On closer inspection he found that she too, had blood dripping down her face.

How ironic. How poetic. Twins! Both bloody!

The only thing he could think to do was an act of panic. It was as if the vision of blood had forced his hand. Before seeing this blood, he had been a little calm at least. Now though, it was as if there was a race against time. Quickly passing over to get some kitchen roll, he broke off a few sheets to touch up his wife.

A bit too much blusher, what you think, Jaggy?

By now, tears of sadness and confusion were bearing down, mixed with sweat, as he worked under pressure and with incertitude.

He opened the patio door fully, cool air from the clear night easing in. He picked up his wife, as if taking her down the aisle.

How romantic!

Not really thinking what he was doing, he squeezed through the patio doors and out into the cool night. Taking a few looks around to check no one could see, he continued. He really didn't know what he was doing, just letting one foot follow the other.

She was still warm, thus he declared she was not dead. The line of blood started once again, as it dripped down from her temple onto her lips and into her mouth. It was as if an external drip or vein was feeding her with blood, her own blood! Concussed she clearly was, but as per Doctor Jag's assessment, still alive.

Why had he taken her outside? He had no idea. He was just trying to take the problem outside of the house. Even after what he had done, however bad it seemed, and in fact was, he still felt an anger towards her. He just sat there, looking up, looking down, anywhere for solutions. Then he looked at her as if asking what to do next.

Still in the back of his mind was the torture of The Forex Group and the way they had fooled him. For months, all he had tried to do at home was hide it from his family. At least that, he had been successful in.

'What to do, Jen? What to do?' he said to his unconscious wife.

At least the clock is working! At least she isn't moaning about the clock now. Look on the bright side!

Then he heard a low moaning sound. He picked her up again, moving her onto the grassy part of the garden. There were still concrete flags, wooden planks, and a couple of leftover bags of compost. It made the garden look like a work in progress set up. A human body now added into the mix.

Again, the moan. The first moan, he wasn't sure about, but the second, well, it was clear she had come back to life!

Welcome back to the jungle, Mrs. Singh!

At first there was surprise on Jag's face, shock revisited. More consistent noises now from her. 'Jaa... Jaa,' were the strained words that she fought out.

Jag just felt awkward. Instead of rushing to her side, he ran behind her head, where she couldn't see him.

He panicked.

He just didn't expect her return, or maybe didn't have a plan as what he would do if she did come back from the dead. Well, she was back! And, as normal, Jag was again trying to hide things from her.

She's back, Jaggy! Give her a hug!

Looking around like a lost man anticipating danger, he quickly headed into the shed, closing the door behind him. In the meantime, his beloved wife had started to move more, her hand moving slowly towards her temple where she felt shuddering pain. It was like she was waking up from surgery, the medication starting to wear off. With the pain in her head, it was more like she had awoken mid-operation.

Coming to her senses she mustered the strength to sit up, whispering some inaudible groans. The pain was so severe, but it didn't stop her keep pressing on the wound as if to self-inflict more trouble upon herself.

There was a noise coming from behind her, a clattering and distant sound of movement and objects falling, but she was too drowsy and concussed to respond at her normal rate.

The noise continued as she tried to get more accustomed to why she sat here in the garden.

'WWWWhat… am… I… doing… in… the… garden, Jag? Wait…? Wait, Coronation Street... television...'

THUD!

CHAPTER 50

Jag dragged the body of his wife along the ground. Nothing was making any sense to him now.

He had been digging a while now and was very tired. Adrenalin was powering him on. All the while he just couldn't get the image of Mark Goldsmith and his Cockney accent out of his mind.

'Gardening Leave, Jag, Gardening Leave. We all need a bit of Gardening Leave now and then, Jag. I'm sure you'll agree. Know what I mean, Jaggy? I think you do, my friend. I know you do!'

The furthest away potato bed was now a mess. An hour ago, four potato beds lay there, nice, and tidy, green leaves sprouting as their young spuds grew underneath. Now, soil and loose leaves were scattered around the bed, along with some small young potatoes. They were clearly not yet ready for harvesting.

Jag had dug out a huge amount of soil from the raised beds to leave a long rectangular pit. The shovel he had taken so long to decide over at B&Q had been busy. It had been worth his while a few months ago when he was fake digging in the store, deciding on the strongest and most suitable one to buy. He realised now it had been a good choice.

At the time, in the B&Q store, he had no idea he would be, not only using it to dig for potatoes, but more importantly, for wider ranging activities. He never considered that it would be used for smashing his wife over her head repeatedly, and for digging her grave. That's just the way things turn out sometimes.

He was nearly done digging but couldn't help continuous glances over to his beloved wife. After the way she woke up last time he was half-expecting her to move again, a female version of The Undertaker. The sane side of him also felt remorse, regret, sadness. But now, a hole had been dug in his mind and he was so confused he didn't know what to fill it with.

'I'm… sorry, Jen, Jenny. I'm so sorry what happened. I just had a bad moment. A real bad day. REALLY BAD! You know, I had been trying to tell you for weeks about my forex trading mess, my… addiction. There, you see, addiction. I just never got around to it. I just feared how you'd respond. I was scared how you'd respond, my love.

'You never listened to me, Jenny. I, I did not mean to have all these losses, problems. Just one thing after another. I had to sort out my problems some way or other. Things… they just piled up and up. I was waiting for my break… my lucky break. Well, it never came, and look what happened now. Look… you're dead, and I'm still in this mess, a big mess. But I'm gonna fix it. I really am.' Tears were flowing freely as he spoke now. There was just no control.

'They promised me so much, the forex people and the Group… They all lied to us, Jen. They all lied.' Jag fell to his knees in desperation, grasping his head, then slapping the front of his head repeatedly as if trying to kill a fly on his forehead. He was engulfed in a mass of sweat and tears now.

It was probably the longest conversation he'd had with his wife for years. When there's no one to fire back complaints at you, it gets easier.

Then, he eventually got up and took a step towards his beloved wife, and for one last time stroked her hair back into position. Her temple area was now matted with dry blood. For a few minutes he sat there in reflection, stroking his wife's face gently.

From the shed, full of tools and bits of rubbish, he returned with a heavy-duty black bag and some plastic zip ties. He had to bend her legs to get her to fit into the black bag, then secured it with two zip ties. She fitted well into the raised potato bed, lying on her side, to become something different for the worms to feast on.

CHAPTER 51

Jag hardly had time to take a breath when the doorbell rang. A doorbell, that to Jag sounded like an alarm bell. A million and one things swept through his mind. It was 10:15 pm, and normally no one came by so late. On this night in particular, he did not need a visitor.

The mixed emotions that had entangled his mind needed untangling quickly. His first thought was the police. Someone may have reported a noise or seen him in his garden. The only saving grace were those high fences he had put up. Those fences should have blocked out most onlookers. It was more hope than anything else that he was depending on.

Who else could it be? Should I even answer it?

Do it, Jaggy!

Safest bet is not open the door, he thought. Then he realised how unsuccessful he was at betting. It did still seem the best option though, as his conscience tried its best to scare him further. They would probably leave any moment, so he ignored the bell.

The doorbell, again!

What are you waiting for, Jaggy?

'Wha... oh, come on,' he whispered to himself. Now what to do? He was still outside and there was a huge mess, not to mention, a dead body, and of course sweat and dried tears all over him. The only positive was that with the garden lights off you couldn't notice if it was a garden back there or a cemetery. The curtains should also hide what lay behind. He just hoped it was not his final curtain call.

Just to be safe, he quickly covered the potato beds with a huge black plastic sheet that he kept for a rainy day like this. There had been a lot of rain recently for Jag.

He hurried inside after performing as much cosmetic surgery as he could outside. There was sweat all over him. Thankfully and amazingly though, he could not find any signs of her blood on him. Quickly checking himself over and over, he realised he should go to the door.

'Just a minute,' he yelled to whoever it was as he headed into the bathroom to wipe away the sweat and tears from a hard night's work. Working furiously, he threw open the tap, only for water to fire everywhere. 'Oh, great!' He quickly turned off the tap and dried himself as much as he could, whilst at the same time removing as much soil as he could from his hands.

His receding hairline and that sweaty quiff he had seemed to suit a sweaty persona. All the same, he ran his hands through his thinning hair to at least try to smooth it out. A deep sigh, as the bell rang a third time. That speeded Jag up.

Jag was completely surprised to see Olivia was his uninvited guest. There was an extended silence as their eyes met. Both were nonplussed. Jag was the first to break the silence. 'Hello. It's Hannah's mother?... Olivia?' Two questions side by side from Jag.

'Oh, hello... Jagat, Jag? Yes, I'm, Olivia.'

'Jag, yes. Okay, how you doing?' There was a lot of awkwardness already, but understandable. They last met a few months ago at Hannah's party. As Jag's mind went back to that visit, he remembered smashing their mirror in frustration. Wow, he thought, I wonder if she ever found out that I smashed her mirror?

'So, How's Hannah?' asked Jag, holding the door half-closed behind him. It was a little obvious he was trying to hide something behind him.

'Good, good... First of all, I know it is late and, I suppose it is a bit stupid of me now, but is Jenny around? I just had something I needed to give her. Maybe I should come over tomorrow if it's not a good time now?'

Not a good time! You can say that again!

Oh dear. Oh, no. That's all that went through Jag's mind. Is Jenny around? That's an interesting question, he thought to himself. How to answer that one?

Well, she is around, she's around the back, the back garden, actually!

'Jenny, of course you came to see Jenny. Jenny, she... she wasn't feeling too good. She sometimes gets migraines. Well, she got a bad one tonight, so she went up early to bed. I could wake her if you like?' Olivia noticed Jag was breathing a little heavily. She had the feeling the timing was clearly bad and couldn't even begin to think what was going on.

'No, no... not at all needed. Its fine,' replied an awkward Olivia. 'I hope she gets better though. Migraines can be terrible.'

'Yes, thanks so much. Please come in, even if just for a couple of minutes. Sorry. I should've asked sooner.' Jag wanted to act normal to avoid any suspicion.

'No, it's okay. I better get off,' returned Olivia. She felt a little uncomfortable because of the time and had hoped to meet Jenny for a chat.

'Please, I'll go up and check, maybe she is awake now. Please make yourself at home, I'll be back in a second.' Jag was already heading off upstairs, despite Olivia trying to step in to stop him.

It was a little unexpected for Olivia who felt more uneasy by the smell in the house. For a few seconds she took tentative steps, then headed over to the dining table rather than the sofa, just to add more formality to her visit.

'I'm sorry, Olivia, Jenny is still out of it. She took some medication, so I didn't want to wake her, you know? You said there was something you needed to drop off?' Jag, whose mind was still in bits from what he had done tonight, was trying to paint a picture of normality. 'Where are my manners? What would you like to drink? Juice, water, something stronger?' He was simply living word to word now, no idea or plan to get himself out of this new mess he was in.

'No, no, nothing really, nothing at all. I... I shouldn't have come this late anyway.'

'Well, you're here now. Drink?' questioned Jag.

'Err, juice is fine. I'm driving as well.'

'Not a problem, just a min.' Jag turned to the kitchen and Olivia noticed how dirty his clothes were, especially the jeans. They looked either damp, muddy or dirty to Olivia. And she kind of thought, it matches with the smell in here.

Jag returned with the juice. 'Oh yes, I remember, you work for a law company, don't you? I remember you mentioning that when we came to Hannah's party. How are things going at work?'

'Work is... work, really. Quite busy at the moment. I remember at that party you mentioned you had a friend who fell for some fraudsters. You said you were going to call?'

'Oh, yes, Olivia, my friend. Yes, he was having financial troubles. I think he's going to figure things out somehow. I think he'll be fine. He'll be fine.' Jag was a little calmer now, less frustrated. 'Yes, he will be fine,' reflected Jag, looking at the wall, thinking about his own condition for a second.

'That's good. You know it's still hard to believe how busy our cybercrime division is. Even busier than when we met last time. The gullible nature of people. Pathetic really. Some people really need to wise up a little. The types of stories they mention in the office, unreal.' Olivia was not holding back in her trivial dismissal of the vulnerable. 'Nice wall clock by the way.' There were remnants of blood on the clock, but Jag had done his best to remove most of the evidence.

The smile had disappeared off Jag's face, and the calmness, too. 'Yes, I'm sure there are lots of stories, some must be worse than others.' Jag spoke through gritted teeth. 'You said when you came there was something you needed to drop off?'

'Ah, yes, I almost forgot. Well, I did forget. It's this.' Olivia delved into her coat pocket, then the other. 'Oh, can't find it. I must have left it in the car. Just give me a second please, Jag.' Olivia got up and headed out back to her car.

'Oh… you dro…' Jag begun, but Olivia had already set off.

He bent down to pick up the rectangular card that Olivia had just dropped onto the floor as she had been looking for whatever she brought over that evening. On closer inspection, Jag found it to be a business card. An even closer inspection sent his already lacerated mind into a million pieces.

He whispered the words in disbelief, reading the business card in his right hand.

'The Law plc... Elizabeth Sharpe… Cybercrime Investigator…'

After reading those few words he just looked to one side. He felt a cold flush overtake him, almost forgetting to breathe as he tried to take in information he could not believe. 'How is this possible? Wait… what is this?' Memories of the past started to make a little sense. He thought back to sitting in his car and those Zoom meetings. 'Olivia… Elizabeth… she is the angel that was supposed to save us!?' Jag couldn't think straight.

The angel... or a devil?

Finally snapping himself back to the present, Jag put the business card in his pocket and headed out into the garden hastily. He came back in a rush, then went into the kitchen area. A few seconds later Olivia was back with a half-empty Tesco bag. As she returned, she noticed Jag, a little out of breath coming from the kitchen area. It wasn't a particularly large room, open plan kitchen, dining, living.

‘It’s maybe just something small but I remember last time Bunny came over to see Hannah she kept talking about this spinner that Tinkerbell had lost. Well, guess what turned up inside Hannah’s toy box? I'm sure it means a lot to Bunny, so it means a lot to me too. Here you go. Hope Bunny can sleep happily at night now. That is the spinner, isn’t it, Jag?’

That was it!

Long live the spinner!

But Jag was in no mood to offer thanks. Not knowing how to respond without letting on that he knew she was the one who had just pulverised Jag’s evening even more, he tried to keep up the charade.

‘Oh… wow. That's nice of you. Yes, that's it. We've been all over the house looking for that you know. So that's where it was. She won’t believe her eyes! Thanks so much, Eli… Olivia. You deserve some more juice for that.’ Jag picked up Olivia’s glass and headed back into the kitchen. There was genuine disbelief as Jag took hold, then put the great treasure that was the spinner, on the table. At that moment though, the spinner was not at the forefront of his mind.

‘No, it's fine,’ interrupted Olivia. Something on the sofa took her attention as she spoke. It looked like dark dots of various thickness. Looked fresh also. Then she noticed a few more dots on the cushion. Olivia rubbed the dots inquisitively.

CHAPTER 52

The semi-circular sickle came down like a whip. It's force only slowed down due to impact, impact with bone and muscle. The first impact was straight into the left side of her neck. It almost came out the other side as blood sprayed out like water from a sprinkler, hissing in the process.

Queen Olivia/Elizabeth scrambled... for her life... for her breath. The more she tried to breathe, the more the red sprinkler watered Jag's house. She was like a squirming chicken after decapitation. Hands flailing, as Jag continued to scythe his way through the warbled wails of a former Queen.

This was a much messier situation for Jag, a watershed moment. His fortunes had turned his life from bad to worse, and he had bought himself a one-way ticket.

This time there was less remorse for Jag as he knew he was killing the woman who had deceived him and the others so much. He had no idea how he felt as confusion ruled Jag's lack of normality.

She ended up on the floor with nowhere else left to go. A pool of blood had formed like a red garden pond with no fish. The occasional shake of the head from his lawyer friend, who only came to give her daughter's friend what was rightfully hers.

Convulsions and spasms continued as her heartbeat was beaten, the body trying unsuccessfully to say no to inevitability. Olivia was morphing from a person to a body, then rapidly into a corpse, each breath shortening. Soon to be a slab on the butchers table, she had conceded to the butchers' knife.

'And that, Queen Olivia, is the last time you are gonna make fun of me!' Jag brimmed with vengeance as he looked the erstwhile Queen in her eyes, open, but nobody home. He looked at the clock that was used to part-kill his beloved wife earlier. 'See, Jen, working like clockwork now. Time flies.' There was a madness now to Jag, now far from the rational man he once was.

His receding bands of hair were starting to look messy as his clothes now were a mix of soil and blood, with the morning aftershave hardly evident. He used his dirty fingers to reshape the parting in his black thinning hair. Then he got down to the familiar task of dragging the body into the garden. The second of four potato beds now came into focus.

Jag was so tired, digging his second grave of the night. So much had happened he never got chance to consider or reflect on exactly why things had gone so far. His tipping point had been The Law plc fraud he had suffered. Hard for him to imagine that it was only the morning when he found out about that unfortunate development. Things just broke apart then and with Jenny's continuous grievances with the clock, he flipped into another dimension.

So, he sat there, leaning against the new graves, head lost in space somewhere. Then he dozed off for a few short minutes. It seemed like a lifetime, but he only dozed for a few minutes. And in those minutes, he tasted a strange and horrible dream.

In his dream he was sitting down to dinner with James Balden, his old friend. They were laughing and joking about office times and really were best of friends. After dipping into their drinks, they prepared for dinner served under a cloche. It was so shiny and reflective that Jag didn't want to remove the cover. It was so perfect. He even waved at himself in the silvery reflective coating, making scary faces. Jag really didn't know why James had invited him.

James was confident as normal. He had been to these types of restaurants many times and was telling Jag to lift the top. Eventually Jag did it. Underneath were all the cooked parts of his murdered victims. It was shocking and extremely disturbing for Jag, who sat there frozen into disbelief. He looked around for help and answers. James, at the other end of the table, just smiled back as normal, his eyes twinkling in the lights of the restaurant.

Then all the waiters came over and surrounded Jag. Each of the waiters goaded Jag, prodding him, and looking at him. It was horrendous pressure and fear he felt. Then, when he looked at the waiters and waitresses, he saw they had no eyes. Where their eyes should be there was just empty blackness. It made Jag think back in his mind to the darkness that plagued Jag sometime in his past. He had a flashback of the frog and when he was locked in the blackness of the utility room. That horror engulfed him each time he looked into their evil eyes.

The waiters and waitresses forced him to eat everything, the fingers, ears, and tongue included. Even though it was like eating poison he had to do it. It was either face these dark, black, empty eyes, or the plate of human body parts on the table. Those eyes just terrified him so much that he chose the body parts, though he retched many times throughout his ordeal.

Jag was crying uncontrollably throughout all this. He didn't want to eat anyone, let alone his wife and her friend. He didn't want to eat anything again in his life after this.

Finally, the only things left were the eyes. The eyes sat on his dinner plate. Then the eyes started moving around like imbalanced eggs on a table, like jumping beans. They started jumping up and down frantically, eyes locked on Jag. He screamed so loud as they jumped up at him, slime dripping and dropping off them.

Then he awoke. He awoke with fresh tears.

Jag found himself bent down at the graves of his victims, as he woke up, sleeping next to his wife. It was a terrible experience. He rubbed his eyes, checking that he still had his own eyes, and trying to erase that darkness. He got up, shaking himself and mostly his head in disbelief of the situation he was in. Sleep did not help him, it only made things worse.

Chapter 53

So, he headed inside again, now not even noticing or considering the late-night chill. It was the same chill that greeted him when he went to look at his sprouting potatoes before Jenny made her last complaint about the faulty clock.

He went in through the open patio door. Inside was also cool now from the open patio. 'Wow,' he said to himself, head shaking and looking around. The whole place around the sofa looked like an abattoir, and probably smelt worse. Blood, some dry and some drying, was like spray paint decoration.

He went over to the table, the Tesco bag sitting there. It still housed the spinner, the sentimental spinner of Tinkerbell, and of course, Bunny. Tinkerbell to the rescue he thought. More tears. 'Where were you before, my friend? Where were you?' Regretful and painful words as tears filled Jag's eyes. Without physically having to curl his eyes and face he was crying full, painful tears.

Remorse and penitence overtook him. New feelings he never knew existed ploughed into him. Sadness dug into the roots of his emotions. Pangs of contrition had sowed their seeds deep inside him now as he held that spinner. He'd cried before, but this spinner had brought out a stronger emotion he never had felt before.

Slowly and thoughtfully, he made his way upstairs. Each step was like a mountain, feet heavy and adrenalin all used up. Clutching the spinner tightly, it was as if that spinner might just be his way out of this mess. He entered his daughter's room with a tranquillity that had betrayed him of late.

Bunny was sleeping peacefully, oblivious to the passage of time. He didn't wake her. As he approached her, he couldn't help but notice the fluffy Russian Blue cat in the middle of the room. Eyes wide open, it looked right at Jag, as if tracking his moves. The way it was positioned made it appear to be a bodyguard for Bunny.

Jag refused to take his eyes off the cat. He went over to Bunny and quietly removed the duvet. The cat seemed to peer higher to get a cautionary view, or was that Jag being overzealous?

There it was. Tinkerbell was in her hands, still clutched, even in sleep. He picked up his daughter inside the duvet, as she picked up Tinkerbell and headed out back to the stairs. She was in deep sleep.

It didn't feel right... something.

Returning to her room, he looked inside. The cat, still there and still beaming a smile at him. He looked around the room, then sighed and headed for the cat. It turned out to be tricky, but he decided to pick up the cat with his free hand, his daughter, wrapped in her duvet in the other. It was a bit of a juggling act to get back down but he'd been through tougher than this over the past few hours.

It was past 2:00 am as Jag made it back downstairs, clumsily. The patio was open, and he headed straight out. It had been one of his daughters long standing wishes to get that spinner back. Jag had done it, by hook and by crook, despite not in fact doing anything, that spinner had returned.

That gave him a sense of satisfaction though, to have finally given his family what they wanted. It made him feel a sense of pride and value. His daughter was a large part of what he lived for and getting that spinner meant a lot to him, more than his daughter could imagine.

He put the cat down in the middle of the garden, and then put Bunny down on the fourth potato bed. He had already dug out the potatoes from the soil of the remaining two potato beds. His cracked and sore hands were evidence of that hard work. Hands that normally worked on the computer had been employed elsewhere this night.

Noticing how damaged his hands looked, he lifted them up so that he could see their shadow against the gibbous moon. They shook and shivered uncontrollably.

After a moment, Jag removed the spinner from his inside pocket, protecting it with all his might. It was the one thing that now meant a lot to him. No Goldsmith could take that away from him. Heading over to Bunny, he took the spinner and placed it in the area between Tinkerbell and the shoulder of Bunny. There, it was perfect. Finally, Jag's daughter, Bunny, reunited with a fully functioning Tinkerbell. Jag again started to cry, this time sentimentality the cause.

The Russian Blue watched on; eyes transfixed on Jag as he wrapped Bunny up a little more to avoid the chilled summer night. Then, he headed over to the shed... again.

CHAPTER 54

An exhausted Jag returned from the shed.

His garden was starting to look like a nursery, only not the agricultural type. The cat was on watch, checking on proceedings, protecting Bunny. Tinkerbell had her spinner. She was ready to sprinkle some pixie dust. For Jag, the relief and satisfaction in putting Tinkerbell and her other half back together meant a lot.

Potato spuds and leaves were dotted around. By the time Jag had reached the fourth potato bed to dig up he was so shattered that he would just dig up soil and throw it anywhere. It had become a life hardly worth living.

The darkness was peaking. Jag, of course hated darkness, but given his situation and actions he just had to be as quiet as possible to avoid becoming conspicuous. But that darkness that had plagued him all his life, as well as the claustrophobia that, at times molested him, made his life miserable.

He used what little light there was from the glistening moon to check the sharpness of the blade. That saw had treated him well over the years. It had been especially useful recently in the creation of his raised potato beds and the planks needed for that project. He just needed it now for one last project as he looked over at Bunny and Tinkerbell embracing in sleep; a family reunited. They were a family now, all back together to spread their magic.

The shed offered much success and many memories. His time in project planning and management had its place, but to Jag, gardening was what he was born to do. From a young age, even when up against the odds he always took the good from his gardening experiences. His family greenhouse during his childhood was like his private world at times, where he felt most comfortable.

Jag went over to Bunny, wrapped her up a little more and moved some of the soil that had dusted itself onto her duvet in the recently converted raised potato bed. Then he went to the neighbouring potato bed to lie down himself.

Ruskie, smiling nearby, was inactive and calm, but watching. Jag lay down on his back in his potato bed, put the saw horizontal across his chest, and folded his arms. He was lying directly in front of Ruskie who was staring right back at him, into his eyes.

'What are you looking at, weird cat?' Jag never saw eye to eye with that cat. It seemed to wag its tail, but in the darkness Jag could not be sure.

Then the moonlight caught the eyes of the cat. Jag stared in. There was always some familiarity in those eyes that he didn't like. Something in there he didn't trust. A mechanical cat in a world of its own. Jag just wanted to sleep for a very long time. He wanted to wake up after that sleep and have his normal life back. A time when he didn't have financial trouble and when he loved his wife. That's what he wished for.

Jag looked into those eyes, never allowing himself to blink, hypnotising himself into submission. He saw a familiarity but didn't see any solutions. He tried to think back to when he was happy but couldn't. His life had become so polluted that the good times had been blurred by dirty grey smog.

The silence around him. Complete silence. Only the eyes of a stranger and misty memories of those happier sights and sounds.

That mean cat. It was all his fault.

None of this was your doing, Jag. That bloody cat! It was the cat!

A lot of bad I've done, thought Jag. A lot of things that could've been done different. We all deserve a second chance, don't we? I will sort things out, explain what happened to the police. Things will be okay. He looked into the eyes, deep. They'll understand it wasn't really me. The Forex Group, Goldsmith, all the haters and those who just don't understand. It can happen to anyone. ANYONE!

Then another voice in his head.

You should have done your DUE DILIGENCE, Jag. You know that, right? You can't just go around killing who you like! This was your test. You failed!

And Jag cried silently to himself, more mental wounds to deal with.

And the cat continued to smile at him, watching him, watching Bunny, watching Tinkerbell.

Jag shuffled around in his bed of soil, sitting up. He picked up the saw with his left hand and used his right to balance himself. The night was coming to an end. The moon was lower towards his west. He got up and went over to Bunny.

Jag stroked the beautiful face of his daughter, warm in the cool summer morning. She was well wrapped up in her fairy blanket. Jag then stroked the jagged edges of his saw. Polar opposites. Signs of rust on a well-used blade. His twisted mind just kept going through his recent experiences, blaming himself, then the others.

He lowered the blanket from Bunny's face, down towards her chest. 'It's okay, baby, it's okay.' He felt sorry for her that she must be feeling the chill of the morning, though knew it would not be forever. And Ruskie looked on, a little cautious this time.

The glimmer of the first signs of a new morning appeared, before the inevitable onslaught of the sun for another day would come. A final shimmer of the blades on a dying moon. That darkness about to wave the world away for one last time. Jag lifted the saw to the height of his own self, himself crouching over his calm, sleeping daughter. Then he looked around at the cat, closer, larger, ominous.

Jag turned back, whispered consolations to himself, and then to Bunny. 'No one loved you like me, Bunny, no one.' He closed his eyes and brought the saw into contact with skin. Frantically and almost impossibly he made the saw movements he had made a million times before. A million times before, but never like this.

Movements he had used to make the planks for the very same potato bed that he, his family, and friend lay on. The same movements that he had even used to cut and make his own shed. That shed that he loved like a home.

The blades zipped through painfully, unbelievably painfully. Indescribable pain. The type of pain you only feel once.

And the cat watched on.

Those old heavily used blades jagged across flesh and sinew, cartilage, and soft bone before he could take no more.

Jag dropped the saw as he did not have any life left inside him after bringing the saw upon his own neck. Already in a lying down position, he dropped down into his very own custom built potato bed to become worm food.

The nursery had now become the cemetery.

And, like the others he had killed before him, he too squirmed uncontrollably until there was no fight left inside.

EPILOGUE

The sun arose, like it always does.

The birds chirped, like they always do.

The Russian Blue smiled, like it always did.

There was silence in the home of Jagat Singh, not like there always was.

But there was calm after that storm.

The phone rang. And rang.

No one picked up.

It rang again, this time for longer. Again, no one picked up. The voicemail kicked in this time.

'Hi, Jag. Hope you're okay. This is James, James Balden here. We were wondering where you were. Didn't see you in the office today. Is everything okay? Hope you and the family are well and you sorted things out. You know one piece of advice I've got for you, Jag. My friend... my little young friend… DO DUE DILIGENCE. Oh, and of course, keep up the gardening.'

The line died, and with that, the phone call from the Cockney, James Balden, aka Mark Goldsmith.

Silence continued in the bloodied home of Jagat Singh. On the other side of the line, James Balden disconnected the phone and looked over at his friend, Martin O'Leary.

His eyes glistened as his smile broadened.

After a deep sigh, Balden went over to his computer to switch off the camera connected to Ruskie's eyes.

The Russian Blue's eyes shut as the sun continued to rise.

Printed in Great Britain
by Amazon